THE PECULIAR
MEMORIES OF
THOMAS PENMAN

By the same author

PARANOIA IN THE LAUNDRETTE
WITHNAIL AND I

THE PECULIAR MEMORIES OF THOMAS PENMAN

BRUCE ROBINSON

BLOOMSBURY

FOR SOPHIE

First published in Great Britain in 1998
This paperback edition published 2004

Copyright © 1998 by Bruce Robinson

The moral right of the author has been asserted

Bloomsbury Publishing Plc, 38 Soho Square, London W1D 3HB

A CIP catalogue record for this book
is available from the British Library

ISBN 0 7475 7458 8

10 9 8 7 6 5 4 3 2 1

All papers used by Bloomsbury Publishing are natural,
recyclable products made from wood
grown in well-managed forests.
The manufacturing processes conform to the
environmental regulations of the country of origin.

Typeset by Hewer Text Ltd, Edinburgh
Printed in Great Britain by Clays Ltd, St Ives plc

www.bloomsbury.com/brucerobinson

'It's a strange, unsettling book which is, by turns, grotesque, lyrical, touching and darkly comic. But I would have expected no less from the author and director of *Withnail and I*, the cult comedy about two struggling actors at the fag end of the 1950s. What does come as a pleasant surprise, though, is the quality of Robinson's prose. His idol Dickens would, barring the odd expletive, be proud'

Spectator

'Profoundly moving ... When we first meet Thomas Penman he is emerging into adolescence from the last constriction of a troubled childhood, namely the frightening tendency to defecate at the worst times in the worst places ... A husband and wife wage silent war and an increasingly senile old man nurtures perversity in the attic. Thomas loves his grandfather and even after death the old man helps him understand the mad, passionate world of adulthood ... There should be a law against this being called a début novel. It's far too clever, too assured and too damn good to be a first attempt'

Independent On Sunday

'Living with a family of wittily caricatured eccentrics, we follow in the trail of Thomas's hormones as he learns to smoke and has knee trembles over a vision of loveliness called Gwen. The tone is very Stephen Fry meets *The Darling Buds of May* and Robinson writes with such freshness and brio that it really doesn't matter that there is no plot to speak of'

The Times

'Beautiful . . . Almost every passage of this book hums with particularity and vision ... *Thomas Penman* is the work of a genuine prose-writer – and a gifted one at that'

Observer

'This book is in a league-table of revulsion all its own'

Sunday Times

'It's rites-of-passage stuff (first love, first death), but told with very dark humour (as well as plenty of old-fashioned digestion-related gags), a touch of the gothic and a fine sense of a sad, claustrophobic pre-divorce-reform England strong enough . . . to explain why people of Robinson's age were so happy when the 1960s came along'

Neon

'Robinson careers brilliantly through the illicit fascinations and sickening thrills of adolescence'

Select

'Bringing to bear the same melancholic gusto and off-the-wall perceptions that made Robinson's film *Withnail and I* the distinctive tale it was, he writes here with a movie-maker's voice, more interested in the impact of a scene, the quickfire cutting of image to image, than the precision of his prose. The odd missing verb or illogical jump of phrase doesn't bother him so long as we get the picture. And, once we're used to his rollercoaster style, we do . . . As Thomas struggles to get to the root of the family's closeted truths and free himself from the strangle-hold of a lifetime's misery, he emerges as something of a hero . . . This is fiction that reaches the heart'

Scotland on Sunday

'You have the director of *Withnail and I* to thank for this hilarious, tender novel about dysfunctional family life in the 1950s. What with discovering his grandfather's porn stash and his violent father's affair, these frank, often crude memoirs of a 13-year-old make for compulsive reading'

Elle

'For Robinson, it's all about telling the story. "I don't differentiate between directing, screenwriting or novel-writing. Some guys can tell a good joke and others can't – the whole thing is about being able to tell the joke." Bruce Robinson is a man who can'

The List

WINTER, 1957

It was a dislocated unfriendly old house with Victorian additions and plenty of empty rooms. There was a constant smell of meat cooking. On any day you could open the Aga and there was always one in there, meat was continual, and when it wasn't a joint it might be a tongue or a gut. Plus, there was the enormous ancillary vessel of dog meat, stewing without specification, and cooling through long winter afternoons into ultimate paralysis under two inches of yellow fat.

The history of its meat clung about this house like a climate. Like oil-vapour in a garage. Perhaps the only room immune was an upstairs back bathroom, facing north. Someone once said, 'Let's stop this bathroom being green?' But they ran out of interest, it was green and old yellow. In here were the six toothbrushes of the residents and an egg-coloured carpet with a known verruca. But there was hygiene in here. A smell of cloths provided antidote to the dinners and hours abandoned to them in this apartment of ruined tiles.

It was in this area that his grandfather liked to lurk about, not necessarily in the bathroom, not necessarily excluding it. He rode the toilet like a horse, facing the wall, and crept around in the attic with his penis out. The boy knew this because he was always creeping around too. Sometimes they inadvertently spied on each other. On one occasion he was concealed behind a bedroom door, staring up the hall, and he saw an *eye* behind the crack in another door, staring back at him. The boy and his grandfather shared more than they might have imagined. Both liked secrets and were interested in the secrets of others. Both thought a lot about nudes.

His grandfather carried pictures of nude women and quite often sent away for brassière catalogues. Anyone prepared to scale a fifteen-foot wall could lie on the roof and watch him in his 'office'. Inside were a pair of wooden filing cabinets, a desk with an ancient Olivetti, and two twelve-volt lead-zinc batteries wired into a Morse key. Unfortunately, the only way to observe him in here was by hanging over the gutter and cautiously lowering your head. This meant everything was upside-down, but it was the only way to watch him with his sleeves rolled up and a cigar in his mouth, working on his nudes with a razorblade and pot of gum arabic.

Walter was extremely old and full of cancer, although they hadn't diagnosed it yet. On the day the first cell divided the boy got his first pubic hair. The hair was unimpressive and the cancer just a few miscreant spores in the old man's gut. No one knew anything about either. Except Walter had lost weight. He was two holes up on his watch-strap and his coat hung off him like a coat on the back of a chair.

On summer evenings yellow light bored into the cigar smoke and the part of his head that was chromium-plated shone. Sometimes you could see your face in it, like a hubcap.

'What are you looking at?'

'Nothing.'

He was careful how he combed his hair, manipulating specially grown long bits over the top and securing them with a wad of grease. This wasn't always successful. During sultry weather his plate warmed up, melting the Brylcreem, and his dome would emerge like part of a small bollard. I have to tell you when you were looking at this you were looking at something. That's why he wore a hat.

2

'What are you looking at?'

'Nothing.'

'You're a liar.'

He was right. The boy was a liar. They were both expert liars. In 1914 his grandfather had lied to get into the army. He signed up, lying about his age, and they rigged him out in big boots and gave him a ride to France. He was the best Morse-code operator on the line, he could *think* in fucking Morse. He didn't know it then, but Morse was the only thing he was ever going to be any good at.

They took them by train to a little town in Belgium a few miles behind the fighting. The Germans had been here for a year or more and junked the place up somewhat. Even the school was full of bullet holes. Did they shoot the children? Who knows, there are no children here to tell. They got billeted in some of the downstairs classrooms and for a month or two this is where the Morse came in. Fifteen words a minute if you were good. Walter could send thirty. He could look across the dead-zone towards the collapsed church where they blew up their own God and hear it in a series of electrical discharges – dit – dit – dah – dah – dit – hits in his head like organised flies. But what about the pretty evenings when the weather was pink? What about the girl he fucked in the meadow? Can Morse ever be beautiful? I can't think so. Surely this kind of language is only good for ugly things, like horse blood, and maggots in the horse's head? Kissing tits sounds just about the same as your arse blown off.

—.— .. .. —. ——. — .. — ...

.— .—. ... . .—... .—.. ——— —. ——— ..—. ..—.

Rain all over the town and it felt like the 35th of January. That's what he wrote home to his sweetheart, Ethel, although he didn't write that much. Then the message came, and he was the first to transcribe it: 'We're out of here, and going on some kind of offensive in a place called Passchendaele.'

The officer was a new boy, never heard of it, and looked it up on a map. As it turned out it wasn't too far away.

Walter had never seen a tank before and laughed when he did. It was like an elephant in an idiot's dream. Diesel pouring out of its head, like an elephant breathing like a whale.

But it was big and made him feel so little and realise he was still a boy.

That's why he laughed.

At twenty minutes past two that afternoon half a kilo of shrapnel took the top of his head off like it was opening it for breakfast. Another element of the same shell hit him in the gut.

He heard it in Morse.

.. — −.. . .− −..

I'm dead.

Twenty thousand went into the toilet that day but Walter wasn't one of them. For seventeen days he lay where he fell, buried under a heap of horses and rotten Scottish dead. When the Germans picked him up his eyes opened and they stuffed his brain back in as an experiment.

He lived.

It was a story his grandson liked to hear. He liked hearing about the Germans and magic flies. The hospital in Koblenz was full of both and Walter genuinely never knew which one of them saved him.

His grandson's name was Thomas Christopher Penman, a thirteen-year-old asthmatic short-arse with big ears and an unwholesome characteristic. If you want the picture in more detail, from the age of four he navigated all lavatories and shat himself everywhere else. This was nothing medicinal, there was nothing 'wrong' with him, he wasn't incontinent or anything like that. No, he shat himself because he wanted to, it was wilful, and not a room in the house nor its considerable gardens was beyond his remit. Sometimes they saw him in his workshop, sometimes in the Wolsey, or cross-eyed and ecstatic in the raspberry canes. More often than not he located on the landing, wedged between the wall and piece of furniture called a tallboy. When there was no one around this was his favourite spot. It was a dark, secret place, with bland wallpaper covered in dots. No one else ever got in here. (The only other person who ever got in here was his grandfather who had been known to exploit the isolation to hang his testicles over the banisters.)

When this chosen section was unavailable he set off around the property looking for alternatives. Hypnotics were what he was after and there was a list of them. Moss growing anywhere out of almost anything. Rusting nails and lichen on ancient concrete with weeds scraping a living through the cracks. Mould on fences, and tinsel from slugs, and once, unexpectedly, even the dingle-berries on a broccoli root. (How did that happen, it never happened before?) Holes, he liked too, especially in fucked walls where beetles black as phones eat the bricks. Not that he cared a toss for beetles, or anything animate, as a matter of fact. What he wanted was to imagine he was the size of them and get into their stagnant galleries. Only then in these secret holes of moss and silence could anything begin.

It was a sensation of total security.

When his entrail stirred, an organ under his skull produced a peculiar kind of pickling vinegar that shrank the skin on his brain, and his eyes glazed as a pulse of elation grasped his bowel, like the hand of a ferocious angel. At moments like this his shame was an ecstasy. On the best of days whole afternoons would drift by with him pole-axed in the undergrowth. For as long as it could be held in transit, on remand, so to speak, suffering it to be neither prisoner, nor yet free, then its enchanting authority would maintain.

It was a church in heaven.

There were outlaws of course, sudden rogues that motored

into the gusset with inevitable consequences. Once control was lost the reverie was over and a new circumstance had to be coped with. It was called the Saturday Bag. The Saturday Bag was the bag set aside from the rest of the common laundry. It hung on a hook in an out-house and featured only Thomas's underwear. It was the burden of this hamper that drove his mother into guard-duty outside the lavatory door. There was no other way – if she wasn't out there, he wasn't in there. Ultimately she took up crosswords and said it was worth the wait. Thomas's load meant a day in front of a washing machine with the attendant anxiety of not only dealing with them but first finding where they were hidden.

'Where are they?'

'What?'

Short of hauling up lino there was no place left upstairs that wasn't as well known to her as him. But numbers were down and instinctively she knew he'd branched out somewhere else in the house. He was questioned, he was innocent, and forged an asthma attack as the search began. After the initial shock of discovery in his grandmother's sitting room they were almost always located quickly, usually in a drawer, or vase on the mantelpiece, sometimes down the side of a sofa, sometimes on top of another pair as yet unearthed.

Remember Christmas 1955?

1955, when to Thomas's horror, Uncle Horrie pulled out not one, but three pairs driven down the side of an armchair – that dreadful, stained clutch coming out just after he'd mastered the art of Solo. On the days following his mother took more, and by New Year's Eve she had eight. Two on top of the curtain pelmet, one in the wireless, the three that were Horrie's, and one even flattened under the carpet. She also found a sock under her mattress with one in it that he swore was nothing to do with him.

'I've admitted the rest, why would I lie?'

They took him to a doctor who wasn't interested, said he'd grow out of it, bring him back if he didn't. They brought him back and the doctor looked up his arse. There was nothing up there.

'How old is he?'

'Nearly fourteen.'

He wrote a prescription that was never used, and for the wrong reasons he was almost right. By 1958 something happened, and Thomas had all but grown out of it.

One afternoon he was out drowning flies when he realised he was in love with Gwen Hackett. She was at the same school, half a year younger, but already with a well-filled bra. It wasn't until he was in love with her that he realised everybody else was. Gwendolin was beautiful, stone blonde with sexy teeth, lips like the bit after a knot in a balloon. He drew a picture of her in the nude and wrote numbers on her tits, one and two respectively. Plus more pictures with more numbers and explanatory arrows pointing at her quiff. She had blue eyes, harsh as forget-me-nots, and always sort of sneered when he looked at her. Did this mean something? He knew girls had to hide their desires. He wrote her an anonymous letter signed 'Q' and the next day her friend came up and told him to drop dead.

'We know it's you,' she said. 'Gwen loves Dick Gollick.'

Heartbreak was instant and overwhelming. How could anyone love Gollick? He tried to put the pair of them out of his head but Gwendolin wouldn't go. Whatever the thought, it became a thought of her. Her impact however remained positive, and as he progressed through the third year anything in his knickers but a bit of graffiti was scarce. Risk of a contraction was limited to the classes he loathed: literature (a.m.), algebra (p.m.), a duo of stultifying shits in competition for tedium and both on a bastard Friday . . .

If m equals x over b what's n?

He shoved eyes back at the blackboard and had another look at m. What *was* m? What relationship did it bear to n? How could anyone ever get hold of n when they were clueless about x over b and never heard of fucking m? In certain areas nibs were scratching. How did the others know what it meant? Maybe they didn't. Either way he couldn't get a grip on this kind of stuff. Whose fault was that? He'd been sitting here years and nobody told him nothing. He wrote w and blew it out, fuck it, that might be right.

Twenty minutes past three on the clock. G.P. Norris, maths and music, slumped under it, bored beyond endurance. He was a stale little twot with too many pens, lived with his mother on the western promenade and got there on a motor bike with a side-car that he occasionally took her out in. It was an unfulfilling sort of life. Out of hope. Like a used match put back in the box . . .

You could hear the mechanics of the clock, minute after minute, one gone and another filling it. Thomas had a look at his book. At the back several pages were set aside for lists of cockney rhyming slang taught to him by his grandfather:

> Dog = Phone (Dog and Bone/Phone)
> Maria = Sperm (Maria Monk/Spunk)
> China = Friend (China Plate/Mate)
> Tom = Shit (Tom Tit/Shit)
> Sky = Pocket (Sky Rocket/Pocket)

Here comes one, a complicated one, his spelling so bad he could hardly read it himself:

> Harris = Arse – Harris derived from Aristotle –
> Harris-totle/Bottle (Bottle and Glass/Arse)

Thomas started drawing spokes round the inkwell. His eyes drifted along the desk to a tiny gully filled with pencil leads and bits of India rubber. Winter sunlight cut across them and suddenly they were a shoal of dolphin – they were dolphins plunging in and out of an old and inky sea. Within seconds his eyes slipped focus and his arse was on to it. He could hardly believe it, this was dangerous, he was already carrying a Shakespearian potato and the perils of another if Norris woke up were alarming.

He tried to force his eyes off but couldn't, the dolphins were going a beauty. By now his pupils were so severely dilated any notion of control was fantasy. Suddenly, it half barged out, hot and uncompromising; nobody wanted it, least of all Thomas, and he tore eyes away to check it, and the worst of all worlds was reality. He was staring straight into the eyes of Norris. Now something really unuseful happened, Thomas grinned, grinned like he was sharing something with the cunt. But what else could he do, raised and weeping, staring into the lenses of this myopic prat with something so enormous in his pants it felt like a knee.

The moment was quite awful.

Norris looked away, beating a pen against his teeth, and the next time Thomas looked at him he was on his feet scanning the class for a victim. The question of n was now going to have to be answered. It was Thomas who was going to have to answer it, he knew it, and he was right.

'Pens down.'

Somehow Norris managed to lower his head into the tweed. He was looking amongst them and taking his time. Everything that was wrong with his life was here assembled, a classload of post-war secondary-modern no-hopers – Maurice Potts and Len Gubb, Fanny Shackles and Pauline Pew, plus twenty-seven more assorted thickheads – this was Norris's lot, and this was the end of the line. And there in the middle of them was that foul little oaf with its ears stuck out attempting to look inconspicuous.

Thomas looked back at him, trying to look normal, blend in with the others, so to speak . . .

'X over b, then?' said Norris. 'What's n, then?'

A few hands went up, particularly that of Boles, who was obsequious to authority and looked like he was trying to hang from the lamp.

'Penman?'

The hands kept waving but Norris wasn't interested; stood there under raised eyebrows with his cheeks blown out. He did this when he was waiting, leisurely releasing the air like his head had a slow puncture. And he was still waiting, hands thrust in his pockets like a pair of Colts aimed at a girl in the front row.

'What's *n*? Penman?'

The double question mark was ominous.

'W, sir.'

'W?'

'Yes, sir.'

'*W*?' he said, his emphasis promoting it to a capital. 'What's it got to do with *W*?'

Thomas looked at his book like there might be something in it.

'I meant, k, sir.'

'K? Did you say, *K*?'

'Yes, sir.'

The twat wasn't looking cheerful, stared with magnified eyes and his foolish little moustache.

'Are you trying to be funny?'

'No, sir.'

'*No, sir*?' he volleyed. 'And *n* isn't *k*, is it, *sir*?'

'No, sir.'

The silence belonged to Norris, he didn't have a lot of use for it.

'Do you know what *m* is?'

'M, sir?'

'*M*, boy?'

'No, sir.'

Thomas was facing crisis, fighting the incomer.

'What have you been writing there?' said Norris. He took a pace or two forward. 'What have you got in your book?'

(Some swastikas and the date and a drawing of Gwen Hackett's bum.)

'Will you put your arm down, Boles!'

The eyes were on him, Thomas shook his head. He had nothing.

On your feet.'

It took a repetition of the instruction for him to rise. He went up like an old man with grit in the joints, noticeably at a tilt. Standing for interrogation added a new dimension, he could feel the weight of it pointing at the person behind him. At all costs he had to hang on, and he did so with lips drawn back exposing lightly clenched teeth.

'Something amusing you?'

'No, sir.'

'Then wipe that grin off your face.'

'I'm not grinning, sir.'

'Don't answer back.'

Thomas decided there was only one way out of this, and it was through the door as soon as possible.

'I don't feel well, sir.'

'What?'

'I need to go downstairs, and report.'

'Report what?'

'Stomach ache.'

'How very convenient,' said Norris, turning an eye to the class. 'You sit here all afternoon doing nothing, and now suddenly you have stomach ache?'

'Yes, sir, I need to go, sir.'

'Go where?'

'Lavatory, sir.'

'Shall I tell you something, Penman?' he said, with transparent dismissal of the request. 'You are an idle little chump, a loafer, and a *skiver*. You get yourself into trouble and think you can scuttle off to the nearest lavatory, well, that isn't the way life works, boy! And as you progress through it you will discover there are responsibilities, obligations, disciplines, team-work, hard work, mortgages. Do you think I can pay my mortgage in a lavatory?'

If it was a joke it was unintended, but it got a dull laugh from one or two at the back and Norris suddenly became stage-struck.

'We'd never have won the war in the lavatory!'

More laughter and the dope lapped it up, pranced about like a bit of a wit. 3C was interested in killing minutes, and they seized the opportunity. Not only did it keep him off the equations, it kept that red second-hand on the Smith's Selectric moving all the time.

Norris resumed his seat with hands clasped behind his head. After a pause a finger appeared to come out of an ear pointing at the desk in front of him.

'Book here.'

Thomas shook his head again.

'I couldn't do the question, sir.'

Norris had seen him writing and told him so.

'I did the date, sir.'

'You know the date, do you?'

'October the 25th, sir.'

Norris repeated it with precision. 'October the twenty-fifth?' but couldn't think of anything funny to say about it, so he didn't.

'Book here.'

Thomas moved forward with exacting steps, like he was

measuring a room. Norris watched his approach with escalating incredulity.

'Something the matter with your feet?'

Thomas didn't answer. This was the first time he'd ever been totally out of control in a classroom. Standing there with this awful cargo put him of a mind to panic, fuck the consequences, and run. Norris snatched the book and was evidently enjoying himself: this was job satisfaction, and probably the only pleasure he got in his life.

He sat forward, turning pages slowly, heading for October. Somewhere around mid-September he struck gold. There was a page full of pencilled hearts and swastikas, and Gwen – Gwen – Gwen – Gwen – Gwen. Next page was a drawing of Gwen's arse with an arrow pointing at it, titled 'Bum 4'.

'(4) Bum should be round, available for massage, and perfumed with Yardley's Toilet Water.'

Norris looked up and down again.

'(1 and 2) Tits, should be pert, with no bra at the weekends, and always available.'

He skipped (3) but look at this, '(5) her "spunk cloth"' (a picture of Gwen holding a rag).

The glasses came off and his eyes came up.

'What have you got to say about this?'

Thomas farted with shock, and that was it, it was over, the bastard was out. And he gave stench like water in a jar of dead chrysanths.

'Have you just been unhygienic?'

'I have to go to the lavatory, sir, I must.'

Norris didn't know what to be disgusted about, dropped the exercise book, put on his glasses and stood up.

'I have two things to say to you, Penman. First, you are not going to the lavatory, and second, you *are* going to be caned. You are going to the headmaster and ask him to *cane* you.' All fuses blown and the book back in his hands.

'How dare you come out here with this pornographic drivel, how *dare* you write swastikas in school property. You should have tried a bit of it. You think swastikas were a joke? Do you?'

Thomas shook his head with his mouth open.

'Right,' said Norris. 'Downstairs with this book, knock on the headmaster's door, show him this, inform him I want you caned at his discretion, and afterwards you are to report back to me immediately, do you understand?'

Thomas nodded.

'What does that mean?'

'Yes, sir.'

Thomas walked out on lead feet without looking back. He was on the fifth floor of an ugly yellow-brick tower built in 1953. Noisy stairs with iron banisters and a view of the bicycle sheds as he descended. The situation was desperate; how could he go in there in this state, knock on the door and ask that two-hundred pound ogre to assault him? There was one hope, remove the offending pages, tear Gwen out and leave him a few swastikas. Would Norris discuss what he had seen? Quite possibly not. He tore out the pages, stuffed them in his pocket, and had an idea . . .

What about some kind of psychological act, like Brer Rabbit: cane me as hard as you like, but please, please, don't tell my parents? It was a straw that turned into a log, he liked the sound of it, and went down rehearsing. 'Please, *please*, I know I'm asking a lot, but please don't tell my parents?' He practised a humble smile. That was all he wanted, mercy from the parents. It might work; if he begged hard enough maybe Enright would fall for the concept of 'domestic wrath', let him out with a letter, and that wasn't bothering Thomas nothing, because neither of his parents was remotely interested in what went on in this school, including his education.

'If you insist, sir, I'll accept a letter.'

This optimistic scenario lasted him down the last flight of stairs but collapsed utterly in the atrium. What was he talking about, accept a letter? He suddenly realised what he was talking about; he was talking like there was going to be some sort of negotiation, practically got himself to the point where Enright would be serving them tea. Reality struck with its usual efficiency. He's not going to give you a letter. He's going to give you the rod!

Sunlight on a polished wood floor. He crossed it slowly, fearful for his load, and there was the door, 'Administration'. That's where he was, that's where he'd administer: small eyes and always annoyed, to be avoided even if you haven't done anything. Last time Thomas knocked at this door it was at his mother's instigation. He came home and told her they were having sexual education, and when he told her about the sexual-tube she became unreasonable and told him to tell Enright he wasn't to have it. He went down there and told him and the fucker became inflamed and started shouting about newts. 'Where does she want you to learn it, then? On street corners?' Thomas didn't know; as far as he was concerned she didn't want him to learn it at all.

That was a year ago. If he freaked over that, what's he going to do with this? What apotheosis of rage would he achieve? Simultaneously Thomas got tackled by another truly awful thought. Until now he'd been under the impression he was going to feel it on the hand, six swift and savage strokes. But if the offence was sufficiently grave might he not feel it on the Harris? And if he went for his arse, God forbid, you're talking front row of a major nightmare. Fear rooted him to the floor and it was obvious he couldn't go in there. Of course he couldn't go in there. What he needed, urgently, was to get into a lavatory and do something about his underwear.

Suddenly a bell went off and he looked at his watch and couldn't believe it. How could it be the hour already? Any second now every stairway would be alive with a rush-hour of children as everybody changed classes. Norris would be among them, also looking at his watch. Voices erupted in the tower and feet were already on the stairs. He panicked, he had to get out of here, and quick, and he ran up a dimly lit corridor trying to orientate himself to the nearest cubicle.

He just about made it. They were coming down in a phalanx of pleated skirts and blazers when he hit the red door, crashed through it past a dazzling line of basins and straight into the embrace of a toilet. He slammed the door and tried to lock it, no lock, and he stood there heaving, holding it shut, trying to catch his breath. A moment later he transferred himself to an adjacent cubicle and slid the bolt. A feeling of relative security now, although this coup wasn't as private as he would have liked. The walls and door were green metal, the latter with a two-foot gap, a design feature conceived by the authorities for reasons that are self-evident: i.e. if such is your vocation, you could see who and how many are in there. Cognisant of this, Thomas kept to the rear of the facility, lowered his trousers, and then with infinite care, his inner pants. Inspection was unnecessary to confirm the worst. They were going to have to come off. Struggling to get trousers over shoes he had a leg out and his bum on cold metal when the outer door of the bathroom bashed open and a gang of chattering girls came in.

Jesus Christ, what's all this? Is this possible? Somehow he'd got himself into the wrong lavatory. Any sense of sanctuary was replaced by instant vulnerability. Males simply do not go into female toilets, it was a vice versa taboo, and just didn't happen, ever.

Their voices paralysed him. How many were there – it sounded like fifty. And they sounded like seniors, big girls. One went into the cabinet next to him and he saw her knickers come down around her shoes. If he could see her stuff could she

16

not see his? He forced himself deeper into the corner, lingerie around the ankles with that dreadful, dreadful sight.

With some difficulty he climbed on to the toilet, stood with his head cramped under the cistern and a foot either side of the bowl. His neighbour started pumping at the flush, cranked the fucking thing to death, but still it wouldn't work, and she abandoned it, passing on the information as she came out.

'You don't wanna go in there, it don't work.'

'Don't it?'

'Nahh, it don't.'

'Who's in the other one?'

'Dunno.'

What Thomas knew was that she was now waiting at his door.

There was much coming and going, much combing, and a lot of mirror work. The conversation was astonishing, shot with expletives. Thomas was amazed, didn't know girls talked like this; he thought they were delicate things on plinths. One of them whistled, and another one farted; she was the only one to laugh, said 'Fuck that' and spat.

'Hurry up in there.' The voice behind the door was gruff. 'Who's in there?'

Thomas shook his head, showing teeth.

More young ladies arrived, one or two obviously out of 3C. He heard snatches of talk while they combed. One sounded like Dorothy Nutt, a thirteen-year-old redhead with a chipped tooth and a lisp.

'They're looking for him,' she said.

'He's had it of had,' said her companion.

'If they find him, they'll murder him.'

Thomas was terrified.

'Who's in there?' said the gruff girl. 'Hurry up,' and knuckles wrapped at the door.

'C'mon, Dot.' The girls from 3C disappeared.

Thomas stared wide-eyed at the back of the door. To his horror a pair of eyes came over the top. It was Margaret Ruther, fifteen, with a boil on her eyelid, and she looked at him like a bunch of old women before she screamed.

Still screaming, she kept screaming amongst the general concern for what she'd seen.

'There's a boy in there standing on the toilet!'

'Who is it?'

'I don't know. He's in there with his trousers down.'

'What's he doing?'

'Standing on the toilet. I saw his dick.'

Thomas looked over the top.

'Don't say anything.'

He tried to smile at them. There was a reciprocity of amazement. There were six of them, all fifth-formers, including a vaguely intelligent-looking tall girl and a fat girl.

'Don't say anything,' he said.

'What are you doing in there?' said the fat girl.

'Nothing.'

A consensus developed instantly; they all knew what he was doing and one of them said it. He was a peeping Tom, in there spying on them.

'Is he masturbating?' said the tall girl.

Margaret didn't know, she only got a glimpse, but she definitely saw his dick.

'Listen,' said Thomas.

'You foul little pervert,' said the fat girl.

'I haven't done anything.'

'Then why are you standing on the toilet?'

Thomas stared; there was a perfectly reasonable explanation but they weren't in the mood for it.

'I've seen him creeping,' said the fat girl. 'He's in 3C.'

'Get Mrs Bredwardine,' said Ruther.

'Please don't,' said Thomas, momentarily disappearing and

coming out fighting his trousers. 'Please don't say you saw me in here.'

Did they see his underwear? It was possible. They all screamed and jostled out. He followed in crisis, saw them vanish towards the gym. The corridor was again mercifully deserted and he rushed up it like Douglas Bader.

A haze of mackintoshes came into view and he hit the cloakroom. This was a sort of adjunct to the corridor, high windows and hundreds of hooks. With feet spread like oars he plunged into the rainwear, got stopped by a wall, went up it via a bench, and considered going out through a window.

Somewhere in the depths of the building a door slammed. He froze in its echo. Seconds later the hugely developed calves of Mrs Bredwardine, the games mistress, pumped past. She was wearing shorts and a whistle and had the facility to suddenly run backwards. She did this during sporting-events and was doing it now, buttocks leading the sprint as she glared back up the corridor. Totalling on panic, Thomas cowered in the mackintoshes; the girls had obviously betrayed him and she was off to see Enright. His sighting would invigorate the search: he would certainly be discovered, possibly take stick *in situ*, with consequences as gruesome for the administrator as recipient. He had to get rid of it, distance himself from at least part of the offence, and it was with trembling hands that he rose to have another look at the underwear. It had shifted in transit. Worse than this he'd rarely seen. It was agricultural. He got hold of it with a cycle-clip and stared, at a loss what to do. These improvised forceps were excellent for custody but where could it be dispatched? He went up and down the aisle a couple of times, until, bereft of alternative, he unloaded the lot into somebody's hat. This was perfect. This worked well. He folded the peak inside, secured the unit with an elastic band and stuffed it back into the unfortunate's pocket. Luck struck simultaneously – this was his own cloakroom! Hat on and scarf on and two minutes later he was prince of the air, grinning with fearful elation as he sped away from the cycle sheds.

THE SINS OF THE FOREFATHERS

A dozen miles away a pair of fog-horns put out the doleful news. Winter had come early this year and you could see your breath in it. By night fog would spill off the Goodwins and be all over the town. Thomas had been pedalling hard and was heaving when he arrived. Dumping his bike he walked to the front door and was surprised when he couldn't get in. He had another go at the handle, rang the bell, and looked through the letter box. A middle-aged Dobermann called Maximus was at the end of the hall looking back at him. Nothing else happening except the beat of a grandfather clock. He stood up and looked at his watch; strange they were all out, but he was early. Maybe they'd taken his grandfather to the specialist? As he passed the garage a glance confirmed it, it was without its usual blue Ford.

He disappeared around the back of the house, up an alley where it was always raining, even when it wasn't (some sort of ball-cock stuck in the attic, no one had bothered with it for years). The back door was also locked; he peered through a window and could smell the meat. Newspapers were piled everywhere, at the side of the fridge and on top of it. Max was back in his basket by the Aga, plus there were two other baskets containing Jack Russells. The one with the cataract looked up but didn't seem to recognise him, didn't consider him worth barking at either.

A chunk of birds took off, ravens in elms older than the house. Thomas looked around with a slight feeling of unease. He didn't like this locked-door and letter-box business, it was too reminiscent of a fear he had, half a lifetime ago. He put it out of his mind, and deciding to wait in his workshop, set off through a vegetable garden policed by grapefruit domes on the ends of sticks.

A long time ago, he thought it must have been a long time ago, this isolated building was brewery to the house. He pushed at a door with rusted hinges, full of woodworm and key-holes. Inside was a deep stench of must, flagstones and beams, and walls with some good-quality moulds. Here and there strands of lost ivy came in through the roof and hung down looking anaemic. They made beer in here and maybe it was the ancient yeast spores you could smell? Thomas adored this decrepit utility and had taken advantage of his grandfather's illness to acquire it, gradually extirpating the gardening tools and moving his equipment in by a process of stealth. Although there was electricity he preferred a more traditional illumination, and he struck a match and the brewery warmed in the glow of a paraffin lamp.

You got a better look at it now and everywhere you looked there was stuff. An enormous bench occupied one wall, a vice either end and an astonishing clutter in between. Wires, batteries, components, pieces of pipe, jars spilling bolts, tubs of grease, oil cans, hacksaw blades, rat-tailed files, flat files, and other files of other lengths. There were washers and screws and dozens of keys, old keys, useless keys, a key clenched in the smaller of the vices and presently halfway through getting filed.

At the end of the bench and in contrast to this confusion was a tall glass-fronted cupboard whose contents were displayed in good order. Furnished with jars and flasks, a pestle and mortar and bottles of soluble aspirin, it looked like someone enjoyed the fantasy of pharmaceuticals, except the chemicals in these pots were real. Crystals of potassium chlorate, potassium nitrate, manganese dioxide, bright yellow flowers of sulphur, charcoal raw, and charcoal already ground – they all shared a characteristic that wasn't immediately apparent – they were all potentially unstable and in the right conditions could be made to explode.

He adjusted the lamp and shadows reorganised as he moved to the back of the building. It was here he located his prized possession, oiled and immaculate; it stood on a table of its own looking like the insides of a peculiar clock. An engine of steel, with gleaming cog wheels, and cotton-covered wires feeding the word into a pair of beautiful electromagnets. He wound it once a week with a fat key, relishing the name stamped into its base plate: 'Tishman/Bracknell, Electrical & Telegraphic Manuft. Co. Springfield, Illinois, 1863.' This thing was ninety years old but could have been made yesterday. It was beautiful. And what it did was record Morse code.

The Tishman was given to him by his grandfather who had stored it in a cupboard for forty years. When the old man saw the transformation in the brewery he liked it almost as much as Thomas and offered to wire him up. There was now telegraphic communication between here and Walter's office, copper wires pyloned off a bay tree. Both ends could send, only this end receive. Transmission from the out-station (Walter) activated the clockwork driving a half-inch paper tape, any tape (Thomas made it himself), and as it went through, the magnets worked a bronze punch stamping the dots and dashes. Watching it chatter was joy (oh, the joy of that first day). It could record as fast as Walter could transmit, ten times faster if necessary. The only thing missing was its glass dome. Apparently they were meant to have domes.

Thomas checked the tape. Nothing on it. But wait a minute, what's this?

−... .−.. ..−. . −... . .−.. .−.. ...

'Bluebells'? What bluebells?

His fingers were poised on the transmission key to ask, but he didn't bother. Firstly, because he knew the out-station wasn't there, and second because it was probably some kind of code. Sometimes Walter transmitted in double-code, sometimes back-slang (it was another vernacular altogether), but like Morse, Thomas was fluent in both from the age of ten.

He was thinking about Enright again and that fucking stick. There had to be a way of avoiding it. Illness seemed to be the only exit; would Enright attack an asthmatic? He momentarily had an image of himself in an oxygen-tent, but decided it wouldn't make any difference. There was no way out. Best just to get in there, beg a bit and take it. Plus there was a certain upside to a caning, gave you a sort of status in the place, a distinction amongst one's peers . . .

The fog-horns were still bleating; it would be dark in less than an hour. He moved the lamp back to the bench and lit a candle to go with it. His eyes settled on the work in progress, a length of brass tube about the diameter of a ten-gauge shotgun. This was an 'experimental' scheduled for use on deep-water crabs. Hauling it up, he unscrewed the end and peered into it like a telescope. Midway down was a metal bulkhead with holes in it and electrical contacts soldered into place. He shoved it at the candle and got two pinpricks of light. This thing was an innovation, the first time he'd attempted to construct this type of bomb. It was easy enough with external batteries – anyone could do that – what he wanted was an 'integral unit', neat as a flashlight, with the power-source actually inside.

The pipe clattered back to the bench with problems left to solve. Munitions fascinated him, or more accurately, explosives fascinated him and he was capable of building some serious devices – not all that pimply bullshit with fireworks. These were proper petards; get these bastards wrong and you're dead.

His speciality was underwater work and he thought he might as well use the time to knock up an aquatic fuse or two. These were standard detonators, simple electrical switches utilising soluble aspirin for service in rock pools. They could be timed to trigger anywhere between ten and sixty seconds depending on how thin you shaved the aspirin. Once in water they effervesced; once used, the spring from a cheap pen snapped contacts in a waterproof tube, six volts slammed into a resistor and a hot fuse glowed in the heart of Thomas's primary mixture. At a fathom the explosion was considerable. But these things were tiresome to make and you broke more than you got.

Opening the pharmacy he shook out a few tablets preparing to drill holes in them. It required a 1/32nd-inch watchmaker's drill almost as fragile as the aspirin itself.

'What are you doing?' He heard himself ask the question at least twice before it stopped him drilling. 'What are you doing in here, drilling a hole in a fucking pill?'

Focus on the question had the effect of an awakening. What he was doing of course was throwing time away, and wasn't this precisely the time he'd been waiting for? All previous attempts had been thwarted by the eyes – they were always watching him – maybe this was the best opportunity he was ever going to get? If he could get into the house he'd have the freedom of it; maybe today was the day he was destined to find the key?

A rush of excitement made him careless; he was already halfway out the door. Just keep it calm, will you? Keep it calm and you won't make mistakes. Retracing steps he killed the candle and retrieved the key from the vice. Its number was known by heart, Yale 0500, a configuration that for many months had been his not insignificant obsession.

He hurried back through the cabbage stalks and made a fast circuit of the house. Nothing on the south side. Up the alley in the rain he saw a window, half open and the only way in. Immediate problems. Although accessible via the 'office' roof, it was his father's bedroom and he never went in there, not ever, even through the door . . .

If he thought about it a moment longer he'd have junked it, but he didn't think about it and fifteen seconds later he was up the wall and on the tiles moving north. This part of the building featured an ugly Victorian castellation, but the windowsills were wide, and feet first through the battlements it wasn't difficult to slide down and obtain a perch.

He could feel the oppression of the room from even out here. It smelt of war and rugby balls – hyperbole of course – but that's how he thought of his father, a brute rushing the enemy in a sporting shirt. Unlike Thomas, his father had gone to a toff public school, Rugby as a matter of fact, and the disadvantages were apparent. His attitude towards almost everything was superior and aggressive. Like Walter, he fought the Germans, but paradoxically always said, 'The Germans had the right idea.' Thomas didn't know what the idea was, but if his father liked it, it was almost certain to be a bad one.

He climbed in and stood there in the awful gloom. What if he opened the door and 'Robbie' was out there waiting? He'd run his head up the corridor like a fucking medicine-ball. The consideration was irrational and he knew it. But his discomfort in here put out those kind of thoughts. This wasn't an attractive room. A monstrous wardrobe dominated all. Two sets of oars were stacked in a corner, signed by muscular contemporaries (Rob had rowed at Henley), and in another corner a small basin sported a nail brush and shaving tools. There was a black eiderdown on a single bed. And next to it on a table, the vague graphite-like sheen of a .32 calibre Beretta automatic.

Thomas crossed the carpet on toes trying not to leave prints. For as long as he could remember his parents had slept at opposite ends of the property, he in here, and her far down the other end with no explanations given.

He stepped out into the corridor quietly sealing the door. Just enough light left in the windows to see where he was going. He felt like a stranger in a strange house. Sounds he never bothered with flourished in the silence. He could hear water hissing in the attic and at least four different alarm clocks. Left to itself, the house seemed to have reorganised its priorities. Cigarettes were no longer part of the general atmospheric ingredient, they *were* the ingredient. There was as much nicotine in the air as meat and dog meat and dog.

Passing his mother's room there was a variation of carpet, blue into green, and he turned off into a thin passageway with no lampshade leading to his grandfather's office. Three stairs up to the door, he hardly dared expectation to meet the challenge. For months he'd been working at different keys, creeping along here with fistfuls of butchered Yales, had swivel on a few, but there was always that final obstructive tumbler. Fumbling in his pocket he produced the freshly engineered key, repeatedly in and out of the vice – he had high hopes for this one, last attempt it twisted midnight through six. All he needed now were maybe three more elusive little hours.

He stuck it in and when the fucker made ten he stood there with an assembly of unexpected feelings that added up to something approaching disappointment. Getting this far was little more than a re-establishment of the distance yet to go. He pushed at the door and it creaked open. Deep shadows and gone-out cigars. Outside fog spilled over the garden wall. He could just about make out shapes on the desk, the typewriter, Morse key, and a lamp with a green glass shade. Although he didn't really want the light he had to turn it on for the search, and as he did any residual anti-climax evaporated as quickly as it had come.

There was the prize, or rather promise of the prize, a pair of old oak filing cabinets stuffed with every secret his grandfather possessed. It was pointless trying them, they were always locked, pushed-in Unions at the top right-hand corner, 6631 and 8658 respectively. Once, for one astonishing minute, he'd had access to those drawers. He couldn't remember why he was in the room or why his grandfather had left it. But he got into one of the files. It was pale green, melon-coloured, how could he forget, and inside were about two hundred women with their genitals. Tits the size of buckets. Black women with bums. There was a nude black with old-fashioned boots and her arse in the air, wearing a feathered hat. There were women in here bending over settees and all you could see was their harris and their hat. Almost all these pictures were hand-coloured, Edwardian kind of stuff and the most remarkable photographs Thomas had ever seen. He was barely eleven at the time, and though he realised they were amazing, to be perfectly frank they didn't actually make a lot of sense. It wasn't until a year or two later, after discussions with Maurice, that he understood what this was. This was pornography, the most wonderful of secrets, unbelievably forbidden photographs that he would have swapped for God.

By now he'd completed a frenzied search of the desk and got nothing. His thoughts were blowing about like leaves. If it wasn't in here, where was it? The question was as daft as its answer. Of course it wasn't in here. People take important keys with them. If it was anywhere it was going to be on the same ring that his grandfather used to lock the door. He was on his way instantly, back up the corridor, stairs in twos, heading for his grandfather's bedroom. Since Walter'd got sick he'd slept up here, a room with no carpet and a gigantic iron bed . . .

Thomas barged into the darkness without thinking, made a dash across the boards and stopped so suddenly it hurt his feet. His grandfather was on his back on the bed, fully dressed with hands folded across his chest and looking quite seriously dead. Had they 'laid him out' already? Is that why they'd gone out, to talk to an undertaker? The room was so dark it was difficult to see. He crept forward and leant over the bed, peering hard through the dozen inches that separated their faces. Fucking hell, he was dead all right, one eye open and a face the colour of slush. Hair leapt all over the pillow exposing his dome like a yid's hat. Thomas could hardly breathe. Nothing in the room was moving except the wheels inside an alarm clock. It was half-past five and his grandfather was dead. He continued staring, wondering what he was supposed to do. Then, to his horror, the right eyelid slid down over the ball as though he were winking. That broke the spell. Thomas lunged back, paralysed with terror. This was the most horrible thing he'd ever seen in his life. For an instant he felt like shouting – flee the room shouting all the way out into the fucking fog. He knew that corpses are capable of extraordinary feats. His best friend, Maurice Potts and a vicar's son, said they'd been known to fart in transit, blow off as they entered the ovens. He'd even heard you have to shave some of them, but he'd never heard of one winking before. As the shock settled he said a prayer. He said, 'Lord accept him into your court with praise.' He couldn't think of anything else, couldn't weep uncontrollably either, which surprised him. But he did feel sad, sad mostly for his mother. After all this was her only dad.

When he got off his knees he noticed coins on the table, also a key. He picked it up, it was steel, not the one he wanted, but it looked familiar. What was this? Still wondering he stuck it in his pocket, his pupils now adjusted to the darkness.

One of Walter's eyelids was half up; they weren't supposed

to do that. Shuffling the coins he selected a pair of pennies (large copper discs in those days) and leaning in he carefully positioned them in the old man's eye sockets. Fuck me, he looked twice as dead now, didn't he? Fucking horrible. Should he still search the room? No, and he shook his head in agreement. He couldn't do it, not with his grandfather so recently died, and he retreated backwards into the silence preparing himself for what might be the next best thing. If this was its key, already back in his hand, he'd hit the sideboard and get into that ebony box. There were keys in there, he'd seen them less than a year ago, maybe even duplicate keys to the cabinets?

Were it not for his grandfather's death his good fortune would have meant elation. Since Christmas he'd been after another go at the living room, but until now a thorough search had been impractical. He was watched all the time. He knew they were watching even when they pretended not to. They were concerned with his obsession for prying. 'Why can't you keep out of other people's things?' they said. But he could not, nor would not stop.

He was back at the outskirts of his mother's bedroom with no previous, but the prospect looked too good to waste. He'd just have a quick frisk of the dressing table, put a time limit on it, and with this in mind he made an entrance.

This was the oldest and most ruptured part of the house, floorboards so warped the back end of the room was almost uphill. A double bed fought the tilt with bricks under its downside feet – that's how she kept it level. But you couldn't see the bricks. Everything was covered in rose candlewick.

The dressing table was Victorian mahogany, big as a shed, with filigree handles and enough mirror for a roomful to get their face in. As he opened the drawer he caught himself in it, the mirror, that is, and for an instant he looked like his mother. Resemblance was principally in the eyes and eyebrows, dark crescents and deep green. He never really thought about it before but perhaps once she'd been beautiful? A hint of her past wafted up from the drawer. Is that what all these empty bottles were about, once being beautiful? He extracted a stopper and sniffed it. It contained dead perfumes, sediments of forgotten days. Is that why she kept them, to remind herself perhaps that even she was once young and desired? Pushing deeper he found more bottles, and in another drawer, instruments of manicure, and some birthday cards stuck to the wood with nail varnish. The leaking bottle was blood red, called 'Coty'. It had a dried-out brush and he sniffed that too. It didn't smell of anything. Did his mother really wear red nail varnish and this cerise-coloured lipstick? The lipstick still smelt of his childhood, like a wonderful kind of soap they put kisses in. He could remember little of them now. He had a photograph of his mother sequestrated from somewhere on a previous search. She was dressed in shorts, about twenty years old, sitting on a rock with round sunglasses, white as icing-sugar. On the back it said: 'Bournemouth, Summer, 1938', seven years before Thomas was born. He wondered what she was thinking at the moment that picture was taken, what the sweet smile was for. He couldn't imagine. One of the curiosities of his mother was that she had no history – nothing of her past was up for discussion. She never talked about how things happened, how she met Rob, for example, or why she would have married a maniac like that. It was a different time, and she was a different woman from the girl in the photograph, that's for sure. Yes, she was beautiful then – hope in that smile – but in recent years she'd put on some girth, more necks, her expansion particularly noticeable since the controversy of the driving lessons.

Previous to petrol, she'd motored around on a bicycle, kept herself taut on a Raleigh with a basket on the front. But now the bike was shoved in the garage with flat tyres, barely used if at all. Last time she'd gone on it – and he couldn't remember why – the saddle practically vanished, a phenomenon that didn't go unnoticed by his father. 'Look at that saddle,' he said. 'Up her arse like a fucking suppository.' It was evident he didn't think much of her, said appalling things right in her face, like the earful she got when discarding this bicycle. 'You never get any exercise,' he said. 'Look at you, you're like a mountain now.'

It bounced off. She bought a Ford Anglia.

Rob didn't actually care about her arse, what he didn't like was her having a car. Virtually all communication was conducted thus, as though deep into argument, irrespective of whether they were arguing or not. (As a matter of fact, it was impossible for them to have an argument, neither would have noticed.) It seemed to Thomas that this reciprocal animosity was the gel that bonded them; if she couldn't have his love, she could at least have his rage, a tirade about the best she could get. And that's probably why she encouraged him to shout. Communists, students, and the unions were the commonest detonators. She planted them like cues in a crap theatrical. Plus the Labour Party. The Labour Party could bring him to his feet at the dinner table in a foaming apoplexy of mustard and cold beef. 'Let me tell you something about the fucking Labour Party,' he said. And he told you, and you listened. And if you dared tell him he'd already told you, he'd tell you again.

Mabs, for so she was called, had initiated and absorbed so much aggression over the years she was immune. The crust had thickened. Nothing got through. But you can't prune off bits and pieces of emotions you don't like and expect the rest to survive. Emotion covers all, that's the deal. Denial of certain unpleasant realities denies everything, and more than anything, the truth. This was constant war, and truth was the first casualty.

But ain't that life for everyone? Stuck in bullshit, talking the tosh like a TV? It certainly seemed so to Thomas, and either way, he was too much part of the picture to see anything else. In reality he never gave his domestic arrangements a second thought. This was the house he lived in, and they were the parents he lived with, and that was that.

He was looking at himself in the mirror again and couldn't help inventing another prayer. 'Lord, O Lord, receive him into your house with joy.' Still staring, he rose into a kind of religious ether, indulging the melancholy, allowing morbid thoughts to develop, and develop they did but in a most disturbing way. With Walter gone, who would be guardian of the pornography? His grandmother wouldn't want it. Neither would his mother. What would they do with it? Sure as hell they weren't going to give it to him. They'd probably sling it out like so much junk. What an awful thought. The prospect was actually alarming. Maybe today really was the day he would have to find the key. So what was he doing, lurking around in here, sniffing a dressing table?

Suddenly he wasn't in there any more.

Embers were still glowing in the grate but it was cold downstairs. He added coal from a copper scuttle and carefully locked the living-room door. A sixty-watt bulb got wasted by its altitude: this was a dull room with an oil by someone who couldn't paint over the fireplace. Everything else was a zoo of reproduction furniture. For some reason his mother couldn't take antiques, they were disappearing all over the house. Genuine walnut would get replaced with a genuine-walnut finish, a modern copy of the furniture she already had. It was as inexplicable as it was despicable, it was also the reason Thomas could hardly get into his bedroom. Anything that got the Mark from Mabs, he'd do his best to haul up.

One of the few original pieces left was the sideboard in here, its intrinsic mediocrity guaranteeing its permanence.

Plus it belonged to Walter, and he liked it, probably because he made it. Thomas went for it with the key, and as hoped for it twisted. Within seconds he had the ebony box out and up on the nearest table. Walter had won prizes for carpentry and this was another example of his handiwork. Two feet by two feet by one foot with a brass plate on the top. He read its hieroglyphic: 'Walter Furseman, 14th London Signals, 1914.' Walter had made this box just before he'd taken off for France. Thomas eased the lid; it was better than he remembered, everything in tight little boxes and tobacco tins, everything fitted like a jigsaw.

He worked quickly, top layer out, tins opened, tipped into their lids. Such a cornucopia of objects appeared his hands began to shake. There were eight cigarette lighters in one tin alone. There were penknives, there were watches, wrist and pocket, tie pins and hat pins and here come some keys, quite useless, like a tiny bunch of musical notes. In bundles of fifty, there was every cigarette card W.D. & H.O. Wills ever issued: Big Ships and Cricketers and Moths. A wad of photographs came out, names he'd heard of were suddenly given faces: Ernie and Hilda Halfpenny; Uncle Stan in Togo Land with a fern behind his helmet (who would subsequently go into the toilet with cancer of the entire head). A photograph of Bob Knowles. Blocks of invitation cards, and foreign money, Belgian francs. And now medals, medals from the war on fragile rainbows, propelling pencils, pens the size of chisels, a box of wishbones, and a fifty-year-old silver tin containing a pellet of marzipan.

But no key.

The items continued to mass in front of him, so much it was difficult to classify objects of importance, those out or those that were coming out. By the time he reached the final layer he was opening boxes and operating cigarette lighters with the same hand.

The stratum he was now into evidently hadn't been touched for years. It had a good smell of old ink about it, a single big envelope and pair of tins covering the floor. First out was a lozenge-shaped container bearing Walter's initials and engraved with oak leaves, 'The Mystic Order Of The Veiled Prophets' completing the inscription. This was a high-quality item, you could tell as you touched it. Black velvet upholstered its interior, and inset, like presentation pieces, were two pairs of dividers and a gold ball-bearing. It was a weird-looking set whose function wasn't obvious: what was the relationship between these mathematical instruments and the gleaming ball?

He extracted it, it was substantial, big as an owl's egg and apparently solid gold. As he studied his reflection the ball suddenly leapt in the air, clattered to the table, and reassembled itself into a crucifix with a diamond at its hub. Its mutation was awesome, like some shocker out of the Bible. For an instant Thomas thought he was having a miracle. The jewel glistened like the Ruthless Eye, and he put distance on it, stood gaping in a state of dread. What if he'd let something out, unleashed the vapours of his grandfather? Was he now a servant of the Prophets? The only one he could think of was Amos; was this his Orb? He stared, waiting for something else to happen. What happened was a fog-horn. Persuading himself at last that the cross meant no immediate evil, he picked it up again between thumb and some other finger. An examination of hinges and pliant arms drove out the holy phantoms. What this was, at least what he thought it was, was some kind of religious training ball. What it was actually for he didn't know, and was now too fascinated by its ingenuity to care. Somewhere behind the diamond was a mechanism of spring-loaded cams designed to trigger at the slightest pressure. It was a masterpiece of ecclesiastical engineering and he worked it several times. It had a satisfying click. Finally crushing it, he vacillated over keeping it, but a gnat of annoying conscience intervened and he reluctantly put it back in its box.

Next box out was waxed cardboard, full of used cartridge cases, .303 and 7.63 Mauser. All dated 1913. These may well be useful, and seeing as no one else wanted them he emptied the lot into his pocket.

No hope of the key, and nothing left now but the envelope. He approached this last item with a wane of enthusiasm, concerned about the tedium of packing it all in again. But the stamps were interesting, so was the postmark, good-quality 1931 stuff. It was addressed to his grandfather, who at that time lived in London EC2.

Thomas wasn't ready for this. Feet first, she came out in a pair of socks, wild veins and tattoos on her thighs. One thing can't be overstated here, this was an enormous woman, legs like people, she was gargantuan, look at those tits, her nipples were the size of tits, and stuck out of her arse was the head of a live duck.

This picture was entitled *The Temptress*.

Thomas couldn't believe it, of course, it couldn't be real. It had to be just the head of a duck, stuffed, on a stick? Yet in the next photograph she'd managed to get up a tree and the duck was still in there looking down with its beak open like it didn't like heights.

Eve and the Forbidden Apple.

The apple didn't actually appear until the next and last picture, clamped in its beak and offered by the duck. Reaching up into the tree for it was a thin man, age about the same as the postmark, hair ironed flat to his head with an unguent and a not entirely convincing grin. But no one was looking at that. He was animal-rigged, huge balls needing a tidy scrotum, and this one hung like a sporran.

The picture was entitled *Adam Takes Her Sin*, and the man in it was unquestionably his grandfather.

A kaleidoscope of questions, not least of which, what happened to the duck? He went back to the envelope, no more photographs, but a wad of papers. Typed in black, and occasionally red with lots of revisions and crossings-out, this seemed to be part of a manuscript, twenty pages held together with rusty staples . . .

'Chapter One' (and that's all this was), 'Jonnie Thomas's School Days'. This boy, Jonnie Thomas, arrived with his trunk at a railway station in the middle of nowhere, winter rooks over the farms, wondering what his new school was to be like, and who would pick him up. It was 1912, and he was fourteen . . .

Car?

Thomas got the freeze and listened and he was right. A car was coming up the drive, sounded like the Ford and he leapt up and killed the light instantly. It wasn't a long wait for a key in the front door and coats off in the hall. His grandmother, mother and sister arrived. Nothing said, but he knew it was them; he didn't need their voices but got them anyway as a second later the dogs arrived in a ritual explosion of joy.

Leaping and licking he could hear that Jack Russell, levitating in sycophancy, yapping the glad tidings, its entire body wriggling in airborne ecstasy. It was his mother's favourite and Thomas loathed it. It was useless, lick anything. It spent most of its day licking her feet, and when these weren't available, hours licking walls.

Coal light the only light in the room now. He waited with eyes on the door knob, knew it would twist, and here come the footsteps and it did. His mother rattled the door, no luck, and she knocked at it.

'Dad? Is that you in there?'

Thomas shook his head. He knew they'd all come up and have a go, all ask the same question, and all have to go away.

'Wally?'

This was the name his grandmother used for his grandfather. Her name was Ethel. Sometimes she called him Wol.

'Wol? Is that you in there?'

More swivelling of the knob followed by a brief exchange of possibilities. (a) He was in there, and the door was locked from that side, (b) He wasn't in there, and the door was locked from this? They fixed on the latter as most likely, although they couldn't understand why he'd done it. And neither could Thomas, he thought they were stupid.

'I'll go and look upstairs,' said Bel. She was Thomas's sister, she was sixteen. But first she needed a pee.

They vanished up the hall and Thomas had to move like a demon. No time to repack the box in any decent sequence – speed was the order, he literally threw it in. The lid wouldn't shut but that didn't matter: now he had the sideboard key he could take care of that later. Creeping back to the door he stuck an ear on it and listened. Nothing. A plan was formulating and he was already in it. He unlocked the door and was about to travel when he remembered, Christ Almighty! the photographs were still out.

A relock. Gathering the lot, including the manuscript, they returned to the envelope and then down the front of his trousers. Back to the door and the key took another twisting. He opened it no more than an inch.

A wireless had gone on in the kitchen. Radio Newsreel. The coast seemed favourable. He followed a foot into the hall and as he did there was a horrible scream upstairs. Before its resonance was absorbed he was again in the living room assisting the door with a silent slam. The scream repeated, more of a yell, he realised his sister had found the corpse. Simultaneously, there was action out of the kitchen, scuttling feet as his mother and grandmother hit the stairs. It couldn't have been better for Thomas, part one of the plan was up and running, and so was he, up the hall and out through the front door.

Fog had thickened around the house, cold and glum. He made a yard or two and looked up at his grandfather's room. A light had gone on and you could hear the conflab from out here. His sister was screeching, Thomas didn't get it. No one loved his grandfather as much as he, no one else could read Morse, so what was the fuss about? He waited a while and looked through the letter box (that same feeling), they were already coming downstairs. As soon as his mother arrived he put on his cycle-clips, rang the door bell, and started panting. It was two miles, eight hundred and fifty yards from his school.

She didn't believe one of them.

'What have you *done*?' she demanded, lividly opening the door. And if such an action wasn't possible then neither was Thomas's expression. He walked in, making sure they saw the cycle-clips, overdoing it a bit on the breathing. There was quite a lot of emotion about, weeping up the hall. He looked quizzically at his sister.

'Is something the matter?' he asked, balancing innocence with concern and failing at both.

'Don't pretend you don't know,' said his mother.

'What?' said Thomas, and two paces towards his sister, he again asked, 'What?'

'He sat up with coins in his eyes,' she howled. 'You put coins in his eyes.'

'*Me*?'

'It was *you* in there, wasn't it?' said his grandmother.

'In where?' said Thomas.

'In the living room. Why were you in there? Why did you lock the door?'

'I've just come home from school,' he said, taking off his hat to prove it. 'Science Club.'

'The boy's a liar,' said his grandmother.

'He sat up,' wailed Bel.

'Is something the matter with Grandad?'

His mother responded with an angry shake of her head.

'He's alive, is he?' said Thomas, genuinely surprised.

'Of course he's alive, he's had his *pill*.'

'What on earth do you think you were doing in there?' said his grandmother.

'I haven't been in anywhere,' said Thomas.

'Don't lie,' said Bel, still crying. 'We saw your bike.'

That blew it. He opened his mouth to say something but said something else.

'I have to admit, I was here briefly,' he said. 'But I couldn't get in.'

'The boy's a liar,' his grandmother said again.

'I might be a lot of things,' said Thomas, moving about with affront, 'but a liar, I am not.'

No one bothered to listen. They'd had their go and attention returned to Bel. She was escorted into the kitchen to be fed tea and Ethel and the dogs went with her.

Thomas was poised to follow when he noticed a business card on the hall table. He was trained to read at a distance: 'J.T. Brackett, Private Investigator (thirty years in the Met).' His mother saw him looking and snatched it away together with a blue handbag.

'Where have you been?' said Thomas.

'Nowhere,' she said, disappearing into the kitchen. 'Nowhere.'

The grandfather clock struck seven. Thomas tramped after her looking at his watch. It was six. Even the clock tells lies in this house.

THE BUSINESS

Friday was a bad day, Enright caned him. Saturday was worse. On Saturday he had to get up and meet the newspaper train. Rob came around the door at 5 a.m. He wore a surgical-collar and shades – 5 a.m. I'm telling you – he came into the bedroom with cream-coloured hair and brown bifocals, and when the light went on you sat up and saw your shock in them.

Why Rob wore sunglasses in the middle of the night wasn't questioned. Rob was six foot and combed, formerly blond but greying now. He had enormously developed arms from lifting newspapers, and it was newspapers that shagged his neck. His head came out of the collar with a curious resignation, like he'd been born with it. He was deft, but it impacted his movements, gave him a weird gait. If he wanted to look anywhere but straight ahead, his whole body was required to turn.

Thomas descended into the kitchen and his father boiled the milk. Rob always took his tea with boiled milk – it was a habit he'd acquired in India. Thomas drank the tea with a hot feeling travelling down from his head; it was bilious, a fist in the gut. He hated newspapers, and he hated this – even the fucking Dobermann was still asleep. Rob went out to fire up the Wolsey and two minutes later they were in it, flat-out through the silent town and heading for the railway station.

Neither had spoken yet.

Drizzle around street lights in last night's fog. A row of gas lights and a Morris van parked in the station yard with 'Furseman's Wholesale Newsagents' painted on its side. It was dawn, and a cold wind was coming down the track from Ramsgate.

Twenty minutes to six.

'Rob's boys' were already on the platform, barrows ready. The only thing that ever dared to be late around here was the train. Rob's boys were in fact Bill Bing, thirty, sucking a Woodbine, and Arthur, sixty, half dead.

He said good morning to Rob and got no answer.

If the train was late, and this morning it was, Rob would get on the wristwatch. Anger was instant and woe betide any railway worker in the vicinity. He'd give them what he called a 'hammering', get into a strut offering 'hammerings' up and down the platform, sometimes to passengers who had nothing to do with it. It was probably quite unnerving if you saw him coming – a muscular man in dark glasses and a surgical collar – claiming the property and telling you off before dawn. (The reason the train was late was the laziness of everybody on earth, drivers, coalmen, guards, but above all those indolent bastards at Margate. They took ten minutes to unload a wagon – Robbie could do it in two).

You heard it in the rails before it arrived; the train came in dragging its weather. *The Maid of Kent*, choking on coal-fat and enormous asthma, sparks heaving out of its chimney and a face in the driver's cab catching an earful from Robbie as he went past. Trucks the size of houses followed, thirty-eight-tonners with wooden doors. The name of every town in North Kent was written on their sides – Bromley, Chesterfield and Swalecliff, Herne Bay – they kept on coming, and kept on going, Rob started shouting, and everyone had to run after Broadstairs.

The driver had purposefully overshot his brake-line. This happened not infrequently and it was done to annoy Rob.

When the train stopped and the doors opened, Rob rushed the wagon like he was leading a boarding party. Bundles of *Telegraph, Mirror, Financial Times*, sixty pounds apiece, trussed with sisal, on fire with their weight in your hands. Thomas could barely drag the bastards to the barrows. Rob came out with one at the end of each arm, sometimes with a 'spare' in his armpit, totalling a hundred and eighty pounds of newsprint. Arthur was at the other end of it with a face the colour of a Stilton rind, buckling under the onslaught – how could he survive another morning of this? Rob plunged deeper into the wagon, arms going like cranes, moving at the velocity of an armed robber. He was out-sweating them, out-lifting them, out-loading them, his personal quest to be the single greatest unloader on earth.

Meanwhile, Bill Bing had been ferrying barrows to and from the waiting room. The last load was now loaded and Rob was back on the platform, hauling up and off. It took clenched teeth and every ounce of Thomas's body weight to get his barrow on its wheels. Fighting it up, with a foot on its axle, was an effort equivalent to digging a hole in one with an enormous shovel. Sometimes it threw him into the air.

Pulling, rather than pushing it, he went after Rob like a dwarf in a rickshaw, speed was of the essence, size was no excuse. The temperature rocketed as Thomas laboured into the waiting room; a potbellied stove stuffed with brimstone put out the heat. The premises were tall and gas-lit, wooden benches either side, and a parquet floor filling the rest of it that no one had polished for fifty years. Christ forbid anyone should be sitting on the benches. From eight minutes past six, to forty-five minutes past the same hour, these benches belonged to Rob.

And so did the floor.

The bundles were split. Rob used a razor-sharp carpet shiv with a blade like an eagle's beak – severing fast, just below the knot, and ripping out the string that was to be used again.

There were about a dozen titles, some in huge numbers like the *Telegraph* and *Express*, and some just a few, like *Lloyd's List* and the *Manchester Guardian*. The counting started now. There was a board with the names of sixteen newsagents, and columns of numbers designating who got what. By now one or two of the local retailers had probably turned up – Tucker, a squat bloke with a pointed head and nothing much in his mouth but a pair of front teeth, and Eric Stopper, whose shop was opposite the station . . .

Rob was counting and no one spoke. They stood at the sidelines terrified he'd make a mistake, and then they'd have to tell him, 'I'm sorry, Rob, I'm two *Sketch* short.' And he'd rear in disbelief, and they'd get wrath, and on one occasion, the Bunny got knuckle, and that's why they were silent and let him count.

The piles were growing on the benches and it was Thomas's job to knot the recycled strings. At three yards each they hung over the arm of a bench. The next and most loathsome process in this most loathsome of mornings was to begin.

They were going to tie these fuckers up.

Walter had taught Thomas the 'packer's knot'. Its mechanics were special, known only to the newspaper trade. Like a garrotte it couldn't slip, only get tighter and tighter. Thomas could tie a parcel so tight you couldn't get a fingernail under the string. But the problem with the packer's knot was the hatred in the sisal. To do it right would all but cut your hand in half. Bing and Arthur put on the glove. And so did Thomas. The only one to shun protection was Rob. His right hand was like a hoof. Years of packing had created a six-inch callus down the karate edge, split like concrete, and the colour of a cockerel's foot. Any tissue still living had escaped round the back of the bone.

A last wrench on the final knot and Rob led the charge into the station yard. Sudden cold, harsh in the lungs, and half a ton of prints crushing the Wolsey's suspension. Boot slammed, and doors slammed, and a hair-raising race with the dawn to a dozen different newsagent's shops.

Rob's maniacal pace made little sense to Thomas. This was a commuter town, and in half an hour's time people in bowler hats would buy these papers and take them all the way back to London. What was the point of that? Why couldn't they buy them when they got there, or sell them the fucking things on the train? It was a question Thomas never asked. They had to get to these shops before the commuters did and that's about all there was to that. Arthur and Bill went round the town in the van. Rob and Thomas made the 'country run'.

They still hadn't spoken yet.

It wasn't until the last delivery was made about a mile from North Foreland lighthouse that Rob might light a cigarette and talk. If he did it was most likely to be about something he'd seen headlined in one of the morning's newspapers – Archbishop Makarios, for example. Rob's neckwear precluded any eye contact, which suited Thomas because he knew what was coming, had heard it before and wanted to go to sleep. No chance. Rob hit the Rothman's and put out the smoke. Apparently there was some murderous Greek on the loose in Cyprus called Archbishop Makarios and Rob wanted him hanged. Makarios led a group of anti-British terrorists on the island called EOKA and he wanted all of them hanged too. In Rob's view there was little social, economic, or political problem that couldn't be solved with the rope . . . hang the bastard . . . hang the Irish . . . he could solve the Irish problem overnight . . . get into Dublin and string up some Micks . . .

'*They* wanna get tough?' he said. 'Well, let-me-tell-you-something, *I* wanna get tough. And I'm just the boy.'

In Rob's lexicon of jurisprudence capital offences were myriad: you could get hanged for almost anything, hanged for vegetarianism. Endless streams tramped to Rob's scaffold, Communists, trade unionists, the Labour Party – he hanged the lot of them, and it wasn't even 7 a.m.

'I'd like to see that fucking idiot bishop Makarios hang.' A fist came off the steering wheel for a thumb to peck at his chest. 'And if they want someone to do it, *I'm the boy*.'

Rob was the boy all right, sixty up the Margate Road heading back into town. First light on the slates and an awful sick feeling in Thomas's gut. Fresh newspaper has a sickening aroma, stuff of the night, and to Thomas it smelt of insomnia realised.

'Out of the fucking way!' A milkman got full horn. 'Lazy cunt, he's home by eight, I work all the hours God sends.'

And it was true, Robbie did put in the hours. Up at five seven days a week, even Sundays when he didn't have to. He had nothing else in his life but this business, no holidays, and no friends. His management of Furseman's happened suddenly some years ago when Wol first got ill. Rob turned up out of the blue – or rather South Wales, or Fulham in London – Thomas wasn't sure which. 'He's not driving my car,' said Walter. But Walter had no choice and they all moved into the big house and Rob drove the Wolsey. That didn't mean to say that Walter had to talk to Rob, or even acknowledge his existence, and he never did.

Thomas wished they were going home, breakfast and bed, but first there was some business at the depot. Furseman's was situated at the dark end of a yard around the back of the high street. Its entrance was piled with SOR (sale or return newspapers), hundreds upon hundreds of bundles reaching to the roof of a corrugated-iron porch. It was a sort of cellar without stairs; even so you had a feeling of descending as you went into it. It stank of magazines and sisal, there were no windows, and not once since its construction had it known daylight. Three other businesses operated in its precincts. There was a greengrocer above who kept out of the way (Rob wouldn't let him use the toilet), a bicycle seller and repairman called Monkton, who had lock-ups, and opposite him at the other side of the yard, underground, a fortune teller called Madame Olanda.

Olanda worked her Ball in a shack on the seafront next door to a fish-fryer and it cost five shillings to get in. She had a picture of the All-Seeing Eye in the window and a photograph of a celebrity who had visited Thanet. She wore a turban and drank too much and her face was the colour of a brick. It was only in summer months, when some tourist might wheeze by for a reading, that she sat in her hut. But this time of the year she was in her vaults, underground, and here she resided alone, spending most of her life in darkness, like a tongue.

Madame Olanda thought her dead husband lived on in a pigeon, at least, his spirit lived in one. Her problem (and everybody else's) was which one? So she attracted them all and that's why she put bread on everybody's roof. There was bread on top of Monkton's garages, and this pissed the bicycle repairman off because the pigeons shat on his bikes. On any day there were hundreds of husbands in the yard, but complaint was futile. To communicate you had to go and shout down her grid . . .

'For Christ's sake, there's bread everywhere. They *can't eat it*,' said Monkton, and he was right. There was so much bread on his roof grass grew out of it. It would have taken every pigeon in Kent to clear his loaves, and they didn't want it. She'd built up bread outside the foyer of her subterranean hovel. There were abutments of bread, thousands of decaying grey-green crusts stacked a foot high like a wall.

Because of the threat to her husband, Olanda hated cats

and put curses on them. And it was said (when she could) she'd catch them in hessian bags and throw them off the jetty. Local cats were often missing and on occasion someone might call the police. But they couldn't nail her, couldn't prove it and couldn't get her out. She was always in her psychic hole.

Pigeons took off as Rob turned the Wolsey into the yard, headlights on although there was just enough daylight around to see. Suddenly he hit the brakes, tore at the door and exploded out with the engine left running.

It was still night under the depot's awning. Madame Olanda was partially concealed behind the SORs. She wore a wool kaftan, high-heeled slippers and a turban the colour of methylated spirits, and what she was doing was spraying down the newspapers with a hosepipe. It wasn't the first time she'd done it, but it was the first time she'd been caught. She did it because she didn't like Rob. When Walter ran the business he used to give her free back-numbers and went down her basement and possibly had some kind of awful relationship with her. As soon as Rob arrived – irrespective of what else she was getting – she no longer got the magazines.

She heard him coming and spun around and started hosing him like the bundles. This wasn't a good idea, and she realised it and ran with her water spouting. This wasn't wise either. She should have dropped it but foolishly didn't and didn't get very far. Rob seized the pipe and hauled her back, all but had her off her feet. She said he was a cunt and aimed a stream of water into his face with a thumb on the nozzle to increase pressure. There was a brief but frantic contest for the end of the pipe. The advantage was quickly Rob's, and he was now hosing her with his lower teeth exposed in a horrible malice of pleasure, saturating the bitch, how do you like it? She didn't, and got a knee up, missed his balls and he knocked her turban off. To Thomas's astonishment she was totally bald. Howling mad, she went in again, grabbed him

49

by the surgical-collar and somehow got on his back, kneeling there, like a rucksack.

'You fucking witch.'

And they spun around with water spraying out of their conflict, centrifugal-force finally throwing her feet out. His rigid neck and the pressure on it seemed to impede him; he was trying to punch her off but it was difficult to land one on something that high up. But then he caught her, and she flew backwards clutching her tit. She went down; he'd winded her with a shattering right hook. Shades askance and heaving, he stepped back, and for a moment Thomas thought he was going to put the boot in. He re-hosed her instead, and laughing loud and hysterically, drove her up the yard like litter. Wailing imprecations, she got back on her feet and made off through the sodden loaves.

'You'll die in the month you were born,' she screamed.

'Not as dead as you,' said Rob. 'I'll dance on your fucking grave.' And he did a little dance on his toes there and then in demonstration.

'Beware of November,' she shouted.

'Wrong month,' retorted Rob. 'Get back in your hole.'

Clutching her turban like a crash helmet, Olanda retired to her basement without looking back. Rob killed the tap; whipped out his blade and severed the hose, launching half of it after her like a dead snake. He was grinning maniacally but said nothing, returned to the depot and went about the locks. As he got a key into the second, Olanda reappeared from her hovel with her hat back on. She was carrying a large chunk of concrete which she elevated above the turban before slinging it through the windscreen of the fucking Wolsey.

It took out the lot.

Suddenly there was no windscreen and no Olanda either. Rob went after her like there was a murder coming up, but the barricades had already gone into place. He pummelled her door but, like everyone else, was soon on his knees and forced to shout down her grid. Her appearance under the bars at the bottom of it inflamed him more, and this obviously was her intention.

'Beware of July,' she said, pointing a finger at his face.

'You half-witted fucking gypsy,' hollered Rob.

'The third Sunday,' she croaked with some pleasure, and disappeared.

'You ugly bastard witch,' he bellowed. 'Granite cunt! You'll have to come out sooner or later, and when you do, I'll be waiting for you!'

Threat delivered he returned to the car and pulled out the offending rock. It must have weighed twenty pounds. Backing off, he took the measure of it, and then rushed violently up the yard, bowling it like an enormous cricket ball at her front door.

It landed on the door bell which rang in curious anti-climax, but the frame shook, and the concrete shattered, and Rob motored away looking reasonably satisfied.

Thomas was still watching in amazement. As he turned to follow his father into the depot he noticed someone was watching him. There was a weaselish-looking geezer at the mouth of the yard, about sixty years old. He wore a mackintosh and a tweed hat, and trousers tucked into his socks. Thomas didn't know why but he was immediately suspicious of him. He looked right into the boy's eyes before pedalling away.

It started to drizzle, quite hard.

Thirty minutes later they were hunched in the rain doing sixty up Pyson's Road. Thomas thought loss of the windscreen might have slowed Rob down, but it had little effect. This was open farmland with feeding gulls and it felt like sitting with them on a cliff. It was easier for the driver, he was behind shades, but Thomas could hardly see. As he drove, Rob cursed the mystic; he had plans for that bitch. You could tell what he was thinking, his thoughts were in his fist, clenching spontaneously as he relived that difficult backward punch. It was Olanda's lucky day. If she'd taken full force of the same thing from the front she'd never have got up again . . .

Black fields turned into clumps of abandoned woodland and the road divided into a choice of towns. What happened now was half expected. Rob's gigantic thumb hit the indicator. He pulled over, telling Thomas he was taking the Ramsgate Road and he could walk home from here. This had happened before, always at this junction. What was his father's business at seven o'clock in the morning in Ramsgate?

'I've got to get this windscreen fixed.'

Maybe he did, but it wasn't broken last week, nor the week before that, so where was he going? Thomas didn't ask and got out and realised it was hardly raining.

'Did you shit in someone's hat?'

No pause.

'No.'

Rob was staring although you couldn't see his eyes, and a second or two later the Wolsey belched away. So, the school had spoken, and he was suspected; how much of a problem was that? Not much of one, he concluded, they had no proof. Even in the fullness of his rage Enright had made no accusation. His biggest problem was Thomas in the female toilet. Arseholes to it.

He was a mile from home and started walking. Hadn't made a dozen yards when a man with a bicycle broke cover rapidly from the trees, mounted his machine and rode off.

Thomas stared after him as he disappeared, travelling in the same direction as Rob. It was *him*, the weaselish-looking man with suspicious eyes he'd seen outside the yard. This time he hadn't looked at Thomas, but cycled off without a glance. Obviously caught unawares, he was forced to pedal towards Ramsgate pretending he wasn't interested – it was the oldest trick in the book.

But what did he want, who was he, and why was he following Thomas? The answer came almost before he'd asked the question. He was the 'Investigator'. Thomas couldn't remember the name on the card, but based on 'thirty years in the Met', had already assembled the implications. (a) They watched him all the time in the house, and (b) They were now having him followed outside of it by a professional.

But why?

What did they think he was going to do?

THE BOY POTTS

It could have been the same Saturday but in fact was several later. Thomas got on his bike and rode over to Potts' vicarage. It was a stale, leftover sort of day, leaves dragged in clusters by the wind. He pedalled through the deserted streets of St Peter's, a village named after the church that was almost the only thing in it. Virtually everything else was a cottage, at most a small villa, and almost everything was built of flint. The vicarage was an exception, a tall Victorian dwelling with melancholy windows, privet cutting out the light in downstairs rooms.

Thomas parked his bicycle, walked up the path and put two small taps into the knocker. The reason for his timidity answered the door. Fifty-five years old with violent eyebrows looking over his face: as expected, the Reverend Potts did not seem pleased to see Thomas. He was still chewing a mouthful, like cud, and had harboured a negative attitude towards this boy since he'd shot holes in his rhubarb with an air rifle.

Thomas waited for him to swallow before explaining he had an appointment with Maurice to play dwarfs in the attic.

'Dwarfs?'

'I meant, darts, sir,' said Thomas nervously.

'He's having his lunch,' said Potts.

Thomas said he'd wait outside but got ushered into the hall with all the usual get-thee-behind-me attitude he'd learnt to ignore. He always had a special face for Potts, a sort of daft grin signifying his awareness of suffering. Suffering was Potts' trade. You couldn't get a doughnut down without being told about the millions who hadn't got one. Potts reminded him they were still eating lunch and told Thomas to wait where he was. He got a nod in reply and the Reverend disappeared back into the stench of his kitchen.

If Potts didn't like Thomas, Thomas didn't like Potts. He was a typical self-righteous religious prat. Because of the lack of applicants he'd been accepted by the town council and got into speech days at schools. He thought Thomas was a malign influence on his son. But what he didn't realise was that the influence was the other way around. It was Maurice who taught Thomas to flob – and was trying to teach him to smoke – an expertise he had almost certainly acquired from his father. Nobody could have smoked as much as Vicar Potts, his fingers were tangerine to the knuckles. And he had a hacking cough, like one of those unfortunate dogs who've had their bark surgically removed. This house, as was Thomas's own, was always dense with cigarette smoke, a smell of ashtrays and unwashed things. Soiled items were hidden, no doubt of it. Thomas had a nose for that kind of thing.

He continued to wait, scrutinising the trash Potts had picked up in German East Africa. He'd been a missionary before the war and the natives had given him dried animal heads as symbols of their affection. The hall was decorated with shields and Senegalese crap – the back foot of an elephant filled with umbrellas, and a tusk that may well have come off the same animal. There were horrible elongated voodoo heads hacked out of black wood, a dagger, and a couple of spears. Along the picture rail there was a six-foot snake with stitches up its gut: Thomas couldn't believe the natives had really cared for him.

The rest of the walls were covered in pictures of religious maniacs in crisis – Ezekiel on the floor, Moses bent double –

the blind were opening their eyes and cripples tossing sticks away. There were ten miracles on one wall alone. At the end of the hall there was an impressive print of Jesus knocking on heaven's gate. It was called *Lux Mundi*. What was worrying about this picture was the obvious state of neglect of the entrance to paradise. All the hinges were rusted and the path overgrown. More disturbing was the ethic of the painting. It was the Son of God knocking at the door. If he had difficulties getting in, what about the rest of us . . .

A moment later Mrs Potts came out wearing oven-gloves. She was an ex-nurse and looked like one. She was followed by Maurice, a chubby boy with chewed fingernails and blond hair. Susan Potts was also of some weight, it widened her, a bra-strap showing through her blouse like a girder to keep her shoulder blades apart.

'We're having baked jam-roll,' she said. 'Would you like some?'

Thomas declined, scratching an ear; no way did he want to sit with the Vicar.

'I've already eaten, thank you.'

She smiled without meaning it, and informing Maurice she was about to serve, turned back with a pause at the door.

'How's your grandfather, Thomas?'

Thomas shook his head, didn't really know.

'He's having tests, Mrs Potts. They think he might have to have another operation.'

She absorbed this news nodding slowly and retreated into her kitchen.

'Come along, Maurice.'

Maurice repeated his mother's invitation, said it was raspberry. When this got another negative he also said he was going to be ages because they'd probably make him do the washing-up.

'I've got some photographs,' said Thomas, flashing his

envelope and instantly converting both their voices to whispers.

'What of?' said Maurice.

'A woman with a duck.'

'What?'

'Up her arse. You won't believe it.'

He didn't.

'Let's have a look?'

'Fuck off,' glared Thomas, teeth clenched and almost inaudible. 'I'll show you outside.'

'Pudding, Maurice,' ordered a voice from the kitchen, followed by the appearance of Vicar Potts' head.

'I'll wait in the orchard,' said Thomas, smiling somewhat obsequiously for the benefit of the head. And he edged backwards to the front door, Potts watching until he'd gone through it and it was again closed . . .

St Peter's Church was hundreds of years old, perhaps seven hundred, and like the little cottages in its shadow, built of flint.

Thomas walked around it towards Old Moules Orchard, eyes up at the menacing sky and looming tower. He had a feeling he was being watched, but churches always made him feel like that. He didn't like religion, hadn't liked it for years, but he adored churches, loved them like old scientific instruments whose time is long past but are nevertheless fascinating and strange.

He tried a side door in the tower but it was locked. It was almost like the door in the picture, he thought, studded oak and rusted hinges and you couldn't get in . . .

Turning away, he walked through ancient graves and had another thought. Maybe Susan Potts was interested in his grandfather's health because it meant business? Maybe they wanted to bury him in here? Thomas didn't really know what was wrong with him, but he wasn't well, that's for sure. He'd been in and out of hospital in the last two or three weeks, and a week ago one of the doctors had made the tactless suggestion that he might have to have another operation. He didn't like the idea. Suggesting another operation to a man who could hardly get up the stairs because of the last one was understandably upsetting. They'd been inside him already. About a year ago, a specialist from West Kent made an 'exploratory' and removed something. But what distressed Ethel was that two years before that an accomplice of the specialist had prescribed pills for anaemia. These pills didn't work. Despite weight loss and deterioration, these pills that didn't work were defended by the specialist's friend with the plea that 'they should be given the time to work'. In the time they took to give them the time to work, they kept not working, and Walter continued his inexorable decline. By the time the specialist's friend spotted this Walter was the colour of a banana, but apparently this wasn't unusual in cases of chronic anaemia. This bloke knew all about it and reiterated his diagnosis. Everyone except Thomas, his grandfather, and the specialist's friend knew he was dying of cancer.

It started to rain and Maurice was nowhere to be seen. Thomas decided to wait for him in Head of an Angel Hole. Angel Head was a secret meeting place they'd constructed some summers ago at a derelict end of the orchard. It was made of apple boughs with a skip-sail stretched over poles and camouflaged with ivy and brambles. During the past couple of years the undergrowth had grown so thick it had become impossible for anyone to find it who didn't know it was there. The canvas roof made it waterproof, and despite backing on to Potts' graveyard – even using a headstone as one of its walls – it was completely invisible from either the church or vicarage. Its existence, they believed, was unknown to Maurice's parents, and apart from a few selected friends, nobody but he and Thomas ever went near it.

Potts certainly didn't. To Thomas's knowledge his forays into the graveyard stopped short at the fresh end where the lawnmowers went. He was uninterested in anything other than modern acquisitions where a few chrysanthemums might turn up on a Sunday. As far as the Reverend was concerned, if you'd gone in before he'd relieved the last incumbent (who incidentally, together with Moules was in the fresh bit) then you had to look after yourself. His concern for the dead depreciated as their monuments collapsed, and when they finally lost care of anyone left living, they lost with it the attention of Potts and his gardeners for ever.

For Thomas and Maurice it was the reverse. As the dates went back the graveyard became more interesting, and by the time they got into the pre-Victorian section, it was sacred. Here was an enchanted wilderness of run-down crosses and headless angels, an estate of tombs. Wild attacks of elder and crooked oaks demolished the paths and desecrated the graves. Faceless saints lurked in holly and seemed to tramp about the place like ghosts, sticking their heads out of the undergrowth in places they swore they'd never been before. They called this domain The Plot of Sycamore Dick, named after Simon Edmond Dick, Dearly Beloved of Rose and (worn away) Dick, who actually had a sycamore tree growing through his slab. He died in 1851, a year after Thomas's favourite author published *Copperfield*, and Thomas liked to think Sycamore might have had the chance to read it.

Once, a winter ago, Maurice had a crowbar working on his grave, and for one wonderful, terrifying moment, they thought they'd got up his stomach. Atrophied, Maurice said. But examination with the end of the bar revealed the skull of a granite angel that stood headless at the end of the plot. This noseless Victorian was now kept in Head of an Angel Hole, thus giving their den its name.

Rain battered at the roof as Thomas crawled in. White

moths and rain in blackberries tangled as wires. He wiped his face on his sleeve and squatted on the boards. They'd built a platform of fence-slats and no matter how fierce the weather it ran underneath leaving the floor quite dry.

Thomas pulled an apple box to the headstone and took out his cigarettes to wait. Once a week he was a heavy smoker. On Saturday mornings his first stop was Tucker's where he bought a packet of Park Drive filters for half a crown, blowing his entire wages. Park Drive were not only the cheapest twenty you could get, they were also the strongest. Maurice rated them a 'fair snout'. He was a better smoker than Thomas, stealing his old man's Player's and smoking regularly throughout the week. With a father like Potts it was easy to practise – Thomas found it harder to pinch cigarettes because they were always watching – and not smoking anything like the quantity of the Vicar, his parents noticed their loss.

Six skulls were positioned on a shelf, five adults and a child. They grinned the grin as he struck a match. As yet, Thomas couldn't inhale properly, had to hold the smoke in his mouth, pumping it down nostrils to simulate penetration. Asthma got in the way, that's what he told Maurice, who would then demonstrate a full open-mouth drag, keep it down if necessary, then expel it with that kind of furious velocity that can never come from anywhere but deep in the lung. He could also inhale a cigar, and by some fortuitous deformity, blow smoke out of either ear.

An easterly moved on the graveyard, rattling vegetation, playing bramble-ends on the sail like a drum. The belfry joined in with a slow three and Thomas shivered – it was already getting dark in here. He looked at his watch to confirm it, he'd been waiting the best part of an hour. It didn't look like anyone was coming and was looking like time to leave. He'd give it five more minutes, push off in five, but he didn't have to wait for one.

Maurice burst into the hole like he'd been shoved from behind. His hair was stuck to his head and half of it seemed to have gone missing in the wind. He wore a brown plastic jacket, like a safari jacket, black jeans with zip pockets, and his school shoes. Dragging a hand backwards through his hair, he slumped on the box opposite, sniffing rain hard into his sinus.

'Why didn't you light the fire?'

'Coz I didn't think you were coming.'

'I said I was, didn't I?'

'I was talking about *today*,' said Thomas, and he said it a bit miffed. Firing a match on the side of the angel's head he lit a candle stuck in wax on the top of it.

Maurice produced his pipe, cigarettes, and dog-end container, and nodded towards a crude-looking grate made of bricks and a biscuit tin.

'You wanna light the fire,' he said. 'And let's have a look at those pictures?'

'What d'you think I am, the fucking butler?' said Thomas. 'Why don't you light it?'

They lit it together. Thomas tore off strips of damp newspaper, rolled them into balls and threw them in the tin. In reality he was in no hurry to get his photographs out – they gave him some currency around here. Maurice had the edge in this relationship. Firstly, because he was six months older, nearly sixteen, and second, he'd been into Piermont Park with Freda Pew and nearly made it, something Thomas was entirely jealous of.

Some twigs and one or two partially cremated potatoes went on and Maurice lit the match.

'Cold in here,' he said.

'What took you so long?'

'They made me feed the rabbits,' said Maurice, blowing at the tin and getting smoke.

'What rabbits?'

'Norfolks,' he puffed. 'My mother's started to breed Norfolks, there's five hundred.'

'Five hundred?' said Thomas. 'What does she want five hundred rabbits for?'

'Table rabbits,' said Maurice. 'She's got an outlet in Margate,' and at last the twigs flared.

He threw on more sticks and a clutch of leaves and the flames started to poke through. Momentarily they were both engulfed in smoke.

'How do you snuff 'em?' said Thomas.

'Butcher comes round every Thursday, smashes them on the head with a coal hammer.'

'All of them?'

'Nahh, fifty, sixty, fuckin' horrible.'

Dry holly cracked in the flames and a log went on and they sat back on their fruit boxes to watch it burn. Holes in the tin threw light like a lantern, and though their arses were cold their faces were warm and it was a good place to be in a gale.

Maurice flipped the lid of his tobacco tin.

'Let's have a look then?'

'Give us a minute,' said Thomas, about to have a cigarette and sticking a Drive to his lip to prove it. 'I'm having a fag.'

Maurice smiled derisively through the smoke, sorting through his butts. Two dozen or more, plus some half-smoked cheroots he kept moist with a cabbage leaf. Selecting his finest dogs, he cracked them open, stuffed them into his pipe, paper wrappings and all.

'I bet you haven't got anything.'

Thomas lifted an eyebrow and they both lit up.

'I thought you said you couldn't find the key?' said Maurice.

'I can't.'

'Then where'd you get 'em?' Thomas smiled through a nice little silence. 'You're telling me you've got a photograph of a woman with a duck up her arse?'

'That's right. A mallard.'

'I don't believe you.'

'How much d'you wanna bet?'

He didn't want to bet anything and his eyes returned to the fire. At intervals he tossed out great lungfuls of smoke with unconscious ease. Thomas did his best to copy him, turning the cigarette over in fingers with a sneer. Maurice knew the optimum way to hold one for premium staining. Conventional smoking, with the cigarette held out between forefingers, was useless for stains. Maurice always smoked with the hot end in towards the palm, like a policeman, even with his briar. And although Thomas couldn't inhale, with the covert technique his knuckles were almost as yellow as Maurice's and he looked like a proper smoker.

'You wanna suck it straight down,' he said.

'I do,' said Thomas.

'Go on then, let's see you.'

'I've just had a drag,' said Thomas, rather limply.

Maurice laughed down his nose and the expression of derision was fleetingly back. They sat listening to the logs snapping and brambles scratching harder with every change of the wind. At the end of the tunnel the afternoon had decomposed. Angel Head ejected its smoke close to the ground. Thomas watched it dodge across the orchard, twisting in a riot as the wind grabbed it and raced it invisible through the apple trees.

'Take that down!' ordered Maurice.

Thomas had been caught midway through a massive drag that inflated his cheeks like a bassoon player.

'Go on, take it down! It won't hurt ya!'

Thomas stared back. There was no escape. Maurice had 'called' him and he was going to have to inhale.

He did and suffocation was instant. He stood up and tried to say he couldn't breathe, but he couldn't breathe so he couldn't say it. An arm appeared in front of him, it was his, pointing nowhere in particular. He dropped the cigarette and opened his mouth and the arm started waving. The smoke had entered his lungs and somehow sealed them. Very slowly a sound developed in his throat, like baying. It transformed itself into a rhapsody for two bagpipes, Thomas going it alone with one. He went down blind for the cough and hacked at the slats.

He had exhaled, and collapsed forward gasping for air.

'That's it,' said Maurice. 'That's the first time I've ever seen you smoke.'

Thomas tried to communicate but couldn't.

'Flob,' said Maurice. 'Flob in the fire.'

A demonstration plug of sputum left his lips at high velocity and smacked into the side of the tin. Thomas cleared tears and on hands and knees, spat the last part of a cough. Its fruit hung pathetically from his chin and was misinterpreted by Maurice as an attempt to join in the spitting.

'Nahh,' he said, launching another sizzler off the side of his tongue. 'Before you can flob, you gotta suck in, you can only get flob from your lungs, and you can't get real flob unless you smoke properly.'

A vicious circle.

Humiliation was total with no exits. When he could speak he told Maurice it was asthma. Their eyes contacted but it didn't wash. Both knew the asthma-angle was bollocks and one of them said so.

'Just keep practising,' said Maurice. 'It takes time.'

And retrieving Thomas's cigarette he hit the bastard so hard it looked like he was living off the vitamins in it. Tilting his head he dropped a grin, put out a perfect smoke ring, and destroyed it in blue.

'You'll get there,' he said.

Thomas tried to say something useful to himself but his tongue was engaged. Embarrassment had replaced asphyxiation with no change in the colour scheme. He was drowning in shame, felt the blush boiling in his head like paint. His inability to smoke had been confirmed by an expert, and all his previous inhalations publicly demonstrated as fake. Maurice looked at him with the grin still loitering. Tossed the butt in the tin.

'Yeah, a reasonable smoke.'

Rehabilitation would not come easy. There was but one hope, one ace for Thomas to play in restoration of his dignity.

Was it possible the Bird could redeem him?

'Maybe it wasn't all asthma,' he said. 'But it was half asthma.' And he produced his envelope in expectation it would be alibi to a face-saver. In this he was correct. Maurice had eyes on the stash and allowed him to get away with it.

'I'll tell you what asthma's like. Breathe out as far as you can, then try and breathe out some more. That's what it's like trying to breathe *in* with asthma.'

His companion just about nodded and Thomas was halfway off the hook. But when the 'Temptress' came out and Maurice got into that, the blush let go and Thomas was mercifully free.

'Fuck me dead,' said Maurice.

Fruit boxes were shifted in more favourable aspect to the light. Maurice stared in genuine astonishment, his principal interest of course, the Duck. Its head stuck out looking freaked. Was it real? Yes, it was. Was it alive? Yes, it was . . .

'Wait till you see her up the tree, she's got eyes looking out of her arse.'

'Fucking Ada!'

Maurice was commenting on the next picture, *Eve and Her Apple*. Eve up the tree.

'How the fuck did they get her up there?'

Thomas shook his head.

'How did they get the duck up?'

'They oil them,' said Maurice.

He studied the photographs from many angles with all the fastidiousness of an art-historian examining a work for authenticity. This snap definitely readdressed the balance. They were equals again, and as a matter of fact, possession of the next picture put Thomas somewhat on top.

'Christ!' said Maurice. 'Look at those fucking balls!'

This was *Adam Takes Her Sin*, featuring Walter, and Maurice repeatedly couldn't believe the size of the balls. Thomas almost told him it was his grandfather, but decided against. In truth he was surprised and not a little disappointed with his friend's interest in the man. The testicles stimulated more expletives than the bird and several wild comparisons, notably to a pair of African gourds.

'Look at the tits on it,' said Thomas.

Maurice nodded but he'd seen the tits, and to Thomas's dismay seemed increasingly more occupied in tearing at a fingernail. The photographs had gone off like fireworks, and like fireworks their glory quickly died. Maurice was up for more, but there were no more, and with palpable diminution of enthusiasm he finally went full-time at the nail. He spat it reaching for cigarettes and handed the pictures back.

'What else you got in there?'

'Part of a book,' said Thomas feeling drab. 'About a boy at a boarding-school, weird stuff with a matron, but I don't like it.'

'Let's have a look.'

'You don't wanna read it now.'

'Why not?'

'Coz it's twenty pages with no girls in it. You can read it another time.'

He replaced the pictures and Maurice sniffed, lighting his cigarette. Another magnificent inhalation.

'I bet your grandfather's got some fantastic young stuff.' A probability confirmed by Thomas.

'That's what I like,' said Maurice. 'I like 'em young, not weird, just rude, underwear and that, and they have to be pretty.'

This led to further discussion of the filing cabinets and Thomas's inability to find the keys. He further confided his concerns about the pornography, should his grandfather actually die.

'What's the matter with him?'

'Something with his stomach. Maybe something to do with the war.'

'What war?'

'First World War, he got hit on the Somme. Unconscious for seventeen days with his guts hanging out. The flies laid eggs in him, bluebottles, and it was the maggots that kept him alive.'

'Bollocks.'

'I'm telling you,' said Thomas, and he was telling him. 'They ate the gangrene, kept him alive.'

Magic flies.

Maurice didn't believe it but didn't bother to say so and they sat in silence until the moment became a minute. Maurice threw another log on and a mass of brilliant sparks leapt in the air like burning confetti.

'You know what I'd like now?' he said, without taking his eyes off the fire. 'A pot of tea on top of that and a shag.'

Thomas agreed.

'Do you realise it can take up to a year of constant shagging for a girl to achieve orgasm?'

He didn't, but went along with the prognosis. After all, Maurice had had an experience in the park.

'You know what my dream is?' said Maurice, and he sat back, sucking his cigarette, taking time to put it together. 'A fifteen-year-old girl, with lovely long black hair, and a red dress with buttons, right up the front. And you lay her down in the long grass, have a fag with her, and then you undo the buttons, slowly, starting from the top, and she doesn't move. And she's got blue eyes and you take her bra off, and she doesn't say nothing, and then you give her tits a good feeling-with, and she likes it.'

'Like Freda Pew?'

Maurice glared like he'd just woken up.

'Freda Pew hasn't got black hair, you cunt.'

'I'm talking about on her thing.'

'What thing?'

'Her clump.'

'Flies!' snapped Maurice. 'I was telling you my fuck-ing *dream*, wasn't I? Last thing I want in a dream is Freda Pew.'

'She goes, though?' said Thomas.

'She's a fucking mess. Hannibal. Anybody could do it to her, she's a dog.' His vituperation ultimately made him smile. 'She said, you can do what you like, as long as you don't kiss me. All right, I said, feeling fucking grateful. Tell you the truth, I couldn't wait to get out of the house.'

'House?' said Thomas. 'You said it was in the park.'

Maurice swallowed looking a bit shifty, pulled out a fragment of eyebrow and ate it.

'Yeah . . . well . . . it was . . . first time.'

'You mean, you've had another go?'

'Yeah.'

'When?'

'Week or two ago. We all went back to her house.'

'What's all this *we*? I thought she was alone.'

'Hard to be alone when you're that fat,' sneered Maurice.

'Was she with someone?'

'Sort of.'

'Why didn't you tell me?'

The question got no answer and the question was repeated.

'Why didn't you tell me?' said Thomas.

'Because you like Gwen Hackett.'

'Gwen Hackett? What's she gotta do with it?'

'She's Fredda's best friend,' said Maurice.

'I know that, what's she gotta do with it?'

'You don't wanna hear.'

'Don't I? I fucking well do.'

Maurice considered spitting, but didn't.

'I didn't tell you, coz I know you like Gwen.'

'No, I don't.'

'Yes, you do.'

'I don't.'

'All right then, you won't mind hearing that Ron Shackles nearly fucked her.'

'*Shackles?*'

'See?' said Maurice. 'I said you liked her.'

'I thought she was going out with Gollick?' countered Thomas, quite yellow.

'She is . . . just that me and Shackles took Freda in the park, and we're sitting there on this bench, sharing tit, and who rides up on her bicycle, Gwen Hackett? . . . And we're all wondering how to get rid of her, when Freda says, let's go back to my house. . . . Her mother's working in a bakery.'

And while the bread was boiled they were in the front room, and the lights were off and Shackles got his hand up Gwen's skirt . . .

And worse.

'She keeps saying, have you got anything?'

'Who does?' said Thomas.

'Gwen.'

'Anything what?'

'Condom.'

'Condom?'

'All he had was this condom he'd found on the beach. It was three feet long and she didn't like the look of it and she wouldn't go.'

Horror pressed at the inside of Thomas's face.

'I tell you,' said Maurice, 'I wish I'd known then what I know now . . . Shackles could have had Freda, and I could . . .'

Thomas managed to go deaf, couldn't bear to hear the conclusion of this scenario. Shackles could have had Freda? And his best friend Gwen?

It was too painful. Too awful.

'She's a goer,' said Maurice. 'You should ask her out.'

'I told you, I don't *like* her,' said Thomas.

There was sufficient animosity in his voice to shut this down. Or maybe Maurice regretted telling him? Either way, neither continued with it. Thomas put out enough silence for them both, stuck eyes at the fire and saw awful visions . . . what was she wearing, school uniform, or a dress? . . . whichever was worse was that he saw . . . it didn't bear thinking about . . . but he could think of nothing else . . .

'You know what we should do?' said Maurice.

Thomas hauled himself out of it to look across. Maurice dumped his butt, adjusted the fire with a stick.

'Get down the rock pools and fuck up some crabs.'

'I can't,' said Thomas.

'Why not?'

'I can't really discuss it. But I'm under surveillance.'

Before Maurice could take the piss, Thomas produced the

70

business card he'd extracted from his mother's handbag: 'J.T. Brackett, Private Investigator (thirty years in the Met).'

'They brought in the professionals,' said Thomas. 'I'm watched all the time.'

'Why?'

'I don't know, but I've got to be careful.'

The solemnity of his tone convinced Maurice who handed the card back and listened as Thomas detailed sightings of the detective, six or seven in the last six weeks. Indeed, he'd seen Brackett that very morning, but a long way off, pedalling east on the Ramsgate Road . . .

'He's always there, I think he's been in my shed. If we hit the beaches, we'll have to use regular stuff.'

'Why would they want you followed?'

'Your guess is as good as mine,' said Thomas.

There was a silence before Maurice went on to speculate. It was probably the explosives. Maybe they thought he was about to take something out? Bomb a building in the town? Thomas agreed, and that's why he'd ceased work on the 'Big One', the one with the internal battery. He was going to give it some time, possibly relocate, and get back to it after Christmas.

Another silence, and Thomas's eyes were already gone, staring again at the fire. Seeing as nothing else was happening, Maurice retrieved the manuscript, got some light on to it, and in the next few moments, silently started to read . . .

The day roared down and it really was getting dark in here. Thomas went back to the disaster. He would never forget this day of rain and misery and leaves . . . How could she? . . . At least with Gollick you knew where you stood. He'd come to terms with Gollick, ugly prick that he was . . . but *Shackles*? . . . a lout, pure and simple . . . prone to boils . . . red hair . . . red eyelashes . . . always disgusting . . . a huge unleavened chancre on his nose . . . How could she? . . . Her

71

eyes, so beautiful ... like bluebells ... her beautiful hair, drenching the pillow ... How could she allow that lout up her clothes? ... Did Shackles kiss her? ... Did she kiss him? ... The thought hurt in his brain ... If it hadn't been for the second-hand rubber he'd found on the tide, she'd have 'gone', shagged in the seaweed ... anywhere, with anyone ... except him ... She must be a tart ... What could he do? ... He was already not looking at her ... He wished there was a way of not looking at her even more ... What else could he do? ... A letter to Gollick, perhaps? 'Dear Gollick, are you aware that on the 13th instant' ... No ... no, forget it ... forget her ... His darling angel, fouled by that rusted yob ... He would never look at her again ... *never* ... She was a tart and a prostitute and a slag ...

A sudden laugh brought his eyes up and he realised Maurice was reading, his merriment sustained in oblivion to Thomas's agony.

'Fuck a pig,' said Maurice, and he laughed again as he read out loud. '"The head of his penis throbbed like a turkey's heart. She attached the lead at its end, and led the naked boy silently along the chilly corridor ..."'

'Yeah, I read it,' said Thomas dismissively.

'Who wrote it?'

'My grandfather,' at least he supposed he did, he didn't care, and looked at his watch. 'I gotta go.'

Climbing into his coat he went about doing exactly that. A bit of a sticky moment followed. Maurice was reluctant to give up the half-read story, and Thomas was reluctant to leave it. On any other day he'd have said no, but he hated today, today had fallen to bits. A solemn promise was made for its safe-keeping, and against his better judgement, Thomas allowed his pal to hang on to it.

'What about the pictures?'

'Keep them in the envelope,' said Thomas. Right now, he

didn't want them, they were just another part of this dreadful afternoon. He finished with his last button, and on hands and knees prepared to crawl up the tunnel.

'And if you get caught with any of it, it's yours, right? Nothing to do with me?'

The oath was repeated.

The very ruins of daylight were behind the church and you could just about make out its tower. Rain was already in Thomas's face. He looked back, realising how harsh the weather and how warm it was in Angel Head Hole.

'Aren't you coming?'

'Nahh, I'll stay a bit,' said Maurice. 'Wait till the fire goes out.'

He poked it with his stick and Thomas was in the gale.

RUBY ROUND THE CORNER

Something strange was happening in the house. It started, or at least, Thomas finally became aware of it, on the first day of the Christmas holidays, a Wednesday morning, about 10 a.m.

He was on his way downstairs, and turning into the hall noticed something behind a sofa in the living room. There was a twist to it, terminating in a turret. It was a turd.

It is well known Jack Russells are capable of shitting up to two-thirds of their body weight a day; it was probably the work of one of them. But it was a peculiar sight, because whatever else they were, the dogs were house-trained. What was additionally curious was that this wasn't the first time it had happened. Presented with another he recalled one or two more in unusual spots, in fact, now he came to think about it, they were increasingly common. For some reason the dogs seemed to be becoming unhouse-trained. He wondered why, but left the question with the turd.

It is extraordinary, is it not, how so trivial, albeit unpleasant, an event in the living room could carry such enormous significance, although he didn't know what the significance was of course, or indeed that it was to have one.

He wandered into the kitchen for cornflakes. All dogs were in their baskets, and as he fixed his bowl he told his mother about what one of them had done. She was at the other end of the table mincing meat

with a hand-cranked machine and seemed totally uncon-
cerned.

'I'll have a look later,' she said.

This surprised him, but what surprised him more was that
that evening the turd was still there. It had actually remained
in situ all day until Rob came home and saw it, and then she
entered with a coal shovel and snatched it.

Rob was pouring Scotch and watched it go out.

A day or two later there was another halfway up the hall, and
again it survived until six o'clock and discovery by Rob.

The same shovel then arrived but nothing was said.

Something was up. There seemed to be an agenda somewhere, but what? Thomas assembled fuses in his workshop and
pondered it, wondering whether it was something he should
worry about. The house seemed to have acquired a more
negative charge than even a place as receptive as this could
tolerate. There were weird evenings. Conversation between
his mother and grandmother would abruptly terminate as he
walked into the room, and on recent occasion, precisely at
the moment the name 'Brackett' was articulated.

'Brackett?' he whispered. Could the turds be something
to do with Brackett, some sort of 'evidence' set up on his
behalf? He'd never actually seen any of the dogs in action
and the thought suddenly occurred to him: Maybe the turds
not only went *out* on the shovel, but also came *in* on it?

Was she planting them?

No, that was absurd. More likely the dogs had simply picked
up on general anxiety over illness in the house and couldn't
control themselves. But then why were the turds always left out
for Rob to 'witness'? They were clearly evidence of something,
but of what, and in respect of whom?

Surely they weren't planning to accuse him?

It was true he had a record for hiding shit, but they were
always wrapped, and since Gwen had come into his life the

Saturday Bag was history. Gwen had changed everything. It was a one-way love affair, that he acknowledged, but from its inception everything about his life was different. It was still changing and (Walter included) was his major worry.

Lately, his voice was all over the place. Sometimes abnormally high, then abnormally low and then just abnormal. He'd grown three inches and had the beginnings of a moustache, like a baby's eyebrow, plus a couple of blackheads and a boil on his back.

And he started writing poems.

Powerful undercurrents were at work, both in the house, and in his head. The poison of puberty was in his veins no less than the poison of illness in the veins of his grandfather.

Walter was thinner than ever, on that same yellow diet that had carted Uncle Horrie away. He was so frail he looked like he could float, like a breeze could blow him off the bed. He rarely got out of it these days, travelling no further than the bathroom and only infrequently to his 'office'.

Coincidentally the Tishman began to chatter.

−.. − − − . .− ..−. .− ...− − − − ..− .−.

Traffic on the wires was unusual these days and Thomas was mildly surprised. He'd already deciphered the message in his head but moved in with the lantern anyway to get the pleasure of reading it on tape. His grandfather wanted a 'favour', but didn't say what it was. Thomas flipped the lock on his transmission key and pulling up a stool hit the brass, confirming he'd be there in less than ten minutes.

.− −. .−. . .− ... . −.−. − − − .− −. −.− − − − − −.−

He waited but there was no reply and the light finally led the way back to the bench to complete the delicate conclusion of a fuse. An aspirin was eased into place, and simultaneously his thoughts shifted back to himself and his anxieties.

If anyone was planning anything, it was his mother. It was she, after all, who had hired Brackett, she who always made sure Rob saw the turd. But then again, it was his father who asked him about the turd in the hat. Is this what this business was about? Were the school, in association with his parents, trying to prove it was *him*? It didn't seem credible. The hat was weeks ago. Surely no one's going to hire a detective to find out who shat in someone's hat?

The munition was finished and joined half a dozen more on the bench. He looked at his watch. Ten minutes had already become twenty and snuffing the lantern he called it a day. His worries went with him across the vegetable gardens. There were so many facets of this he didn't understand but it all conspired into something unpleasant, like the uneasy feeling he got looking through a letter box, that same fearful remembrance of being a little boy and staring up the hall of an empty house.

He went in through the back door and straight upstairs. A radio was playing in his sister's room. By the time he was around the corner at the end of the corridor the skiffle had evaporated into shadow.

The door to the office was open, but Walter wasn't in it. Strange he'd left it unlocked, that was a first. He must have nipped out for a slash and it couldn't have been more than a moment ago? The air was yellow with cigar smoke and there was a half-smoked butt in the ashtray. Thomas picked it up and sniffed it, damned good, he wanted to light it, but was worried about catching anaemia. His smoking skills were improving, he was working on it. If the opportunity arose he wanted to inhale in front of Gwen. He sniffed the butt again, it smelt delicious, but he decided against and returned it to the ashtray.

Still no Walter. Perhaps he'd gone to his bedroom? He was on his way to check and made three paces back up the corridor before he realised what he'd just seen.

They were stuck in the lock. Hanging off the door. Was this

real? His eyes flashed up the corridor and returned to the keys, Unions, gleaming in the flat afternoon light. He could barely believe what he was looking at. But elation was tempered by the appalling circumstances. Why such fortune at so inopportune a moment? This was the worst of moments, his sister only seconds away and Walter probably closer than that?

The seconds were passing. Could he take the risk?

No question. He grabbed the keys and hurried into the office, his body thumping like a heart. He closed the door and then opened it again – better to leave it open? 6631 went into the lock and he silently drew back the top drawer. Expectation was overwhelming; he'd never undressed a girl but it had to get close to this. There was file upon file of pale-green folders and he extracted and opened the first . . .

The shock paralysed him: like the best of contractions, it was a tide of joyous needles in the scalp. This wasn't like the other stuff, this was modern, gangs of nudes all leaning over and grinning. There were partially dressed secretaries on the phone wearing spectacles and high-heeled shoes with their knickers pulled down. There were policewomen and nurses and a farmer's wife with her tits in a milk churn. But most amazing were the collages of naked girls, all young and pretty and showing their twats, and all with a startling amendment . . .

They all had nipples on their arse.

Bosoms had been acquired from some other source, pruned of all but their ends, and grafted on to these girls' bottoms. Thomas suddenly understood what the glue pot and razor blade were about. They said he'd gone weird after the war – that's what his mother said – is this what she meant? He'd seen his grandfather in the lavatory with these files, propped on the toilet cistern like a lectern. Is that why he always faced the wall? So he could sit there and tom and fiddle with himself?

Thomas was in a state of such alert he would have heard the cough a mile away. It was a lot closer than that and coming up the stairs. His panic was chauffeured with astonishing competence. By the time his grandfather made the corridor the pictures were refiled, the drawer shut, the keys back in the door.

Thomas gazed nonchalantly out of the window as Walter shuffled in. He had an elbow stuck out, like he was accompanying some extremely frail old person, although he was walking with no one but himself.

He carried a tray with two bottles and two glasses, wore slippers and an open dressing gown, which looked strange because he was togged underneath. His neck poked out of a shirt with a gold stud, but no collar, and trousers that looked enormous, like he was standing inside them rather than wearing them. He put the tray on the desk and eyes at Thomas, and he knew he'd been in the filing cabinets and Thomas knew he knew.

How did they know? They knew.

Travelling as far as the kitchen had wasted him, and he sat in the chair heaving a bit, took a minute before he could find the muscle to unscrew his Guinness bottle.

'Your mother's bought a Christmas tree.'

'Has she?'

'It's on the roof of the car.'

Thomas perched behind the desk on the window ledge with his back to the weather and Walter poured the Guinness, mixing it fifty-fifty with tonic water. It was an unpleasant-looking brew, black, with effervescing scum. He liked gin, but they told him Guinness had 'iron'.

There was a silence and a question Thomas wanted to put, but the moment wasn't right, and when Walter looked up he asked a different one.

'Can I have a taste?'

'I brought you a glass,' said Walter.

And he had, a spare on the tray, and that's what he loved about his grandfather. He made no judgements, no rules. His philosophy was always kindness, and since Thomas could remember, Walter had been kind to him. He made bridges for the clockwork trains, put headlights in his pedal-car, and now he had long white earthworms instead of veins and Thomas felt sad for him.

'What do you want for Christmas, Grandad?'

Walter poured a seventy-thirty fix and just about got up a smile.

'To feel slightly better than dead.'

'You'll be all right, when spring comes.'

'You think so?'

'Give the pills time to work?'

'On what?'

'Enaemia,' said Thomas, pronounced incorrectly as he would have spelt it, with an E.

'I been kind enough to the pills already,' said Walter, and you could hear the wind in the roof and the beer in his throat. 'I'm dying, Thomas.'

Thomas was genuinely surprised. Felt almost embarrassed.

'No one's said anything like that,' he said.

'Not to you, they haven't. And not to me.'

What they had said, and said repeatedly, was that this was chronic anaemia, and referring to it, Thomas mispronounced it again.

'It's enaemia. Gran says so.'

'You want two and a kick on it?'

Starved fingers fumbled coins in his pocket, found a half-crown, and when it came out the bet had turned into a gift.

'Here, have a beer on me.'

An accurate toss put the coin into Thomas's hand, and wind put rain on the windows.

'Why don't you go and help your mother with the tree?'

Thomas nodded and drank, didn't like the taste of the Guinness; it was bitter as piss and he almost gagged. It messed up his question. His intention was to drop it casual, slide it in under something, but instead it came out curiously high-pitched and direct.

'Do you know anything about a man called Brackett?'

'Who?'

'Brackett?' said Thomas. 'He's a retired detective.'

Hard milk in the corner of Walter's eyes; his expression wasn't easy to read. Did he know Brackett and wasn't saying, or was his head-shake the genuine thing?

'Never heard of him,' he said.

'Mum hasn't said anything about him?'

'No.'

Walter's lack of interest seemed to contradict his denial. If he didn't know Brackett, why wasn't he asking who he was? Surely the notion of a 'retired detective' would stimulate some sort of enquiry, but it didn't.

Despite dislike of it, Thomas finished the Guinness and put the glass on the desk next to the Morse key. Another thought surfaced: – ... .–.. ..– . . –... . .–.. .– .. .. ., and he almost didn't ask.

'What's Bluebells, Grandad?'

His grandfather looked up but didn't answer.

'Sometimes you just send Bluebells?'

'Bluebells are a memory. And some memories are secret.'

There was a silence that developed into a stare.

'When you're out hunting secrets, Tom, make sure you go after the right one.'

His stare maintained and Thomas felt uncomfortable. What did he mean by that? Was he referring to the secret of Brackett, or the secrets of the filing cabinets? If the latter, he was worried Walter would ask questions, and then he'd have to lie, and he wouldn't get away with it. It was impossible to lie to Walter. You can never lie to a liar better than yourself.

Using the Christmas tree as means to leave he landed an affectionate hand on his grandfather's shoulder and made for the door. He'd go and get the tree, but what was really on his mind was his mother. She knew who Brackett was, hired the bastard, and he was determined to confront her with it, here and now, no excuses accepted.

Pausing on the exit, he slipped a glance back at Walter. The cigar-stub was in his mouth, a match already lit.

'You said you wanted me to do something for you.'

The old man exhaled and answered through smoke.

'I wanted you to get me a Guinness.'

Thomas smiled a weak sort of sorry and vanished up the corridor. Lonnie Donegan came and went. As he descended the stairs he put it together, tuned his strategy. Confrontation would not be profitable – he abandoned that, stair one. It was no good going in there demanding information about Brackett; he wouldn't get it. What this required was 'an approach', a dance around the houses. What he would do was suck her into discussion, perhaps mention that he'd seen a man on a bicycle at the end of the drive, and then tell her that he happened to find this card somewhere. Where had he found it? Well, on the floor, he'd found it on the floor. And if this old man on the bike is the same man on the card, it's something they should discuss, because frankly, he was worried . . . no, not worried . . . concerned, he was vaguely concerned . . .

It sounded good and it was with confidence that he walked into a kitchen full of steam and dogs and his mother manoeuvring a dish of half-cooked hot potatoes.

'I'm vaguely concerned.'

She either hadn't heard or decided to pay no attention.

Either way she didn't look at him, and he motored into the heat of her potatoes and said it again.

'I'm vaguely concerned,' he said.

'I'm cooking, Thomas.'

She turned away, already annoyed, not necessarily with him, probably with something else. The potatoes took a basting of animal oils and she opened the Aga with her toe. There was a part in there, trussed and skewered, spitting at the onions of hell. The potatoes joined it and she slammed the door.

'Would you get the tree for me?'

Thomas fixed her with an expression of profound affront. Get the tree? Humiliation and anger welled in his head, fused into anger, and before he knew it he'd lost it.

'Why are you having me followed?' he barked.

There was emotion enough for reply but he didn't get one. If she looked at him it was only in process of looking somewhere else. The lid came off the dog's casserole releasing a smog of unwholesome and thrombotic vapours.

'Don't be ridiculous,' she said.

'I know you are, yes, you are,' said Thomas, plunging forward and forced to abandon any notion of subtlety. 'I've seen him, every Saturday for months; he'd always in a hedge, or cycling past pretending not to look at me.'

'Who?' she said, with an indifference that was throttleable.

'Who?' said Thomas. 'Who? *Brackett*.'

'Brackett?'

'Don't pretend you don't know Brackett,' said Thomas, and he hit her with the twisted smile of a prosecutor that unfortunately had precisely no impact. 'What-does-he-want?'

She finally looked at him, but the look didn't last. She took off around the kitchen escaping into dangling saucepans. He went after her, frustration demolishing any coherent presentation of his questions.

83

'Why do you always show the turds to Rob?'

'Turds?'

'Yes, yes, turds,' snapped Thomas.

'What turds?'

'What turds?' he volleyed, his voice both flabbergasted and fracturing. '*Their turds.*'

And he stuck an accusatory finger at the nearest dog, on its pins because of the imminence of meat. She plucked a saucepan from the ceiling and scuttled in the general direction of the sink.

'I *demand* to know why you're having me followed.'

'You have a very vivid imagination.'

He had her. Her *had* her.

'Oh, no I don't,' he said, and he whipped out the card and read it: 'J.T. Brackett, Private Investigator (thirty years in the Met).' It's *him*. He's everywhere. I've seen him on Pyson's Road with binoculars.'

For the first time in these proceedings his mother showed an emotional response.

'You took that from my bag,' she said, snatching it back. 'You really must learn to stop prying into other people's business.' She tore the card in half. 'Stop lurking around.'

And that was thàt, she was out the door. It was pointless to pursue either her or it. No matter what the evidence she would deny it, as she denied almost everything. Thomas longed to confide his anxieties to her, but that wasn't possible, because, in a large part, she was the reason for them.

He went out the back to get the tree wondering which worry to worry about. Walter with his dying? Or Brackett with his bike? Brackett took it. Why the interminable discussions late into the night between his mother and grandmother, sometimes with his sister involved? He'd tried to tackle her but she said nothing, you could never get anything out of Bel. She was in love with some drip from Ramsgate and had been to the pictures with him. He was a vegetarian and Rob didn't like him.

'Ugly cunt,' said Rob. 'I'd rather look up his nose than at his face.'

Rob was always in bed by nine for the 5 a.m. get-up. As soon as Thomas heard him retire he was out of bed and downstairs, standing in the hall with his ear pressed to the living-room door. But the geography of the house and, more often than not, the wireless, made it difficult to hear . . .

What he did hear was the volume of exchange in the mornings, always after Rob had arrived back from the station . . .

'I will be there,' he shouted.

'I've made the puddings,' she bellowed.

'I will be there,' roared Rob.

Thomas heard this through his bedroom floor. There was nothing particularly unusual about it, just the frequency of it, and as Christmas approached, more and more in reference to that day . . .

And then it came. Christmas 1958.

It was a peculiar day, a feeling something iffy was up, that something was going to happen.

The house was full of relatives and poison, undercurrents camouflaged with cosmetic mirth. Nora and Reg drove down from Basingstoke in a new Humber. He wore double-breasted suits and had been somebody at ICI. His wife was a sixty-five-year-old rheumatic Christian Scientist with ugly hair. A slave to her back. They stayed in the creepy room down the end next to Iris, Horrie's widow. Iris had a weird pupil requiring glasses with one dark lens. She wore two cardigans at once and liked sherry.

Pink and green bells flashed on the Christmas tree. There were Brazil nuts and jokes and double gins. Everyone laughed at everything, and everyone's festive agenda converged into the dining room at about 3 p.m.

Six red candles had just been lit. There were paper napkins with holly on them and it all looked very pretty. Reg was the Christmas joker but it was Rob that got the laughs. He carved in his green paper hat, farted, and got a laugh off even that.

'My Christmas message to the nation,' he said.

Everyone laughed except Thomas. He couldn't share anything with Rob, not even worthless merriment, not even on Christmas Day.

Walter came down for the dinner and sat in silence; didn't have the strength to pull his cracker.

'You're looking better, Wally.'

He acknowledged Iris's compliment with a vapid smile. She was the only one who could have made it because everyone else could see.

Walter didn't want to eat but took a glass of Riesling to go with his cigar.

'Where are you off to then, Bel?' said Nora.

'Germany,' said Bel. 'Dusseldorf.'

'Bombed it,' said Rob, and they all laughed again.

Rob hardly ate anything either, surreptitiously back-handing most of his turkey to Maximus. All the dogs were loitering for feed, Fabius finally throwing itself up at the far end of the table and hanging off Mabs like a colostomy bag.

It got turkey.

'He says: "I like that,"' said Reg. 'He says: "I wouldn't mind some more of that."'

It got some more, and so did the Dobermann. Max was practically sitting there with a knife and fork. Everyone knew why Rob hadn't eaten, except Thomas . . .

'Here's to those that wish us well, and those that don't can go to hell,' said Ethel extending her Riesling.

And they all drank and read the mottoes.

A truce was declared at Christmas.

Thomas pulled the wishbone with Bel and she won. After lunch everyone retired to the living room half cut and full of bird. There was a group autopsy on the excellence of the meal, but the atmosphere was brittle and Mabs went round again with the Gordon's. When Rob left the room, Auntie Nora said something and there was a sudden freeze. Various eyes put the clamp on her, and it was only when that happened that Thomas realised she'd said something important. Silence was broken by the crack of a nut.

What had she said?

When the opportunity came, Thomas asked Reg in the kitchen and his uncle smiled.

'Two gins, and she's Reuters,' he said.

But he wasn't saying anything else.

'Is Grandad dying?' said Thomas.

'He hasn't got a cold,' said Reg. And he'd amused himself and started picking through the debris of the bird . . .

> *December 25th 1958*
> *Here's to those that wish us well*
> *And those that don't can go to hell . . .*
> *And I shuddered at my first taste of gin . . .*

They sent Thomas out for another scuttle of coal. In the coal shed he blew his nose into his Christmas hat and it happened. His voice finally broke.

He tried to hum, but couldn't hum high. That was worth a mention in the new diary. Also something else of note on his way back in. Reg had returned to the kitchen with a mouthful of port and turkey skin, and as Thomas arrived with the scuttle, both he and Reg watched Fabius squat under the table and shit itself, bold as you like.

There was no excuse, the back door was still open.

'Got no class, that dog,' said Reg. 'He's all arsehole and maw.'

Rob wasn't a witness. He'd gone out in the Wolsey to take the Dobermann for a walk . . .

> *And Auntie Nora, in front of the fire*
> *Half asleep*
> *Religiously driving the ghost of a sprout*
> *Deep*
> *Into the dog-rotten upholstery . . .*

It was a peculiar day.

At the end of it Thomas sat upstairs re-examining his presents and reflecting on events. His bedroom was oil- and candle-lit, smelt of paraffin and beeswax and was stuffed with antiques. There were two beds, a brass double, and an early nineteenth-century French single piled with books and broken wireless sets. A bookcase and gate-legged table formed a corridor in between with elderly dining chairs hanging off an adjacent hat-stand. On the walls there were plates, blue-and-green Masons, Minton, very old Willow pattern, and clocks, both square and round, some ticking, most not, plus pictures and prints of curious people, predominantly Victorian engineers, damp in their mounts, and woodworm in their frames . . .

The fulcrum of this assembly was against a wall by the window. Here was a rosewood desk with an antique oil-lamp and shelves of important books. Random volumes of the *Encyclopaedia Britannica*, *circa* 1810, with their covers hanging off. There was a book about viral infections in cattle. Two books about Charles Dickens and, Thomas's second most important possession, a book written by the man himself. It was a first edition of *David Copperfield*, 1850, with only two pages missing, but all the drawings were there. How lovely was the frontispiece. You could smell the seaweed and wind blowing sideways across the beach. Peggotty's house, in an upturned boat, with a chimney sticking out, and the most beautiful girl, Little Emily, the second most beautiful girl on earth . . .

He took out his new pen and rewrote his name in the front, and then wrote out a list of his presents in the new diary, rating them one to ten. He'd got a cricket bat from his father: three; a pullover from his mother: two; a Timex wristwatch from Reg and Nora (no quality): four and a half; a plastic mathematics-set from his sister: nil; a penknife: seven; a set of drills: seven; and a fountain pen from his grandfather with a genuine fourteen-carat gold nib.

It was his only ten.

He adored the pen. It was fat and black with a gold band and he loved reading 14K on the nib. He decided in future to use it only for love poems to Gwen, and was distantly annoyed with himself for already writing with it, compiling his lists, and scratching bits and pieces of a poem about the day . . .

> *Mabs and Nora, Ethel and Rob*
> *And all the relatives who come out*
> *Once a year*
> *Who were famous as film stars*
> *In our house at Christmas . . .*
> *Playing games I didn't understand*
> *And playing cards I didn't understand*
> *With a greasy pack much older than me*
> *And every year Christmas was dying . . .*
>
> *They taught me how to play*
> *And they taught me to learn*
> *That those unlucky in cards*
> *Are generally unlucky in everything . . .*

He called it 'A Dying Christmas', and he called it that because Christmas wasn't like it used to be, or how it should be. It was a strange day, what with Rob still out, and Walter so ill. But the day after was even stranger . . .

Mabs rose at 6 a.m. and it was still dark when she got into the Anglia. She headed west along Pyson's, turned back into the Ramsgate Road and parked somewhere in the mid-numbers.

Snow was in the air, covering the deserted street like an undercoat of white on black (not a bad analogy in the circumstances). She climbed out of the car carrying a canvas bag and a pint of red paint.

Hers were the first footsteps in the street. Past the hedges of privet, past all the curtained houses with bolted front doors sleeping off their puddings, she arrived at number 61.

She opened the gate, quietly, and shut it with equal precision. Temporarily shelving her can of Dulux on the head of a concrete dwarf, she put on gardening gloves and opened her toolkit, selecting a hacksaw.

It was a metal saw, and a bad choice. She had difficulty cutting down the central magnolia tree but passion drove her on. Now she got into the roses, shunted up the flowerbeds heaving with effort, took out half a dozen and kicked them up the path.

She uprooted and trampled. 'Bitch,' she growled, smoke curdling out of her mouth.

Meanwhile, upstairs, a middle-aged couple were in the middle of a critical bit of intercourse. Ruby loved fucking, any hour of the day or night, set the alarm for it. She was a handsome woman, although fleshy, and you wouldn't want to trust the lower side of her face.

'Whore.'

On the second rendition of this sentiment they became aware of something going on in the garden.

'Cunt.'

Ruby was concerned, but the orgasm, like the blush, has a point of no return. Their guts clapped. Her partner shot. As soon as he'd terminated he hauled his vast behind out of the bed for a look.

From Ruby's perspective, tits flopped over the eiderdown, this was a sight. Muscular shoulders and a pocked arse like a map of the moon, and nothing else on but a surgical-collar . . .

And now shades.

Rob pulled the curtain aside and looked down.

Mabs saw it move and glared up from the garden. She knew why Rob hadn't eaten her dinner, because the bastard had come round here to eat another one, with her, the whore.

She tried to throw paint at him. It didn't get anywhere near the upstairs window, but hit the bay below where a small artificial Christmas tree blinked coloured lights . . .

Everything was red.

An old man on a bicycle noted these events via binoculars. The time was 7.16 a.m.

HEAVENLY BEACH

Two winds came off the north.

It was a day of bitter cold, clothes to be worn like weapons. Thomas coasted down the hill on his bicycle, past the deserted tearooms and dark little sea-shops of York Gate. Hardly a person about, only he and gulls on the jetty. In the night the gale had washed over it, left seaweed and huge shivering puddles. There were lobster pots, a lot of them, upturned rowing boats, and iron rings rusting in the walls. The jetty stuck out like a benevolent arm embracing half the beach and had been doing nothing different to that for half a thousand years. It was made of oak, tarred six inches deep, black as your hat with black gloss on the railings. By a process of gravity and nowhere else to go, everyone who visits Broadstairs will end up here, leaning over this balustrade and looking out to sea . . .

The tide was on the turn and conditions perfect, and Maurice as usual was late. Thomas watched a pair of cormorants flying fast just inches above the waves and, as they disappeared to fish, the sun threw sudden gold all over the sea. Shafts of light, pink and blue like a bomb blew out the side gate of heaven. But it didn't last. By the time the birds resurfaced the clouds had closed and the sea was grey again.

He took out cigarettes and the wind made work of it, had to shelter a match in his jacket. He lit up, raising eyes. Not too far away a girl rode by on a new bicycle. It was red and obviously a Christmas present. She wore a fur hat, and Thomas was jealous of it, and a coat with fur at the collar, and he was jealous of that too.

It was Gwen.

As she cycled past she looked at him. Her eyes were intensely blue, blue as flowers, and sent a pulse through his head like sweet electricity. It was the first time she hadn't looked away.

In the crisis of the moment it was Thomas who did, inhaling deep before looking back to blow his smoke in her direction. But he'd mistimed it, and Gwen was already gone . . .

> *You tell me of ecstasy*
> *In our love's complexity*
> *But while loving me*
> *Think who your next will be*

He'd written it a week ago and liked it, except she didn't tell him anything, and didn't love him either. But she had looked at him. He wandered up the jetty smoking his cigarette thinking about the look. Why had she held the gaze like that? Maybe she didn't recognise him, thought he was someone else? That was possible. After all, she barely acknowledged his existence, so how would she know it was him? The hypothesis evaporated as he constructed it. Of course she knew it was him. He barely looked at her either, but instantly knew it was her. He walked on through puddles trying to relive the moment. On the positive side, she must have seen him before he saw her, so there was no reason for her to look at him at all. How long did the look last? He stopped in two inches of water for calculations. With a blink at the beginning and end, he tried to reproduce the length of the look. This wasn't successful. All he could remember were her eyes and that wisp of golden hair blowing across her face . . .

How could she be so beautiful, and how could beauty be so unkind? The fantasy was already decaying. He couldn't think about Gwen without thinking of Shackles with his hand up her kilt. That was reality, and he didn't want to think about that.

A last drag at the cigarette and he jettisoned it over the weather side of the pier. Just enough tide to take it. The beach stretching from here to North Foreland was as bleak as it had ever been. Dirty chalk cliffs collapsed haphazardly into the sands, white into green, and green into endless brown of the rock pools.

Thomas stared at them with a curious feeling of emptiness. He'd blown the shit out of these pools so many times, slaughtered without thought, but today, for some unfocused reason, he wasn't sure he wanted to go on with it. A week or so ago he'd put a bead on a pigeon with his .22. It was a certain kill. He didn't know why but he couldn't snuff it, and the feeling he had then was the reticence he felt now.

The cruelty-to-crab season had opened some months ago – mid-October when the fireworks went on sale – and fizzled out late November when all the fireworks were gone. During the season the squads invaded the beaches, regiments of wicked boys with all the explosive they could afford. Thomas held them in contempt. They went about their business with ridiculous little crackers at a penny apiece – 'Cannon Crashers', 'Thunderclaps' – commercial rubbish all. Even so, for a month or more, unspeakable atrocities were inflicted on anything they happened to come across on the shoreline. Starfish, limpets, shellfish, were systematically routed out and destroyed. Mussels were atomised on the rocks, flat fish disembowelled as they slid in assumed safety across the shallow sands . . .

But the agonies of this lot were as nothing compared to the pogroms the squads directed at the crab. The crab was persecuted for a menu of reasons, not least the very quality that appeared to give it advantage over its neighbours. It had legs, therefore chance of escape, therefore could be 'hunted'. No whelk would make a bolt for it, but the crab would run and fight while it had a leg or claw left to do it with.

There were other factors that worked to the crab's disadvantage. It had eyes and could look at you. Better still, its multi-coloured interior made for an impressive reaction to explosives. When a crab went up there was a mess. A bull crab buckled like an armoured car, or a tank, and even the lousiest imagination could convert its smoking hulk into a catastrophe on some battlefield. And crabs were stupid. Were they not, the oafs that scoured the rocks for them would have had little success.

The animals they targeted were removed from the pools with hooks. There were two species of enemy: the smaller edibles, and big green bastards with claws the size of secateurs that could weigh up to a pound and a half. They were taken to the beaches where they usually collected a badly placed charge in the under-belly, followed by maiming, or if they were lucky, instant death. Those that survived with enough limbs intact to attempt escape were the most unfortunate creatures alive. A unit of hysterical boys would encircle the victim, stimulating its interior with injections of hissing phosphorus. Matches penetrated every fissure of its wrecked armour like explosive-head bullets, animating whatever was left inside either to get up and run or make a fight of it. Thomas had seen blasted crabs fencing for their lives for half an hour, twisting in the sand like unwinding springs, seizing the air with dislocated claws, and all the time dragging themselves in hopeless circles back towards the sea.

After the trauma of explosion a crab will grab at anything, scissoring off even its own limbs, should the blast have twisted a foreleg in the way. The more inventive of the squads capitalised on this phenomenon by offering the poor fucker an unexpected chance of freedom with a Cannon Crasher to take home to the wife and kids. With the fuse sizzling and death in its fist, it would haul for sanctuary as fast as a couple of legs could shift it. Not a great deal of imagination needed now: with exhaust streaming in its wake it really did look like a tank. Some seconds later it went up, massacred in its tracks, its horrible orange interior of rotten rubber bands blown all over its bomb-proof face.

'Beauty,' they screamed. 'Beauty.'

But this was about as good as these thick-heads could get. They used torture and brutality to destroy their victims, whereas Thomas, and to a lesser degree Maurice, practised a combination of sophisticated techniques, undeniably as cruel, but with a bias towards strategy and science.

They were the cream of this game. The elite.

Maurice pitched up about ten minutes later, wore a wool hat with a white bobble, an anorak, and a rucksack on his back with half a dozen sticks thrust out of it. His nose was remarkably red.

'We're gonna miss the tide,' said Thomas.

'Sea's looking slow.'

'No it isn't, it's coming in.'

'All right,' said Maurice. 'Let's move it.'

He stashed his bike on top of Thomas's and they clattered down wooden stairs that got more and more treacherous with seaweed. From down here the jetty looked like a black ship that never went anywhere. Gulls were motionless in the air, standing on the wind. As they crossed the beach, Maurice hooked his briar under dirty front teeth and he looked like a kind of mole.

'I've got some sherry,' he said, and reached over a shoulder into his rucksack, producing a half-full bottle of some fortified wine.

'That's not sherry,' said Thomas.

'What is it then?'

'I dunno, but sherry's not red.'

'Isn't it?'

'Don't you drink?' said Thomas.

'Course I drink.'

'Don't you drink sherry?'

'Not much.'

'Sherry's yellow.'

'Tastes like sherry,' said Maurice, popping the cork. 'Fuckin' handy stuff.'

And he took a swig that snatched his breath away and handed the bottle across.

'I only drink gin,' said Thomas. 'Or port, I'll drink a port.'

'This is port.'

'You just said it was sherry.'

'Yeah, well, I got it wrong, didn't I? It's port.'

It was offered again and declined again. In reality Thomas didn't like the taste of booze, made him feel queasy, and on a day like this he didn't like the cut of it, not with enough explosive in his coat to blow the pair of them to bits.

'Not for me, not with this lot.'

He slapped hands on his pockets.

'How many you got?'

'Six, all deep water.'

'We'll do the town first,' said Maurice.

Sand got scarce and turned into chalk and everything else was black flint. You needed the balance of an ape to move at speed on the rocks. Thin seaweed the colour of salads gave way to fat and oily brown stuff, slippery as ice. It spilled everywhere, yards long and full of blisters that popped when you trod on them. Here and there in advance of itself, the tide gnawed in through bottomless gullies and there were sudden secret pools.

They jumped them in convoy, Maurice in front, sucking at his pipe and navigating towards rocks that were already disappearing back into the sea.

The pools were deep here, morbid cisterns choked with weed, pouring water like overflowing baths. They selected a promontory that had but minutes left in it. Maurice shuffled free of his rucksack, dumped it at his feet and started to unload. First out was a ball of string followed by a fishing line, weighted at an end, with knots tied at intervals of about a foot. As he unwound he looked at Thomas with a smile that you might want to call a sneer.

'I've got some news for you, you might well be interested in.'

'Like what?'

'Like I ran into Gwen Hackett at the top of York Street.'

Thomas used the salt wind to avoid his eyes, reached for the rucksack preparing for the worst.

'She says, she thinks you're sweet.' He stuck out his tongue and wagged it lasciviously. 'You're in there, china.'

Thomas stared, feeling something peculiar in his head, like singing and confetti and apple-blossom and lipstick. Her sweet lips said 'sweet' and 'sweet' was him? He felt elation, he felt dizzy with joy, instant happiness that engulfed him and the whole wonderful world.

'Fuck that,' he said.

'Don't you care?' said Maurice.

'Not really.'

'That's good, coz I was lying.'

He cackled with repressed evil, grabbed the bag and went about the mechanics of assembling his launcher. It was made of three lengths of sawn-off vacuum-cleaner pipe that clicked together.

Thomas felt like throwing himself into the sea, to drown, there and then. The day was a funeral and Maurice a shit-house. How could he have said such a thing, even using the slang that Thomas had taught him? What kind of a friend was that?

The tide was beginning to creep around their feet, lifting the seaweed, swelling like breathing in the pools. Maurice found a platform for his device and knelt screwing his pipes to a wood frame with a wing nut. The final assembly projected not far off vertical, like a mortar-launcher. He looked across and knew perfectly what was going on behind Thomas's lousy weather.

'Only a joke,' he said.

'Yeah, very fucking funny.'

'So, you *do* like her?'

'You know I "like" her.'

Maurice elbowed the briar to get vile with his tongue again.

'All right, keep your hair on,' he said. 'She did say it.'

'Said what?'

'Said what I said she said.'

Thomas didn't believe him, might even say so.

'Straight up,' said Maurice. 'By the holy balls of Jesus' (on which he swore) 'she said it.'

'Did she?' dared Thomas.

'She did, and it's bad news really, coz she's the best-looking bird in school. Her fuckin' loss, but she fancies you.'

'How do you know?'

'I can tell,' said Maurice with the light authority of one with experience of this type of thing.

He popped the cork of his VP bottle and took another hit. Handed it to Thomas and this time he didn't refuse. It tasted divine, hot and fantastic. It tasted of the moment, and this was the best moment of his life. He soared like a giant in the air, drunk on love and red sherry.

The sky split again, the sea was silver and gold again, it was heaven, and Thomas was in love with its nearest angel . . .

'Got one.'

He turned into the wind, unaware of Maurice until he shouted from a pool some yards away. 'Red Back,' and he stood with a six-ounce crab above his head like a champion who won the cup.

'Let's do it,' said Thomas.

Was there ever a day like this? They went about their task with enthusiasm. The crab was imprisoned in Maurice's bag and he threw his sinker into a lugubrious trough that got deeper with every wave.

When Thomas worked the pools he thought in Morse, couldn't help himself, it was part of the game . . .

—.. . .— —. — ....

'Depth?' he said.

'Seven feet,' said Maurice.

Thomas unwound about ten feet of string. His true china held the crab and it was secured in a harness like an expertly tied parcel. His Christmas knife trimmed loose ends, the knots slid tight, and no fucker got out of this.

With its mouth frothing and eyes waving about wondering what was going on, the enemy was returned to the pool. It took string with it, down into the deep where the broken seashells are. They gave it time now, a quiet period in which to reacclimatise, convince itself the trussing procedure was no more than an alarming close shave. At last on the bottom the panic was over, and it walked rather than ran into a safe corner of the sea.

Or so it might credibly think.

Up above the boys were at work. Maurice unwrapped his first rocket. These were hybrids, triple rocket heads clustered around one stick with ignition synchronised to a single magnesium fuse. The string connected to the crab was now connected to the rocket via a hole drilled in its stick. This bastard was capable of making thirty-six hundred feet whether crab-towing or not.

He carefully slid the rocket into the launching device and made final adjustments towards the town.

The wind was favourable.

.. − −. −. .. − .. − − − −.

'Ignition.'

Maurice sucked his pipe like he was siphoning petrol, got a glow in the bowl. The fuse fired, then the rockets, perfect coincidence on all three.

For a moment it was static in its launcher, charring seaweed, clouds of khaki sulphur hauled off by the wind. It seemed the sea would anchor it for ever. 'Go, go,' howled Maurice. And then it was gone, with astonishing acceleration, the wretched edible snatched from its world of shrimp and green things, and travelling at two hundred miles an hour above Broadstairs.

'Fuuuuccckkk,' screamed Maurice. 'Yea, they were snuffed.'

This sounded to Thomas like some kind of biblical reference. The crab disappeared over the cliffs on a trajectory parallel to the high street. (Later in the day they would survey the town on their bicycles in attempt to locate the victims. In the past not a few had been memorable. One was found halfway up Gladstone Road swinging above the dental surgery. Just a back with legs, it had been completely incinerated during flight. To their delight it looked like a set of hellish teeth. Others were discovered hanging over telephone wires, up trees in the park, and one, with everything intact, dangling like a loathsome arachnid from the flagpole of the Chandos Tearooms).

The tide had driven them back up the beach. All rockets and the sherry gone, but time enough for the depth-charges.

With the sea claiming everything, Maurice lowered his

sounding-line into one of the last available pools. It kept going down. Meantime, Thomas shuffled his munitions: identical little pipes with external batteries bandaged into place with wire.   .

'Whass the depth?' he said.

'What?'

'Depth.'

'Are you all right?' said Maurice.

'What d'you mean?'

'You sound arse-holed.'

Thomas laughed, enjoying himself, and Maurice kept a wary eye on him as he hauled out.

'It's nine feet,' he said, and by his expression, too deep.

'We'll have it,' said Thomas, and he circled the pool scratching his arse as though calculating, although in reality he already knew precisely what he was going to do.

'We'll put down five hundred grams on a fifteen-second fuse.'

'*Five Hundred*?'

'That's what I said,' said Thomas, and he produced almost a foot of pipe from somewhere about his person.

'What the fuck is that?' said Maurice.

'The big one.'

'I thought you said you'd junked it?'

'There's been a variation of circumstance,' said its inventor, but he wasn't saying more than that. He was smiling again and felt kind of weird, thought of his grandfather and Gwen as one thought, a loving thought, but it was his grandfather who finally took it, probably because he was going into hospital today . . .

'You know what?'

'What?' said Maurice.

'What happened to my photographs?'

'Forgot to bring them, didn't I?'

'Where are they?'

'They're safe.'

'Where?'

'Under my bed.'

'Under your bed? Your bed's not safe.'

'Under my mattress. I'll bring them in next week.'

'What are you, short on cells?' said Thomas. 'I don't want none of that at school. Bring 'em next time we're at Angel Head.'

Somewhere high in the town a clock struck the quarter. You wouldn't have heard it if it wasn't for the wind. Thomas looked at his watch. It was 2.15 p.m. and approaching a special time . . .

It was at 2.20 p.m. that his grandfather was hit at Passchendaele all those years ago. He unscrewed the end of his device with a head full of memories of the Belgian front.

'Flat,' said Walter. 'Flat, with trees here and there.'

And on that day, four miles away in a clump of them, boys not much older than Thomas primed the fuse of a twenty-eight-pound shell. In that war of course the munitions were much bigger than this. There were tanks and horses, Walter told him about the horses, sometimes as many as six, heaving in their traces, dragging eight-inch howitzers through the mud. English horses fighting German horses with no particular difference of opinion, but dying just the same.

Some of them were so terrified, their hard-ons were permanent . . .

'What's going on?' said Maurice.

'Just thinking.'

'Well, come on, lose the cunt, I don't like the look of it.'

A wave almost made the top of Thomas's Wellingtons. He moved to the far side of the pool. With the wind tearing up his back, Maurice watched in apprehension as Thomas wired the device. A nasty moment was coming up from which the inventor wasn't excluded, and it was the eternity it took to ease the wooden safety-pin out of the electrical detonator. The terminals were now connected, and the top screwed on again.

.−.. .. ...− .

'Live,' said Thomas.

'Bung it then.'

Thomas felt the bravado of booze upon him. He was going to let this thing off on the dot of two-twenty, and he toyed with the pipe, smiling at Maurice, who wasn't smiling at all.

'Just thinking about the Germans,' said Thomas.

'What Germans?'

'First World War Germans.'

'You're arse-holed,' said Maurice. 'Come on, you're giving me the shits.'

Thomas returned eyes to his watch. About a minute to go.

At two-nineteen the German boys loaded the shell into a field gun made by Krupp. They slammed the breach and knelt with hands over their ears as the gunner turned away to fire it.

'We don't know what fear is,' said Thomas.

'Don't we?'

'Not really, not real fear.'

'Speak for your fuckin' self,' said Maurice. 'Come on, or I'll run. Throw the fucker in.'

Thomas dropped the device into the pool.

Maurice was already running, crashing through the waves, and Thomas wasn't far behind. He was counting seconds and both were laughing hysterically. Did his grandfather laugh that day? He said he laughed a lot in the war . . .

The shell came out of the barrel at one thousand six hundred feet every second. It landed in a meadow where there were already many dead. And when the fulminate of mercury collapsed into trinitrotoluene, there were suddenly many more . . .

There was an enormous explosion.

A bouquet of seaweed and young fish made twenty feet into the air, sliced off by the wind like a scythe and on into the green sea.

The boys stared in shock: never seen anything like this before. Simultaneously, an echo went up the coast, swallowing itself, and belching out, and swallowing to the steeple of Holy Trinity Church:

.— — — .. .. —

'Christ Almighty.'

The explosion took the head off the horse in front, and behind the white horse was screaming blind, blood hosing out of its nostrils, its face like shattered crockery. A boy from Bow, East London, died instantly: a sergeant in the Scots Infantry died too. And Walter stood there looking at it all, horses dragging dying horses, and the sky full of burning earth. Even as the shrapnel went in he'd been hungry; the passage of metal through his stomach felt like nothing more than a sudden increase in appetite, not really pain, just sudden hunger accelerating into unconsciousness. And as he fell, in that same piece of a second, shrapnel from the same shell hit him in the head.

.. — — —.. . .— —..

I'm dead.

I'm dead.

And death was under an intensely black sky spangled with stars. He felt the night on his face and saw visions more vivid than dreams. His mother came to him in the darkness and kissed him and he wasn't afraid. Sometimes he heard his mother singing, sometimes the sound of horses' hooves on pavements, but far off and muffled, like they used to sound when he was a little boy and the streets were filled with snow. And then he was in brilliant sunlight, walking again across that same dusty square in the village east of Passchendaele. She was fifteen with corn-blonde hair that smelt of bacon and apples, and she was pretty as flowers. He knew he was in a dream, and the dream was her laughter in a plait of burning stars and a language he couldn't understand. 'Je t'aime.' Before he left to go up the line he took her a bunch of Michaelmas daisies wrapped in newspaper. They made love at the edge of a wood in a drift of bluebells. It was the first love for both of them, and he knew she was the love of his life . . .

But he couldn't remember her name. He couldn't remember anything. Where had the war gone? The war had killed him and gone away . . .

On the second day the flies came to lay their eggs. He could hear them crawling over the horses. Their feet squabbled on his eyelids and walked on his teeth. He could hear them inside his helmet and was terrified they were inside his skull. A sound he was barely aware of wasn't there any more. His watch had stopped. There were flies in place of time, and he lost count of the days. Within hours, it seemed, his uniform was full of small maggots. He could see them now, clustered into his abdomen, simmering like a pan of rice.

It had taken all day to lift his head. He was lying on a pillow of horse flesh and the back end of a dead horse was trapping his legs. Its head was to his right. He looked at it with a wave of revulsion. What was happening to the horse was happening to him. Its skull was a brothel of flies, moving in and out of an eye socket. How many days had this been? Had he known how long maggots take to mature he could have worked back to the day the flies arrived. But he hadn't seen them grow, they just appeared suddenly, and a five-to-eight-day approximation was as close as he could get to the day that he was hit. Why hadn't he died of bleeding, or even lack of food? He was too frightened to eat that morning, a biscuit and tea and that was all. He thought that some sort of cycle must have developed, that the maggots must be growing in a functioning part of his gut: as they ate him, he ate them, and he survived therefore by a process of digestion . . .

Birds eat maggots.

Rain came in the night, and in the terrible darkness, dreams. There were fires in his sleep; he heard men yelling and saw the dead come alive again. On the day he arrived in this forsaken land, he'd seen a wall of two hundred dead Scotsmen in kilts, and as he crawled past, a boy with red hair swung an arm out, and he watched as an avalanche of maggots dropped from his sleeve. Some of the bodies were so full of them you would think they were just rolling around in their sleep . . .

He awoke at dawn under a cerise sky closer to the Municipality of Hell than he'd ever been. He longed to die, and he longed for his mother, wanted her to come again and kiss him. Tears welled in his eyes, he wept like a child, his mind in convulsive tangles of Morse and barbed-wire. All day he walked the coast of sleep. In his dreams things that appeared to be part of him began to undulate and shift. But to wake or to dream was no longer his to discern, and he rambled in and out of consciousness, confused between delirium and the enterprise of the maggots. He thought he was a man rolling in his sleep. He thought it was maggots that had raised his head and given vision to his eyes. It was the maggots alive, not him. And from that day he believed his thoughts were nothing more than the activity of the maggots in his brain . . .

Miles above him he could hear bird song, skylarks, high

over the fields. And he could hear her laughter, and he remembered now, her name was Adèle.

She was a girl without history, one of thousands that trekked the flatlands to the towns and villages, most from the farms, either running away or running towards something or other. Beggars begging from beggars. Children of the dead. None could speak English, some were younger than his sister, twelve, fourteen – hard to tell because hunger does strange things to faces. There was famine in Belgium, and quite a lot of the girls would fuck for food.

But not Adèle, she was one of the lucky ones. She lived in a lean-to room without windows and worked in the kitchens of Les Deux Gorey, a run-down hotel at the edge of town where farmers used to eat before the officers were billeted there. Probably she paid the patron a few francs to sleep in the shed where he would normally have kept his wine and vegetables. Apple-racks still lined the walls. There was a musty smell of cider. It was possible she and the old man with the moustache were related, an uncle perhaps, but nobody, least of all him, showed any signs of caring about that . . .

Walter had to wait a long time that day, saluting everything that came in and out. His heart was filled with misgivings, a great sense of foreboding, but he kept it to himself . . .

And then at last she was there.

Hand in hand they crossed a meadow and a little stream sparkling with sunlight. On a distant church a single bell was ringing; it was the last Sunday in the month. She wore a cotton blouse and a blue skirt with patches and her feet were bare. His heart was beating in a crisis of anticipation: he had never kissed her properly, just her hands or her hair. But he ached for her lips, yearned to make her understand how much he loved her, and today, on this last day he was ever to see her, he determined that he would.

There were dragonflies and shoots of new bramble and it

was hot. The path meandered with the stream and then broke away for a stand of woods. At its turning, they climbed a ruined wall and stared across a hillside ravished with bluebells.

What was she thinking? Was she thinking like him? They sat in silence while he smoked a cigarette. He could hear her breathing, smell the apples in her hair. Now was the moment, he was absolutely going to kiss her now, and he turned his face to hers with dizzy eyes, but she put a grin in the way and was waggling her toes.

'Tu transpires?'

'What?'

'Transpires?'

Lifting her skirt she wiped sweat from his cheek with the hem. He looked down at her legs, one knee raised slightly higher than the other. She had pale beautiful thighs, and when she dropped the skirt she left them exposed and hung backwards on her hands, her face angled to the sun as though her hair were too heavy for her head. Her blouse tightened to her breasts, she wore nothing more. At last her eyes rose and locked into his in a flood of blue adrenalin. Walter was intoxicated with love and desire. Her skirt was pulled so high, and her breasts so perfect, everything she was an expression of exquisite sensuality. But why today was it that a girl so sweetly shy as Adèle didn't seem to care?

He stubbed his cigarette, it fell into nettles, there was too much silence.

'I'm going away tomorrow,' he said.

She continued staring without moderation of her gaze, as if this were something she already understood. Slipping from the wall, she explored a pocket in her skirt, and extended her hand to give him something. He followed her down to take it. It was an American silver dollar, for good luck, she said, and he understood too.

'Ça c'est pour toi pour toujours.'

How many more eternities could he squander? He put a hand into her hair and in an agony of longing, kissed her on the lips. So fleeting it was barely a touch, like a dragonfly on the water, and it was a lie. Adèle raised her head in innocent inquisition, as though the kiss had been a pleasure taken rather than given, and when she looked at him she looked deep past his eyes. There were three buttons on her blouse, two white, one yellow. She undid them carefully, pulled the blouse from her skirt, 'Je t'aime, Walter,' and encircling him in her arms, she pressed her slender body into his and made kisses into his mouth. Her hands spread over his back, as his now over hers, lifting the blouse in heavenly trespass from her waist to the nape of her neck. He could feel her heart beat, and she his, delighting in the timorous fingers roaming her body, albeit incompetent of his desire. Her hand went to his hand, a gentle guide, and now his hand was on her breast. Adèle kissed his lips, kissed his face, intense, careless kisses – her mouth seemed untaught to satisfy. At last he abandoned the embrace, took his hands to her hair, her eyes, her neck, a sublime distraction, and all to rehearse the ecstasy of finding her breasts again.

When their kissing ceased of its own excess; they stood breathless, holding each other with eyes closed. Today was theirs for ever, and if it should never come again, it would always be theirs. They could hear crickets in the pasture and cuckoos in the wood, and beyond, almost as an illusion, the resonance of endless war. A new bombardment had begun. It seemed meaningless in the paradise of this moment, but both were listening now, to the big guns, rumbling fifty miles away . . .

Darkness swallowed everything; there were voices in the fields. He could see electric-lanterns and hear voices. Something put intense pressure on his face. He tried to fight, but hadn't the strength to lift an arm. He was breathing black air, suffocating gas. He knew the Germans had come again, to kill him again, and reclaim this promontory of land he'd already died for. But he cared nothing for that. He was with his love, and thought only of her . . .

ROB IN LOVE

Walter had been home about a week and not really awake for much of it. They brought him back from the hospital in the rain on the first day of February, 1959. The surgeon had apparently operated more than once: either forgotten something, or gone in again to get hold of something else. His name was a Mr Vincent Dawson (they always but an 'a' in front of it in deference to his eminence) and he was 'optimistic'. Twice a day a nurse in a green outfit arrived on a man's bicycle and went upstairs with Mabs and Ethel. Walter didn't like her attentions – you could hear him arguing her off through the ceiling. Thomas loitered, always gave it a minute before creeping up in their wake. The door was usually closed by the medical-woman, but on lucky days he got about half an inch of view. It wasn't worth a lot, he could see only the cabbage-green back and its elbows, and his grandfather but intermittently, as she hauled him forward to scrub. He looked like a bar of soap himself, smooth and yellow carbolic that was slowly been worn away. Other than the bed-bath, there was little to look at but pill bottles and the changing of the bandages . . .

'I won't have her in here again,' protested Walter, his public antagonism towards the medicinal-bird reducing her to a presence that conventional etiquette would have required to have already left.

'And that's *flat*,' he said.

Despite this, Mrs Hardcastle, that was her name, was optimistic too. In her view he was 'on the mend'. That's what she told Ethel, and that's what Ethel told Thomas.

'Uncle Reg said he's got something serious.'

'Uncle Reg don't know what he's talking about.'

In these taut days Ethel's sitting room had become something of a refuge for her grandson, and he spent more and more time in there, eating Turkish Delight and peering at the tiny black-and-white television with a kind of aquarium on the front to enlarge the picture. He loved his grandmother, her 'safety' and warmth, and occasionally she let him have a nip of gin. They sat in the firelight, watching programmes Thomas didn't really like, but liked better than the malign undercurrents in the house. Somehow the house felt ill, and it wasn't just Walter, although he of course was its epicentre.

'What exactly is enaemia, Gran?'

Her fingers were clicking knitting-needles with the facility of an astonishing machine.

'It's a disease, gets in your blood,' she said. 'And you can't make iron.'

'Enaemia?'

'Anaemia,' she confirmed.

'How can they operate on it then, if it's in your blood?'

'He's got more wrong with him that that, Tom.'

He asked her what and she lowered the needles and bifocals put firelight in her eyes.

'Oh, I don't know,' she said. 'Stuff going back to the wawer? He's still got shrapnel in him. Everything went wrong for your grandfather after the wawer.'

Like Walter, Ethel was a cockney, but unlike him, had never really lost the accent. When she talked about the war, which Thomas liked to talk about, she pronounced it 'waw-er' – Boer Wawer, First World Wawer – she'd lived through the lot, plus

113

the worst wawer of them all, the Blitz Krieg on the East End of London in 1942 . . .

'Bloody wawer,' she said. 'I've seen too many of 'em, and I've never known none of 'em do no one no good.' Her eyes raised briefly to the ceiling and she lowered the emerging sleeve to take a sip of gin. 'The Great Wawer ruined him.'

Thomas nodded, not necessarily in agreement, but because he liked her reminiscing.

'He was a wonderful young man, your grandfather, smart as a row of buttons. But when he came back I didn't know him.'

'Didn't you?'

'Not like I had.'

'Why not?'

'I don't know, something had gone. Before the wawer, it was all different. He used to write beautiful letters. He was a very good writer, your grandfather, brainiest bloke I ever met. But he always sold himself short.' She looked up again with a memory to confirm it. 'When he was in hospital, two years in Stoke Mandeville, in 1919, he wrote a whole book.'

'Did he?'

'All about his childhood in the East End of London. His father was a fish-coster, worked for a Jew-boy called Herbie Violet, all the chapters were named after fish. Haddock, Eel, it was full of fish.' All this accompanied by a furious clicking of knitting-needles. 'They wanted to publish it. I sent it to a firm in High Holborn – fifty guineas they offered, which was a lot in those days. But he wouldn't.'

'Why not?'

'I don't know. He went weird after the wawer.'

There was a knock on the floor, a lot of knocking of a walking stick on boards. It was two floors up but you could hear it clearly. Ethel looked at the clock.

'He wants his tea,' she said, snapping spectacles in a case. 'That's a good sign.'

'Whisky, Gran.'

'What?'

'He's tapping out w-h-i-s-k-y in Morse.'

A frown in her balding eyebrows. She left and Thomas sat staring at Eamon Andrews on the TV. It would be dinnertime soon, Rob would be home, and they'd all have to get back into the atmosphere. It was like bad music, a sustained sour note, nothing you could really put your finger on, just a bad feeling abroad that hadn't recovered since Christmas . . .

> *A symphony like a gloomy room*
> *With a violin*
> *Going around the top of it*
> *Like a fly . . .*

He couldn't get anywhere else with it, and poems couldn't do this environment justice. To reduce everything to its base constituent, the domestic ingredients consisted of something in the order of: cancer, loathing, puberty, divorce, dog-shit, dog-meat, and death.

'This is your life,' said Eamon Andrews, and he couldn't have timed it better.

Thomas turned the television off and sat staring at the dead screen. He agreed with himself. It wasn't really anything you could put your finger on, the elements weren't really divisible. When he focused on one, another would immediately take its place. It was a concoction, the one bleeding into the other.

Consider cancer and cooking.

Cancer smelt of chops and the meat of bandages. One came down and the other went up, colliding in savoury osmosis somewhere at the top of the stairs. Plus the dogs had got into their stride, legs up and squatting all over the house. Even the Dobermann had joined in. When Mabs wasn't cooking she was clearing it up – in and out with the coal shovel – and then in to skewer the beef.

Meat was now served at both lunch and dinner, a frenzy of roasting that wasn't easy to understand. But somehow Thomas intuitively knew it was connected with loathing, and loathing in its turn with divorce. All this constituted the general malaise, although he was still in ignorance of various specifics. Divorce was a good example. He had little idea this was the gathering momentum of his mother's intention; however, he had acquired certain information in respect of it and its as yet undiscovered association with the mysterious Brackett.

Just after Christmas, Thomas had been fortunate to overhear a conversation between his mother and the detective. By chance he was behind the living-room door. She was on the line for a good stint, and with a bit of imagination it wasn't difficult to extrapolate what was being said at the other end of the phone. Conversation revolved around times and dates in respect of somewhere called the Canterbury Assizes. What she was going to do there, whether alone or with associates, Thomas didn't know, but something was up, and it came to a head, as they say, the day before Bel left for Germany.

It was on this day that Thomas discovered Brackett was nothing to do with him, but his father, and that it was *Rob* who was being followed.

Well, that was a load off. But what had Rob done?

At his earliest opportunity, Thomas rushed upstairs to confront his sister. In the corridor he gave it pause to gather his thoughts. This might well require diplomacy. Bel was in her bedroom folding clothes when he sauntered in. Everything was laid out on the bed looking neat. There was a new sponge bag and a new toothbrush, and he was surprised to realise how many new clothes she had.

'You won't need all those jumpers in Germany,' he said.

'Why not?'

'It tends to be quite warm this time of the year.'

'It's snowing, Thomas.'

'Is it?'

'Yes.'

'Oh.'

Not the most efficacious prelude to the conversation he had in mind, and he dropped the chat angle and walked to the window and looked out across the gardens. There was a bit of watery sun about, like a light bulb behind a shower curtain . . .

'I've just been talking,' he said with a certain *gravitas*. 'To mother.'

The time for reply came and went and he turned to see what had happened to it. A pair of shoes and a photograph of the Vegetarian were looking for a place in the case.

'I advised her accordingly.'

'About what?' said Bel.

'I think you know what I'm talking about.'

'Do I?'

'Don't you?'

'I've no idea.'

He closed the door and the gap between them got conspiratorial.

'If I tell you,' he said, 'will you promise it'll go no further than here?'

'All right.'

'Swear?'

'All right,' she said.

He was losing this. He had her attention but didn't know what to do with it. It was her supposed to be telling him.

'Tell me what you know,' he said.

'You just said you were going to tell me.'

'I know I did, but I've got to be careful.'

117

'Why?'

'Because it's obvious, isn't it? It's Mum and it's a delicate matter. I need to know what you know, so I don't say anything she wouldn't want you to know.'

'I don't know what you're talking about.'

'I think you do.'

'I've just said, I've no idea.'

'All right then,' said Thomas, with precise articulation of a severely controlled mouth, 'I'm talking about *Brackett*. J.T. Brackett?'

She looked at him suspiciously and squashed in a shoe at either end of the case.

'We've had this conversation before,' she said.

'Oh no we haven't, not like this we haven't. I've just been down there, we've discussed it, she told me everything.'

'I don't believe you.'

'Are you calling me a liar?'

'You are a liar.'

She momentarily disappeared into the wardrobe. On her return she pushed past with a winter coat and pair of Wellington boots.

'For the sunbathing.'

'I was talking about *South* Germany,' said Thomas. 'It's a completely different weather system.'

He was talking to the back of her head.

'I'm busy, Thomas.'

'I'm *not* lying,' he said, advancing at the edge of her vision. 'You can test me.'

'Test you on what?'

'Ask me questions.'

'Don't be so silly.'

'Ask me about Canterbury Assizes.'

That knocked the complacency out. She looked at him, mid-zip on the sponge bag. He had more than a toe in the door.

'What's he doing?' said Thomas.

'Who?'

'Rob. Rob.'

No answer, and he went for the probable.

'Is he burgling?'

'What?'

'House-breaking?'

'Don't be ridiculous.'

'Then why is Brackett following him?'

She was poised to say something but said something else.

'I thought you said you'd just discussed it.'

'Let's not start playing games, Bel. I said, we'd discussed Brackett, and of course, the Canterbury Assizes. But I sensed a bit of choppy water, so I didn't push her on Rob.'

There was a pause. She was softening.

'I don't know if I should tell you.'

'Why not?'

'Because, it isn't really any of your business.'

'Isn't it? For three months I thought he was following *me*. Can you imagine what that's like, the feeling of binoculars on your back?'

'Why would he want to follow you?'

Thomas found this vaguely insulting.

'Bombs,' he said.

Another tidy pause. She was ripe.

'I'll tell you the truth,' she said, 'if you tell me the truth.'

'I've told you the truth.'

'No, you haven't.'

'You don't believe me? Go and ask Mum.'

He opened the door and invited her out and she went. Thomas went after her with his hands panicking.

'All right, all right, if you want to split hairs,' he

said, waylaying her in the corridor. 'I admit it. It is possible we haven't discussed it in the way most people might consider conventional, but I can give you a written guarantee, we were in the same room when it was discussed.'

'Which room?'

'The living room.'

'Where were you?'

'Behind the door.'

'You must stop lurking.'

'I will.'

With Thomas ushering they returned to the bedroom and the door was once again closed. He stuck ears at her and tried not to look impatient.

'I'll tell you, only if you absolutely swear not to tell Grandad?'

'Yes, yes, absolutely I won't.'

'He's got enough to worry about.'

Thomas agreed.

Bel continued. 'If I wasn't going away, I wouldn't be telling you at all. If there was anything I thought I could do about it, I wouldn't go.'

His smile was anything but unsympathetic.

'I'm telling you,' she said. 'Because I think it might help you to understand Mum.'

His understanding nod was a mixture of gratitude and raging frustration. Come on, come on, get on with it, he thought, we've been here a week, spit it out. This was like looking for money down the back of a chair . . .

'Brackett is watching Rob.'

'I know he is.'

'It's been going on for over six months.'

'I know. *Why?*'

'Because he's got a woman.'

'A woman? What kind of woman?'

'A lover.'

Thomas felt all expression drain off.

What do you mean, he's having sex with her?'

'Of course he is.'

Thomas was numbed, not because Rob had a woman, but because intercourse was involved. Intercourse wasn't a concept he could associate with his father – or mother, come to that. It seemed of all things you could conceivably imagine for his parents, intercourse wasn't one of them.

'Who is she?' he said.

'I don't know,' said Bel, letting the worry show. 'Mum says she's almost a midget.'

'A midget?'

'I don't know if she's literally a midget, but Mum says she's very short. She lives on the Ramsgate Road, he goes there every morning after the newspapers, and that's why he's putting on weight. He eats two breakfasts, two lunches, and two dinners.'

'What on earth for?'

'To pretend it isn't happening, Tom. He's living in two houses, that's why he's always late. He goes round there and eats her dinner, and comes home and eats ours.'

It suddenly dawned on Thomas that that was what all the cooking was about. She was punishing Rob with meat. Lamb at lunch and then back at night for a further onslaught of beef. She must have loathed cooking it but loathed him more. No wonder the Dobermann was beginning to look like a barrel.

'What's her name?' he said.

'Ruby Round the Corner.'

'Ruby Round the Corner?'

Apparently the appellation by which she went, at least in this house. Bel didn't know her last name.

'Is she old?' said Thomas.

'Widow,' said Bel. 'Her sons are doctors in the Navy.'

Upstairs a walking stick was bashing on the boards. They both listened and Thomas thought it sounded like an exit.

'I better go and see what he wants.'

'I tell you, Tom, apart from leaving Grandad, I can't wait to get out of here. I'm sick of worrying about it, I've got nothing left to say to Mum.'

Thomas didn't care for the emotional side of it. With no further hard information available from his sister, he made his excuses and left.

'I'll see you before you go,' he said.

Two minutes later he was sitting in his bedroom smoking a cigarette. The walking stick was still banging. If he felt anything about Bel's revelations it was annoyance: why had he been kept out of the equation so long? Most of all he was annoyed with his mother. Who did she think she was protecting, him, or herself? He concluded the latter, although he couldn't quite understand why. All that anxiety about Brackett, and for what? Why should she care if he had a woman round the corner? What did it matter? What was the big deal? Maybe he'd move in with her and that would be a good thing. His mother had nothing to lose but loathing. There was no marriage to destroy, that's for sure, they'd all be better off. If he wants to clear off in the Wolsey and fuck a midget, so what? That's his affair.

The more Thomas considered it the less he could believe it. How could Rob know anything about love?

It seemed absurd to the point of impossible, a phenomenon that just couldn't happen. It was unthinkable, and the thought unleashed full verbal grandiloquence of the fledgling poet as he nailed it in his diary. It was like, he wrote:

A ruby in an oyster.

Bel left the next day. January trudged into February and the diary took a sudden wave of entries. More and more were orientated towards Rob and Ruby. Now he was in possession of the information, Thomas made it his business to observe his parents, and things previously unnoticed took on new significance. It was undeniable Rob was staying out later and later of a morning, and manifest he was getting huge. The arse and gut were out of control, and his neck stuffed into the surgical-collar like a cork forced into a bottle. It seemed to trap too much blood in his head. On occasion this could look alarming, like he was in a condition of perpetual rage, which, in fact, wasn't too far from the truth.

Mabs got up to start frying about 7.30 a.m. – eggs, bacon, toast, marmalade – and the Dobermann enjoyed the lot, even got its own bowl of tea. Whatever the malice behind each other's backs, it wasn't expressed in each other's presence. It was a pantomime of abominable normality. Communication was now almost entirely via the dogs. Rob stroked the Dobermann's head and wrote its dialogue: 'That's right, Max, you were wondering where I was, weren't you? The train was late, wasn't it?' And at the other end of the table in a pink dressing gown and hair awry, Mabs and her whelp: 'We needn't have got up, need we, Fabey?'

Thomas sat between them eating RedyBrek.

February 2: Rob went out in a suit (she pressed it) and new shoes that hurt him . . . He's also started to wear scent . . . it's called Old Spice and smells ponce . . .

February 5: Ethel scuttled on approach of the Wolsey and 'the force' arrived in the hall . . . Got all the usual bulletins about 'hammerings' and late trains . . . Didn't eat his breakfast, and for some reason the Dobermann scoffing it initiated smiles from Mabs . . . clearly fake because she was clearly seething, so what was that about? . . . Grandad smoked a cigar and seemed slightly better . . .

February 9: Put my name down for the Drama Society because Gwen's name was on the list . . . We pass each other in the corridor, and today she *smiled* at me too! . . . God, she's beautiful . . . Mumps going around . . . I hope Shackles gets it . . .

Nurse Hardcastle continued to visit twice a day, and on the eleventh there was too much of her to fit in the diary.

Her usual agenda was a bad-time with Walter followed by descent into the kitchen where she would swallow tea and give everyone a run-down on who had what in the vicinity. Thomas had no idea there were so many different ways to die. She had a man down the road with Gaucher's disease that caused him to keep a leg in the air. Distributed amongst the others was lymphoblastoma, heave, scrofula, alcoholic meningitis, and insufficiency of the valves. Mabs and Ethel were the main recipients of this, but of late, due in part to his retarded schedule,

Rob was increasingly present. Some sort of pharmacological union seemed to have developed, marginalising Ethel and Mabs.

'Was it a sarcoma?' said Rob.

'No, no, it was rather more interesting than that. It was a soft fistula.'

Hardcastle was a fat-ankled Tory with a rural head, and Thomas supposed that's why she got on with Rob. On the day in question, a Saturday, he was showing her to the front door and they dallied in the hall discussing a local who'd just gone into the toilet with a luposa.

'In the duodenum?'

She didn't get the chance to answer. For some reason Thomas was at a loss to understand, this medicinal yak suddenly angered Mabs. She came up the hall in a vengeful stoop, the nurse was summarily ejected, and the door closed after her with emotion not short of a slam. Hardcastle didn't understand either and looked through the letter box to say so.

'Bugger off,' said Mabs.

The last view of her was a pair of fat and uncomprehending eyes. She was unwelcome in the house and Thomas never saw her again . . .

Three days later there was an event of such importance the diary could have taken another stuffing, but it got only a few words that evening: 'Gwen, my darling, my darling Gwen.'

It was February the 14th and 'Guess Who?' sent him a valentine card. Who else could it be? It had to be from her. To avoid witnesses he rushed up the hall and studied it in the downstairs lavatory. It featured a pink and a blue rabbit with blue birds loitering in an orbit of half a dozen hearts. 'LOVE IS,' it said, promoting a question it went on to answer inside, 'ME AND YOU.' In corroboration the rabbits wobbled on little springs, kissed each other, and the hearts exploded like bubbles. And that's how Thomas felt, airborne in the toilet, his heart exploding with love. He was the blue rabbit, Gwen the pink – they had captured his emotions brilliantly.

He took the card into his bedroom to measure it. It was four and three-eighths by three and seven-sixteenth inches. 'Guess Who?' was written in green ink on a ruler to keep the lines straight, as was the poem he discovered on the back:

> My Ink is Pale, My Paper Frale,
> My Love for you Will Never Fale.
> Please Don't Think I'm very Cold,
> I know Your name Should be Written In Gold,
> But Gold is Scarce, So Ink Will do,
> Just To Say, that I *Love* You . . .

The last line was enchanting: she was in love, in love with him, and so saying he pushed the hallstand aside to get at a mirror and see what there was to adore. This wasn't as easy as it should have been. The mirror was Georgian and hardly up to it; half the silvering was worn off and he kept losing bits of his face. No matter where he put it his forehead was intermittently wallpapered. When he got his mouth in the right position an eye would disappear, replaced by a bunch of roses in a basket. Plus there was something about this mirror that made his ears stick out: it sort of sucked the nose forward and stretched the ears to the edge of the frame.

He concluded it was impossible to look at himself like Gwen might look at him, and hustling the hallstand back into position, he decided to continue the experiment in front of the best mirror in the house.

His mother was presumed to be out and her bedroom therefore available. In he went, and tilting the mirror he sat on an embroidered stool and got full portrait. It was important not to prejudge this, but to present it like he'd never seen it before. There were things he liked and things he didn't. In terms of the latter, the eyebrow on the lip was a concern. It had acquired certain rogue hairs, thicker than the others, the sort of thing brambles get, 'suckers' he thought they were called, vigorous tendrils that shoot out at right-angles from the rest for no apparent reason. The moustache was a liability and would have to be monitored. Also, as a general critique, he tended to look quite wintery, drab was the word, and there was a bit of dandruff about that he thought he could cure with an egg.

On the positive side the assembly was more encouraging. The eyes were lovable – he could see that she would love the eyes; they were an unusual green and rather intelligent-looking. And the teeth weren't bad either, a bit of khaki hue, perhaps caused by smoking, but that could be dealt with. The challenge was the ears, what could be done with these? The antique wasn't lying – they looked like somebody else's ears, like wing-mirrors on a motor bike. He tried various angles on them with no noticeable improvement, so decided not to include them in the overall assessment.

At either end of the mirror were additional sources of reflection. He had never known their worth before but now understood they could be manipulated to supply alternative views, views that Gwen might get, and it was her view that he was after. Both were adjusted to reveal an aspect of himself that he was startled to realise he'd never seen before in his life . . .

What he saw was his profile, and he could hardly believe what he was looking at. This was a prime set of features. The nose, chin, and forehead were a revelation: this was like looking at some sort of intruder, like a stranger had stuck his head in with sensational news. The nose was superb – he had no idea he had a nose like this – it was a statement of crisp elegance, with a tilt at the end like a film actor's. Even better, from this perspective, the ears had lost their impact, all they looked like now were ears. But it was the nose that was brilliant, and returning attention to it he angled it sort of south, south-west, and brought an eye into the picture. He was now in the 'corridor-passing position', and though the neck looked a bit peculiar he could see what it was Gwen was in love with . . .

It had to be admitted, he was actually very good-looking. The right profile was better than the left, and the mouth better half open, exposing some tooth. The nose worked wherever you put it. This then was the conclusion. In future he would keep her to his right, head down and hair washed, mouth half open and eyes up like he was looking over a book. What the fuck was that in his ear? Jesus Christ, he was going to have to do something hygienic in his ear. A programme of cleaning would begin that very day, as would the shaving of the moustache. He'd have that bastard off and was on his way to do it when he heard footsteps coming up the stairs. Instinctively he got behind the door and watched as his mother and grandmother went by with a tray and bag of bandages. Since Hardcastle got her cards it was their responsibility to deal with Walter, and because these sessions always seemed to take place when Thomas was at school they were unmissable when he wasn't. He therefore postponed the ear and gave it the usual minute before following them up.

There was another plus to the back of Hardcastle. The door was now invariably left open with a consequent improvement of view. Thomas got into position and peered through the crack.

'How do you feel?' they said.

'How do I look?' said Walter.

'Much better,' said Mabs.

Conversation of this ilk drifted around the bed until the reason they were in there surfaced. They wanted to wash him and he didn't like it. Ethel went in anyway, had him up in a kind of half-nelson. Larded with Brylcreem, his hair stuck out sideways and left a dull yellow shadow on the pillow.

'I'll never get out of here,' he said.

'You will if you take your pills,' said Ethel, and she opened a canister containing the heavyweight anti-anaemics.

'I'm not having any more of those,' said Walter. 'I may as well swallow buttons.'

'You need the iron, Wol,' said Ethel, 'You've got to give them a chance.'

'Cant,' said Walter.

'Specialists don't lie,' said Mabs.

'That crank don't know my arse from his elbow.'

'He's a London man,' said Ethel. She got a couple of pills in his head and reiterated something about 'anaemia'.

'It's all cant,' said Walter, and he spat the pills six feet and wanted a cigar. Mabs said he could only have one if he swallowed the medicine. So he swallowed a pair and Mabs crossed the room with astonishing speed and was suddenly following Thomas downstairs.

'What are you doing, Thomas?'

'Just on my way downstairs,' he said.

'Why aren't you at school?'

'I don't know.'

'Are you lurking?'

'Not really.'

'Go and get your grandfather a cigar.'

'All right,' said Thomas, and he continued the descent as though going down was something he had in mind anyway. In the living room he found a box of Coronas and was on his way out when he realised he was in the vicinity of a dictionary. Apart from Walter's office and his bedroom, there were probably less than two dozen books in the house.

This was one of them, a cherry-red *Chambers Twentieth Century* . . .

'En-eem-ha?'

'En-eh-maa?'

His inability to spell brought him to the point of tossing it in, when at last he found it between 'End-ways' and 'Enemy'.

'*Enema*: An injection of liquid or gaseous substance into the rectum: the syringe used.'

An injection of liquid or gaseous substance into the rectum?

'*Rectum*: The final section of the large intestine, terminating at the anus.'

The anus? The arsehole!

That's what Walter meant – Vincent Dawson didn't know the difference between his anus and his elbow. It was the *arsehole* they were after and it was obvious. They were going to inject some liquid or gaseous substance into his arse. Suddenly it made sense. It was no wonder he didn't want Hardcastle to do it. But why did they say it was in his blood? I'll tell you why, because they didn't want him to know what they were going to do. Or more likely, in fact, almost certainly, *they didn't want Thomas to know*. That's what this was all about.

He stuck the dictionary back in the cupboard and raced upstairs. If the enema was going in today he was determined to witness it, even if it meant forcing his way in at a crucial moment. The cigar was an ideal accessory – he could choose any moment he liked for entrance, and with this unexpected advantage, he took up position again outside the bedroom door.

On the nearest table there was an enamel bowl with a bar of carbolic going in and out as Ethel washed Walter's back with a sponge. Sickness stretched across his body like a membrane, confiscating the power of his muscles. Over his knuckles the skin was so transparent you could see the yellow bones, and Thomas wondered if chronic deficiency of enema was causing yellow blood to be pumped through his veins.

Nothing moved. Whatever Walter said was without change of expression, as if somebody else was in the room throwing a voice into him.

'Dog came up here this morning. Messed itself.'

'Where?' said Mabs, without much concern.

'Under the bed,' said Walter. 'I heard it.'

During this exchange they manoeuvred him back down the mattress and everything was suddenly out of sight. All Thomas could see was his grandfather's nose and dishevelled hair above the bed end. The ablutions were terminated and fresh bandaging began.

'I don't want the tube,' said Walter.

'You have to have the tube.'

Thomas was becoming impatient, started mouthing silent instuctions at the door: 'Give him the tube now.'

'That bugger's agony,' said Walter.

'It's either us, or Hardcastle,' they said.

Discussion swerved again into Walter's antipathy towards Vincent Dawson ('that crank from Bexley'), his acolyte, Hardcastle, and practically everybody else in Ramsgate Hospital. He even hated the other patients. If he ever had to go back in there, he'd never get out again, and that was for certain . . .

'You're not going back, Wol.'

'Come on, come on,' said Thomas. 'Give him the tube.'

A drawer opened and closed quickly and Mabs seemed to be concealing something. As she delivered it to the bed, Thomas rose to his toes pressing at the crack to get a better view. He was convinced Mabs had just palmed the enema kit and was getting everything into position, and he scrutinised both her and his grandmother wondering which would be the actual administrator. Logically, it would be his mother. If the sight of the nozzle panicked him it would need a steady hand and straight aim. Ethel had neither and Thomas assumed, if anything, she would act as a distraction and possible anchor-man if trouble developed. Securing a couple of safety-pins in the gauze, Ethel joined Mabs at the same side of the bed. This was it. They were going in.

'What are we waiting for?'

He continued to wait, and minutes went by, and Thomas for one was getting tired of standing outside the door with nothing happening. They had him in the perfect position – surely to dither now was ludicrous? He knew what he was going to get would be unpleasant. We all did. Nobody likes an enema. So what profit was there in this endless procrastination? The foolishness of his grandmother was overwhelming. She started fiddling with pillows – what kind of pretence was this? Who could she possibly think she was helping, certainly not Walter. 'Just hold him down and get it in, that's the way he'd want it.' Thomas felt his frustration welling to the point of open protestation. 'He knows what you're here for, we all do. We are here to administer, witness, or suffer an enema.' Still on toes he mouthed furious imprecations at the crack. 'He wants an enema. Why do you not give him that enema?'

There was an inaudible exchange above the bed and to Thomas's astonishment they hauled him up again, got him in the pillows and Ethel started combing his hair.

'What the fuck's going on?' said Thomas.

Mabs swivelled at the volume, saw an eye peering in and there was no escape.

'What are you doing out there?'

Thomas motored instantly, feigning breathlessness.

'Sorry, I was just having a quick look in. Took ages to find the cigars.'

He put out a general smile but nobody seemed pleased to see him. Ethel resumed her combing and got some strands over the chromium dome. Thomas looked around for somewhere to blend in, but there was nowhere handy and staying in here wasn't going to be easy. Mabs was again busy at the bedside with towels and it was apparent she wanted him out.

'Do you want this cigar, Grandad?'

Walter just about found the sinew to look friendly.

'I'll have it later, Tom, when your mother's finished.'

Thomas nodded sweetly and stood there with the cigar, deciding that to stand there and hold it was a legitimate function.

On the floor by the bed there was a bottle of slash that looked like orange juice from more than one country of origin. This flagon was somehow plumbed into his illness and supplied by a rubber pipe the colour of dolls' bodies. Uncoupling the feed, Mabs transported it to a basin in the corner, and if you saw it, you'd have to hand it to her . . .

Thomas was suddenly confused about the tubes. He'd seen the flagon before, full and empty, but never the tube. Was this the tube Walter didn't like? Obviously it wasn't Hardcastle's tube; after all, you don't get an enema in the penis.

'What sort of tube is that?' he said.

This got no reply, and he sauntered up the bed trying not to look like a tourist. On arrival there was a mix of disappointment and cheer. In respect of the former, a Gillette shaving set was waiting on the mattress, and Thomas realised it was not the enema nozzle but this item his mother had palmed from the drawer. But of the latter, things looked more promising. There was a coil of virgin pipe, six foot of it, together with the latest type of luxury toilet roll. Put together they made sense.

'Is that an enema tube?' enquired Thomas lightly.

'A what?' said Ethel.

'That tube there?'

Mabs was on her way back from the basin with a steaming bowl of soapy water.

'Stop prying, Thomas.'

'I'm not prying, I just wanted to know what sort

of tube it was. I've been reading about them in the dictionary.'

'Why aren't you at school?' said Ethel, framing the freshly combed head with pillows.

'Because there's mumps going around, and I don't want to catch them.'

'You've had mumps,' said Mabs.

'Have I?' said Thomas. 'When?'

'When you were ten,' she said, and he had to shift himself as she returned to the bed. 'Come on, out of the way, I'm busy, and you're not helping.'

'What do you want me to do?'

'I don't want you to do anything.'

'I'll hold the bowl if you like?'

'You can go downstairs and feed the dogs,' said Mabs, delivering her aromatic brew to the bedside table. This was potentially enema-fluid and Thomas was desperate to stay.

'I'd rather help in here,' he said, and smiling somewhat obsequiously at his mother, he put a question through it. 'Is that Persil in there?'

'No,' said Mabs.

'There's nothing for you to do in here, Thomas,' said Ethel, her expression meaning business. Thomas stood in the gathering vacuum and the only way out was the door.

'You can bring me a Guinness later,' said Walter, and even his eyes expected him to leave.

Thomas gave up and was on an exit when he had an idea.

'Would you like me to collect the turd?'

'What turd?'

'There's a turd under the bed.'

Dropping to hands and knees he crawled across the floor and got halfway under the bed.

'It's against the wall,' he said, looking up at his mother

with a useful kind of expression. 'I'll go and get the shovel.'

'I'll deal with that,' said Mabs.

'Go on,' said Ethel. 'Go somewhere else.'

Her stare was non-negotiable.

'Right-ho,' said Thomas, and he got up and backed for the door and reminded himself. 'I'll bring you a Guinness, Grandad.'

'Not till we've finished,' said Mabs. 'And shut the door.'

'Right-ho.'

Suddenly he was outside, damning his luck and listening. What were they doing in there? Was this the abdominal hose or preface to an actual enema? He could hear Ethel insisting and Walter complaining and he pressed his ear at the paint.

'That hurt,' said Walter.

'Sorry, Wally,' said Ethel.

'Christ, this is unfair,' said Thomas.

They were giving him one and Thomas was rapidly becoming too upset to stand out here and listen to it. If he could imagine it, why couldn't he watch it? His exclusion seemed absurd.

There was a bit of morbid groaning, like a ship docking miles away, and the whole scenario became unbearable.

'Fuck it,' he said, and his feet fucked it all the way back up the corridor to his room where he fell across the bed in a huff. For some moments he lay there thinking truly negative thoughts, ultimately focusing and murdering himself with doubts about the valentine card and everything that could be wrong with it . . . What if it wasn't from Gwen at all? . . . Who else could it be from then? . . . How about that puffy-girl with the pink National Health spectacles who kept looking at him? . . . No, no, he didn't want to indulge it, and got up and sat at his desk and re-smelt the envelope. It was genuine all right. This was from Gwen, and he cursed himself for not sending her one.

Rereading the verse, he held the card at arm's length, experimenting with various positions of display on the desk. At last he settled on a spot illuminated by a shaft of red sunlight. From this angle he could see both artwork and poem and from 'Guess Who?'.

'From Gwen,' he said. 'Gwen, my darling, my darling Gwen.' And he took out his pen, and wrote exactly that in his diary.

SOME DRAMATIC EVENTS

Gwendolin had been in Scotland with her mother on some sort of family business, and if you want the truth, that's the reason Thomas wasn't too bothered about going to school. Now he couldn't wait. How wonderful was that first warm Monday – feel the sun on your face and hope in your feet like you're wearing new shoes – Gwendolin was back, and it was no exaggeration to say that everything about being alive was improving. Not only was there a transformation in his appearance (his teeth looked like an advert), it was also academic, this particularly true of English literature. A year ago he'd have been up the back with a contraction, indulging a Malvolio, or Rudyard, in his trouser. Now, he actually enjoyed composition, could see the point of it, and he wrote an essay about David Copperfield and got a B-plus. This was the best mark he'd ever had. The teacher, a comfortable old duck called Mrs Windermere, was especially impressed with his analysis of Little Emily. What she didn't know was that Thomas had written almost exclusively about Gwen. Gwen in Peggotty's beach house. Gwen in the seaside town. And Gwen all over the school.

He'd see her coming down the corridor with her friend, Constance Bancock, or Freda Pew, chattering like a little wireless, all blonde with a pony-tail and sometimes her bra showed through her blouse. But when she passed she was silent looking at him, and he was looking at her. They never said a word but they were in love, and that's what the B-plus was about . . .

The first day they ever spoke was a Friday, at least, that was the first day she ever spoke to him. He and Maurice were on the move between geography and maths. Thomas saw her and was getting his profile ready for the pass, when Freda Pew suddenly pushed Gwen hard into him. They collided and he touched her arm. 'Sorry,' she said, and that was the first word.

'Watch where you're fuckin' going,' said Maurice, chin swivelling as the commerce of the corridor dragged them apart.

Thomas was truly upset that Maurice had used the F word in front of Gwen, and his hope was that she hadn't heard.

'You don't wanna fuckin' idolise her,' said Maurice. 'She's just a girl – they're not angels, girls, they're the same as us. All they wanna do is make sure you fancy them, and as soon as you do, they don't fancy you. They're not trustworthy, girls. What you gotta do with a girl is be totally up front.'

They climbed the stairs towards an hour of tedium in Norris's windy tower.

'I'll tell you what,' said Thomas with a certain confidentiality, 'I'm going to Drama Society tonight and I think you should come with me.'

'What do I wanna come for?'

'Because Gwen's going to be there, and there might be a chance to ask her out.'

'So what's that gotta do with me?'

'I thought it might be easier for the two of us to do it.'

'What do you mean,' said Maurice, 'ask her out with both of us?'

'No, with me.'

'You mean, you want me to ask her?'

'It might be easier, because you know her.'

If there was a logic to this, Maurice had lost it.

'All right,' he said, 'I'll ask her out, and if she says yes, you don't have to come, OK?'

This wasn't altogether the soirée Thomas had envisaged, and he said so and Maurice put him back on the rails.

'Listen, she *fancies* you, all right? It's not that difficult, just ask her out, and you're in. What d'you think that fucking bulldozer's pushing her around for?'

'I can't,' said Thomas. 'I can't ask her out unless I know what I'm going to ask her. We need to share an interest. If we had an interest, I'd have something to talk to her about.'

'Like what?' said Maurice.

'Amateur dramatics,' said Thomas.

Maurice shook his head with over-statement dropping his chops like a lopsided venetian blind.

'You don't wanna go through all that bollocks. Just take her to the pictures and get your hand up, that's what she wants.'

The last flight of stairs was negotiated and analysis continued during seating.

'Take her to the fucking Odeon.'

Norris was in a state of reversed excitement at the front, bored beyond distraction by the last lot, and as compensation, preparing to administer some fresh mathematics to this.

'Quiet,' he said.

'If she fancied me, I'd have her fucked by now.'

'I said quiet, Potts.'

'Yes, sir.'

Maurice was peculiar with women, had no poetry, thought they were all right for shagging, but that was it. In many ways, Thomas envied him, wished he could just go up to her and ask her to the pictures like Maurice could, and would. But he couldn't, and he sat there for an hour watching the clock and thinking about the Drama Society, and it was the longest hour Norris had ever presided over.

At last the four o'clock bell and the school drained, chairs on desks and lights going out everywhere. So were the kids, six hundred and fifty, straight out of the door. There were some of course, like Bowls, who attended Geography Group, and others, like Gollick, who went to Gym Club and voluntarily hung on rings.

But most went home and gladly.

Thomas trod water in the cloakroom until about half-past, then walked down the corridor to the assembly hall where the Drama Society was to take place. He didn't want to be the first, and he didn't want to be the last; either way he was looking at his watch and nervous about going in.

There were some enormous columns out here in the foyer, part of the support structure of the tower, concrete horrors that could only have been thought of by an architect, but they were good cover for loitering. He spent some minutes behind one watching the Drama Society go in. So far there were two of them. One was the girl who had caught him in the toilet, Margaret Ruther, and the other was her tall friend. He waited several more minutes but nobody else came. This didn't seem right at all. He couldn't imagine Ruther being an actress; the only person in the school he could conceive of as being a film star was Gwen. But where was she? Maybe they were all in there already? Maybe he'd left it too late?

He waited another minute and walked across the foyer and opened the door into the hall. It was a big room where assemblies took place, smelt of feet and prayers, and was like looking down the fat end of a telescope. About a mile away was a small group of thespians sitting in a circle of metal chairs. A 'reading' was in progress, and it stopped, and all of them looked at him, and all of them were girls. Thomas panicked. The only male in the room was Shackles, situated next to

Gwen. The teacher, the previously mentioned Windermere, who ran this group, asked him what he wanted. It felt like a question at the door of a party.

'I put my name down,' said Thomas.

'Come in then,' she said.

Thomas stared back at her and the others, could feel an uncomfortable emotion developing along his top lip. It was exactly the kind of thing he didn't want Gwen to see.

'I didn't know it was actually tonight,' he said. 'I was just checking the location.'

In reality he couldn't go in there with all those girls, and the only girl he'd ever adored sitting next to Shackles.

Gwendolin looked curiously ill at ease and looked away, and Shackles looked like the lout he was. What was he doing in there? Nobody could possibly consider him for a part. He had a lisp like a tap and could hardly read. The intention of the shifty-stinker was transparent: it was to walk Gwendolin home with a possible diversion into Piermont Park.

A fortnight of expectation withered in an instant. Had she asked him to come to the Drama Society? Had she sent Shackles a valentine too? Thomas steadied himself to handle the appalling thoughts, a poisonous and offensive onslaught, but most of all the thought that he'd been betrayed . . .

'Either come in, or go out, Thomas,' said Mrs Windermere. 'But please do shut the door?'

Two dozen eyes were still on him, everyone looking but Gwen.

'I've just remembered something,' said Thomas. 'I think I'll come back later.'

He shut the door, and detouring for his coat, walked out into a frail green evening. At the bicycle sheds he stopped and looked back at the school. The last light went out in the tower and there was the thinnest moon ever. Turning away, he put on his cycle-clips, and he rode the bastard home with a feeling that was just a little like love, and a lot like love was lead . . .

> And I never thought that love
> Could by loving, itself destroy
> And while taking pain
> Give it again
> Ten thousand times to my heart . . .

Next morning at breakfast there was a postcard from Bel. Thomas had just got back from the railway station and sat alone at the kitchen table reading it over a bowl of cornflakes . . .

'Dear Everybody,' she wrote. 'Having a smashing time and learning to ski! I can't tell you how my German has improved. I hope you are all well, and hope Grandad is feeling better. I will be home in two weeks with Eva. Love Bel.'

On the reverse there was a coloured picture divided into five sections showing various pleasantries around Düsseldorf. In the middle was a bloke on a plinth. Thomas tore the stamp off wondering what Eva was like. Sixteen apparently. They have big tits, Germans.

But his thoughts were actually elsewhere. He was about to go upstairs and resume work on his communication to Gwen. The completed poem was to be called 'Lead Valentine', and when he finished it he would send it to her in a black envelope . . .

Two noises happened at once.

One was a measure of quite purposeful footsteps upstairs, and the other someone coming through the front door.

'Oh fuck it,' said Thomas, with no time to escape.

A moment later, Rob barged into the kitchen in his brown bifocals and surgical-collar. His blood was up and he was talking in headlines.

'"CASTRO DEFIES THE U.S."'

A sample of every newspaper printed in England was

slammed on to the kitchen table. For reasons that aren't really material, Thomas had managed to avoid the Country Run this morning and had yet to hear it from Rob.

'"U.N. WILL IMPOSE SANCTIONS,"' he said, with a condemnatory gesture at the *Telegraph*. 'As if the fucking U.N. could impose anything else.'

A white loaf took the brunt of it; he carved a slice with eyes on the dog's casserole. It was clear that for some reason Ruby hadn't fed him this morning. He would breakfast now and at this time of the day the kitchen wasn't a good place to be.

Traditionally, there would be a variety of topics to debate – Blacks rioting in Notting Hill – Cyprus – Korea – anything he'd seen in that morning's inks. But this particular morning, full volume was focused at the Cuban . . .

'AMERICANS are too GUTLESS to do anything. There's only ONE WAY to deal with that BASTARD.' He stuck a finger at Thomas as though it were all his fault. 'CARPET BOMBING, that's the only thing he understands. HIT HIM WHERE IT HURTS.'

Rob lifted the lid of the iron pot and plunged a thumb into the fat. A red, gelatinous compound clung to the underside, and this was the stuff he was after. Even at this time of the day it was too good to pass, and he spread it, and ate it. Simultaneously, an oar went past the kitchen window.

Thomas saw it, but his father didn't.

'"The United Nations Will Impose Sanctions,"' he said again, re-emphasising an equality of contempt for every word. 'The United Nations? They've got a SWEDE running it, you think CASTRO cares about the SWEDES?'

He went up and down the kitchen belittling the Swedes, eating like a creeping bugger. Outside, several pairs of shoes belted down, together with a clutch of shirts and a book or two.

'The most the SWEDES will do,' he said, 'is send him

a letter, you watch. That'll be an imposition, they'll all be rushing out of Havana after that.' There was a pause for some chewing, then a threatening memorial, 'I don't forget the fucking Swedes.'

Rob didn't like the Swedes because of their neutrality in the Second World War. That's why he didn't like the Swiss either, or the French for CAPITULATING.

He was still ranting and back in the dog's pot for more dripping, this time with a bit of gristle attached. Meanwhile, the trampling upstairs had become spirited enough for him to hear above his own volume . . .

'What's going on?' he said.

Various bits of bedding were going past. Rob saw it and led the sortie into the gardens with Thomas in his wake. By now the flowerbeds were littered with half the contents of his chamber. A pair of unlaundered underpants hung from an apricot tree.

Rob looked up at his window in speechless astonishment: a selection of items was currently airborne and still on its way out. Here comes a rugby ball and the other oar, followed at last by Mabs' head. She was heaving at the window, struggling to get a mattress over the sill.

'What the fuck is going on?' said Rob.

Finally the mattress got through and once again they were facing each other via an upstairs window, albeit this time with positions reversed.

'I'm moving you out,' she said triumphantly. 'You can take it all round to her.'

A spare surgical-collar whizzed over his head and she waved an arm in the general direction of Broadstairs.

'Have you gone out of your mind?' said Rob.

Her reply was a momentary retreat, and when she came back it was with a substantial piece of furniture. It was exhausting to get it out, but finally it crashed into the daffodils.

'Why aren't you round there now?' she said.

'Round where?' roared Rob.

'Round the corner, with your fat little short-arsed whore.'

An electric razor was hurled with fine aim, but Rob was quick and she missed. His fists clenched like a pair of grins, he almost laughed, and this inflamed her. Tearing at the curtains she broadened her view, discovering to some surprise that Thomas was also out there and witness to all this.

'Get to school, Thomas,' she said.

'It's Saturday,' said Thomas.

'You need a fucking doctor,' said Rob.

Mabs rose in a paroxysm of rage and her expression was not ordinary. For a moment it looked like she'd come out of the fucking window herself.

'Don't *doctors* with me,' she snarled. 'I've had a bellyful of doctors. You think I don't know what Hardcastle was about?'

'Hardcastle?' said Rob.

'Hard–Castle,' said Mabs, like she was two words.

'What?' said Rob. 'What was Hardcastle about?'

'Your harlot's sons are doctors – that's where you get all your medical clap-trap. And that's where she's gone, to Portsmouth, to see the doctors. That's why you're back here for breakfast.'

'I don't know what you're talking about.'

'Ha. Ha. Ha!' said Mabs. 'I've got a *dossier* on you. I know every move you make.'

Rob shunted forward with an arm up in anger, trod on a tube of toothpaste and was beginning to look disturbing.

'If I see that geriatric twat on a bicycle again, I'll get out of the car and waste him.'

'You won't see him,' taunted Mabs. 'He's *trained*. But you'll hear his evidence.'

'What *evidence*?'

'Proceedings,' she said, with a chortle of threat.

The Dobermann came up on paws and stuck its head out of the window next to her: and at the window above that, there was another head. Walter looked down like a piece of discoloured plastic. It was an astonishment he was out of bed. No one saw him but Thomas. Within seconds he was gone and the evacuation recommenced. A cricket bat came down and paperbacks hailed, including *A History of Warfare*, and *Rommel's Desert Strategies*. She threw everything out but his gun. Nobody touched Rob's piece. Getting hold of his gun would be like getting hold of his prick, and that was the last thing she wanted to do . . .

And that's what Thomas found so bizarre. For years she'd functioned in stifling artificiality, empress of it, so why the crisis now? She loathed the cunt, and the loathing was reciprocated, so what did it matter who he was stuffing? Why would she care? It was, concluded Thomas at a time of more tranquil reflection, because Ruby had invaded the LIE. Mabs didn't need real love, didn't want it any more than she wanted real furniture. What she wanted was a facsimile, something that looked like love, because that was the world she'd learnt to live in. And as long as Rob lived in it too, she had something to share with him, no matter how lousy the deal. But Ruby had busted the charade, broken the rules, and Mabs couldn't handle it, because the lie was as close as she was ever going to get to love.

That evening, Thomas finished the 'valentine', but decided not to send it, at least for the time being, and a fortuitous decision as it turned out. Some days later, probably a Wednesday, it was sports at school and Thomas found himself involved in some sort of appalling cross-country run. He abhorred athletics and did his best to avoid this kind of thing with asthma, but given the circumstances at home there was no way he could inveigle a sick-note from his mother . . .

It was a cool day at the end of March and everyone congregated on the field. Various members of various 'houses' were there to witness the event. The course was four miles long in a figure of eight and it was a foregone conclusion who would win. Bowls took off like a whippet. Maurice and Thomas went round at the back with the fat one. His name was Legge and sometimes he fell over and couldn't get up.

Half an hour later they were a mile or two out, going up an alley of trees, and even Legge overtook. 'Screw this,' said Maurice. 'I gotta have a rest,' and he collapsed on a log at the edge of a dirty wood. There were bedsteads and puddles and daffodils in clumps. Although the pace had hardly been punishing it took a while for Maurice to get his breath, and when he looked up, he looked dreadful.

'You all right?' said Thomas.

'I dunno, I feel dizzy.' He ran a hand backwards through his hair and was still panting. 'I'll tell you what,' he said, 'let's sit here and wait for them to come back, then we'll join in across the field.'

'That's not a good idea, is it?'

'Why not?'

'What if they see us?'

'Their problem,' said Maurice. 'I'm not running through that fucking wood.'

Despite sunshine there was a nifty breeze about for those in shorts and Thomas jogged to keep the blood up. Birds were singing everywhere, and everywhere you looked, daffodils about to explode. He picked one and sniffed it. The smell was wet and reminded him of Angel Head. There would be daffodils all over Old Moules Orchard at this time of the year . . .

'You been down the Angel?'

Maurice shook his head and said he hadn't, and Thomas joined him on the log and destroyed the unopened bloom.

147

'I was thinking of coming over Saturday. I wanna get those pictures back.'

'What pictures?'

'My grandfather's ducks.'

'Oh yeah,' said Maurice, 'I haven't seen them in months.'

'What do you mean?' said Thomas. 'Where are they?'

'Nothing to worry about, they're still under the bed,' and it seemed like he had genuinely forgotten them.

'I'll be over in the afternoon. Get the fire alight, OK?'

'OK.'

Maurice's recovery was now sufficiently advanced for him to search out a packet of snouts.

'How's he going, your grandpop?'

'Not too good,' said Thomas. 'But he gets down the stairs, just about makes it to the bathroom.'

'I thought he was having enemas?'

'He is, twice a day, and I wish I could get in there and watch one.'

Maurice slapped his tracksuit for matches.

'I wouldn't mind having an enema.'

He offered Thomas a cigarette which was accepted, and as they lit up, made apologies for something else he spotted in the pack. It was a tube of tightly rolled paper, itself about the size of a cigarette.

'Forgot to give you this.'

'What is it?'

'It's from Hackett.'

He unrolled the tube and handed it across. It was a multi-folded page out of an exercise book, sealed with sticky brown paper.

'How long have you had it?'

'Day or two,' said Maurice, shoving out smoke. 'She gave it to Rumbold, and Rumbold gave it to me.'

Thomas was visibly peeved to obtain so important a

148

document by default, but there was a compensatory lifting of any residual anxiety over authenticity of Gwendolin's valentine. The handwriting here was identical: *For Thomas Penman's Eyes Only*, it said. *Do not open. Only to be Opened by Thomas Penman.* And in further forensic confirmation, it was all written on a ruler in green ink.

'Aren't you gonna read it?'

Of course he was going to read it. But not here, because he didn't know what was in it. Maurice cleared his sinus and flobbed in a puddle. A gang of Crows rose from the wood, followed almost immediately by Bowls.

'Fuck me, here they come,' said Maurice.

Some fifty yards away a phalanx broke out of the trees with scarlet ears and miles of mud. Maurice rose in a kind of stoop, and with the fag *in situ*, started prancing on the spot like a chicken.

'Run on the spot,' he said. 'And as soon as they see us, start running.'

'That won't work,' said Thomas, panicking. 'Dump the fags.'

'Keep down,' ordered Maurice. 'Run on the spot. Run up the wall.'

Dumping cigarettes they ran up the wall with excellent synchronisation, let Bowls pass, and broke into the dishevelled pack. The contestants behind were too blinded with asphyxiation to appreciate what was happening. But Bowls had seen them, and looked back.

'I saw you smoking, Potts,' he puffed.

'Fuck off, Bowls,' said Maurice, and he overtook him. Thomas went too and suddenly they were winning. Faces started cheering as they came across the field. Maurice would come in first, and Thomas second, and if Bowls said anything he'd get a broken neck. As a dramatic finale, Maurice collapsed a few yards past the finishing line. It was a nice touch and

Thomas was impressed. 'Well done, Potts!' They tried to get him up but couldn't, and he was carted off to the sick room amidst accolades from his house master.

Thomas came in for a fair amount of congratulation too. Being second and on your feet was probably worth more that being first and on your back . . .

Someone blew a whistle and there was a movement towards the gymnasium and its horrible bathrooms. In the general hubbub of 'Well done's' clapping him on the shoulder, Thomas felt a hand that didn't feel 'Well done' at all.

'I'm going to report you, Penman.'

They were back in the corridor, Thomas navigating the showers to get into a toilet and read his letter.

'Report me for what?'

'Cheating,' said Bowls.

'We took a different route, that's all,' said Thomas. 'And you don't want to mess with us. Last bloke who messed with us got three weeks in Ramsgate Hospital.'

Boles suddenly punched Thomas very hard on the nose and ran off. It was an unexpected and quite humiliating experience. He snapped forward into a thousand echoes, clutching a cocktail of blood and tears. There were stars everywhere. And then a voice . . .

'Are you all right?'

Thomas looked up through fingers and saw Mrs Bredwardine.

'Got a nose-bleed,' he said, and backed off and ran for the nearest lavatory.

His primary concern was possible destruction of the nose, the nose that Gwen adored. Several minutes were spent in front of the mirror, mopping at the nose with water and toilet paper, checking as best as he could its sideways structure. All seemed intact, and when it stopped bleeding he went into a cubicle . . .

'Darling Thomas,' she wrote, 'Rumbold came up to me and told me you wouldn't talk to me because I like Shackles and Gollick. This isn't true. I *don't* like Shackles *or* Gollick! It is true, I have already got a boyfriend, his name is . . . (PTO)'

His heart sank, and his nose throbbed, and he turned over. 'Cherry Pup! and he's the sweetest little brown puppy I got for my fifteenth birthday, and so *handsome* he reminds me of you. P.S. *Please*, *please*, come to Drama Group this Friday. We're reading *Arms and the Man* and Shackles won't be there. Love Gwendolin.'

Thomas read it and reread it and walked out of the toilet like a king.

Friday couldn't come soon enough, and when it did, it was so warm you couldn't believe it was March. Spring flowers were awash all over the town and all over the fields at school. At four o'clock the bell cleared the tower as usual, and Thomas descended into the foyer determined not to make the same mistake again. His strategy was straightforward – get there early and loiter, and when Gwen went in, he would go in with her. By this means he would be able to influence the seating and make sure he got a favourable position as far as the profile was concerned.

His nose had totally recovered.

At last she came up the corridor: beauty, and that which normally accompanies it, Freda Pew. Gwen smiled with eyes as she passed, went into the hall where a dozen were already assembled, and when they sat, Thomas got perfection with the chair.

It was true that this week Shackles was noticeable by his absence. There were however, several new faces amongst the boys. Prominent was a sixteen-year-old tall streak from the fifth called Waldron, and his friend with a wandering neifus, Sinclaire. Also, to Thomas's surprise, Rumbold and his pal known as 'Flea-Bag' turned up . . .

'I'm glad to see some Hamlets,' said Mrs Windermere.

This didn't get a reaction because in the circumstances it wasn't a joke. These males are a shambles, thought Thomas. Apart from himself, how could any of them ever hope to get on stage?

They all sat in a group and Windermere dished out the books. It was called *Samuel French's Acting Edition* by George Bernard Shaw, and if dull was a longer word, it would be the right one.

The play was set in Russia, and Windermere reviewed the acts. Act One: Raina's Bed Chamber, at night in late November, 1885. Act Two: The Garden, a morning in March, 1886. Act Three: The Library, that same afternoon.

For the first interminable act Waldron was given the lead. He read with Margaret Ruther, and the pair of them put together couldn't have acted their way out of a fucked sack. Waldron's character, Bluntschli, was a dashing officer-type, and the only thing he was any good at was fancying himself portraying it. He mis-stressed every word, waving arms, and at one point went down on to a knee. By page thirty even Windermere had had enough and recast. Thomas was hopeful, but the part was handed to Sinclaire whose absolute and overwhelming inability to act brought no improvement.

'How *many* tablecloths, have you got?'

'Try stressing tablecloths?'

'How *many*, *tablecloths*, have you got?'

'Without the *many*?' said Mrs Windermere.

'How, *tablecloths*, have you got?' he said.

Etcetera. Etcetera.

Pew had a go at Catherine and curiously wasn't bad. When it came to the minor parts, Thomas had been assigned Nicola, a 'servant', who by the nature of his trade got about one line in five thousand. Page after page went by with Sinclaire and his God-awful blot murdering Bluntschli. And then Waldron got in again with his Petkov. Thomas had totally switched off, and by Act Three was using the time exclusively to stare at Gwen.

At the second recasting session she was given the part of Louka, and Thomas watched mesmerised as she read. She sounded like she looked, a truly beautiful voice, he thought, and a real feeling for the words. Gwen knew he was looking at her, and when she wasn't reading, rationed delicious glances back at him. These moments were wonderful, her eyes blue as bluebells, and when she looked away, his eyes were back all over her . . .

She wore pretty blue shoes with quite high heels, and a navy-blue pleated skirt that hovered just above her knees. He stared at her legs and at first it wasn't apparent what was different about them. Then it dawned like dizzy magic – no ankle socks – she was wearing stockings. Stockings and heels weren't actually allowed in school. She'd changed into stockings to walk home with him.

He felt a kind of glaze in the brain and was working out the route through Piermont Park. There was a bench by a fountain, and it was there they would kiss. Then they would sit, and in the gathering shadows, he would put his hand up her skirt . . .

Gwendolin was looking at him again and he gave her full benefit of the right profile, lips slightly parted, his head tilted, and his eyes coming up to meet hers . . .

She was still looking at him, and in the silence of the hall he realised everyone else was too.

'Your line, Thomas,' said Mrs Windermere.

'What?'

'Nicola?'

'Oh, is it, where is it?'

He wasn't even on the same page.

When the line was located Thomas read it, and Mrs Windermere said, 'You really must follow the text.'

Thomas nodded.

'Have you got a stiff neck?' she said.

He hadn't.

'Well then, sit up for heaven's sake, and stop peering like that. You've been peering round some sort of non-existent corner from the beginning – that's why you're missing your lines.'

That did it, well filled him in, and this was the last time he was ever coming to fucking Drama Group. 'I'm missing the fucking lines because I haven't got any!' But he didn't say it of course, and this was good news because his status was about to change. In a further reshuffle the servant was given to Rumbold, Gwen moved to Raina, and having terminated Sinclaire, Windermere put her lenses back to Thomas.

'Why don't you read Bluntschli for the rest of the act?'

This came as a bit of a shock. Suddenly both he and Gwen were opposite each other in the leads. The exquisite Raina, and the handsome Bluntschli, alone in the firelight, in the library.

Almost all of his scenes were with Gwen, and peculiar it was to be talking to her for the first time in his life with somebody else's words . . .

RAINA (*staring haughtily at him*) Do you know, sir, that you are insulting me?

BLUNTSCHLI I can't help it. When you strike that noble attitude and speak in that thrilling voice, I admire you; but I find it impossible to believe a single word you say.

RAINA (*superbly*) Captain Bluntschli!

BLUNTSCHLI (*unmoved*) Yes?

RAINA (*standing over him, as if she could not believe her senses*) Do you mean what you said just now? Do you know what you said just now?

BLUNTSCHLI I do.

RAINA (*gasping*) I! I!!! (*she points to herself incredulously, meaning, 'I, Raina Petkov tell lies!' He meets her gaze unflinchingly. She suddenly sits down beside him, and adds, with a complete change of manner from the heroic to a babyish familarity*) . . .

GWEN Did you get my valentine?

THOMAS Yes.

GWEN Did you know it was me?

THOMAS Yes.

An hour or more had passed and they were sitting on the designated bench in Piermont Park with their bicycles leaning behind it. There were elm buds in the trees and quite a lot of moon and it was warm. All the way from school they had talked about the reading, how good she was, how good he was, and how pleased Windermere was with both of them. They'd also talked about furniture and George Bernard Shaw.

'What do you think of Shaw?' he said.

'I don't know,' said Gwen.

'He's not a writer I like,' said Thomas.

'Who do you like?'

'Charles Dickens.'

She'd heard of him but never read him.

'Haven't you read *David Copperfield*?'

'No.'

He found it awkward at first, walking with a girl, her heels clipping along. It wasn't like in the play when you knew it was your time to talk, and they kept talking at the same time, and sometimes running out of words altogether. There was a bad patch outside the Catholic church and he stopped and offered her a Park Drive.

'I don't like cigarettes,' she said.

'Don't you?'

'Not really.'

Thomas found this a difficult one to smoke. They wheeled their bicycles across the Broadway towards Piermont Park, a shortcut to her home. He'd long abandoned any idea of fiddling about. Touching her just didn't seem possible, how could he, she was an angel. But then Shackles nearly shagged her, and he was thinking about that when she said, 'What's up with Maurice?'

'I don't know,' said Thomas. 'I'm seeing him tomorrow.'

The lights went on in Piermont Street and they turned into the park. Pretty little gas lamps splashed yellow on the paths, there was a bandstand, and it looked like Renoir had just been around with a match. Thomas found a bench and sat with a head full of brassières and those beautiful blue eyes.

'Wouldn't it be nice if you could play Bluntschli, and I could be Raina?' she said.

'Yes,' said Thomas.

They could hear the town going home, and the clock struck. It was seven already. And then she just sat next to him on the bench and said it.

'I love you, Thomas.'

'I love you too,' he said.

AN ERROR OF JUDGEMENT

There was no smoke in the orchard and no fire in Angel Head to make it. White grass and a single daffodil grew through the floor. The only smoke around here was coming out of the vicarage chimney and the sight of it pissed Thomas off. The last thing he wanted was to go in there and run into Vicar Potts. But he wanted to see Maurice, and with no way around it, he walked back through the holly and graves and knocked lightly on the front door.

No response and he knocked again and this time, to Thomas's surprise, it was opened by a short black man with a crucifix slung round his neck. He had a bulging head, similar eyes, and a nose as wide as a knee. His religious credentials were further enhanced by an oversized kaftan secured at the waist with a brown leather belt.

'Oh,' said Thomas, sort of taken aback to see a chap such as this at the door.

'What is it?' said the black man.

'I've come to see Maurice.'

'He's ill.'

'Is he?'

'Mumpos.'

'What?'

'Mumpos,' and he pushed his face at Thomas as though this were some kind of secret. The accent was dense and muddy and Thomas didn't know what he was talking about until it suddenly clicked.

'Mumps?' he said, and this got a nod. Thomas asked if Mrs Potts was at home.

'With the butcherer,' said the black one. 'They will both be back in half of an hour.'

And he looked at Thomas suspiciously, and looked like he was going to close the door.

'Is Maurice upstairs?'

This was the case.

'He *is* expecting me,' said Thomas. 'Maybe I could just go up and see him for a minute.'

Permission was neither given nor denied, so Thomas walked in anyway and the dodgy eyes followed him up carpetless stairs. At the top, he pushed into an attic room full of shadows and ceilings. The curtains were partially drawn and Maurice half asleep on the bed. On the wall above him there was a wooden cross with the Christ missing. One or two model aeroplanes dangled on strings, and there was a table lamp made out of a dimple bottle. A selection of medications was distributed around it. But apart from a bow-fronted wardrobe, possibly French and of very poor quality, there was little else in the room to speak of except some crap books in a homemade bookcase and an Edwardian dining chair . . .

Thomas valued it at about five bob, pulled it up to the bedside, and sat looking at Maurice. His whole head seemed inflated, everything ill from his neck to his ears. His eyes were so swollen, Thomas didn't realise they had opened.

'Hello, Cherry Pup,' he grinned (categorically demonstrating he had read Gwendolin's letter), but he looked too lousy to be called on it so Thomas let it pass.

'What's the matter with you then?'

'Got mumps, haven't I?' said Maurice, struggling himself

up into a position of relative comfort. 'How long have you been in here?'

'Just got here.'

'You wanna open the curtains, don't ya?'

Thomas got up and opened them and returned to the chair. 'Who's that geezer in the hall?' he said.

'What geezer?'

'Religious geezer?'

'The Tan?'

'Yeah.'

'Christopher Jumo. He's a bishop's assistant.'

'Is he from the Tropics?'

'Well, he ain't from Redditch, is he?' said Maurice. 'World Council A-Churches, cunt's here for a fortnight. I wouldn't mind that, 'cept he's up here every day, and I can't understand a fucking word he says.'

'It's all that stuff you stick in your ears.'

'No it ain't, it's *glands*. Every gland I got is swollen. Doctor reckons I'll be in here a week.'

'A week in bed?'

'Yeah, fucking boring it is too. My sperm count's probably well down.'

'What does he come up here for?'

'Who, Jumo?'

'Yeah.'

'To talk to me about blind people, all I fucking need.' He sniffed contemptuously and put a different thought together. 'What would you rather be, blind, or black?'

'What d'you mean?'

'It's a question, innit? Would you rather be blind, or black?'

'I dunno,' said Thomas. 'I haven't thought about it really.'

'Fuckin' blind any day,' said Maurice. 'Except of course, if you were blind, you wouldn't know you were black.'

'I suppose not,' said Thomas.

Maurice yawned and rubbed at his eyes, discovered something in one and swallowed it.

'I'll tell you what,' he said. 'I'm pleased to see you. I been going barmy up here for a fag.'

There was a pause before Thomas said, 'I haven't got any.'

There was another pause before Maurice said, 'Why not?'

'I've given up.'

'Given up? Why?'

He instinctively realised why, and naming no names, an appreciation of the absurdity grew across his face like a bad taste.

'You don't wanna get too involved,' he said. 'You don't wanna get gooey with a girl, coz they got fucking big thumbs.' He held one up, then drilled it into the sheet. 'She'll have you under it, mate.'

'It's not coz of Gwen, it's coz of health.'

'Bollocks,' said Maurice, and he pointed at the wardrobe, said his pipe and dog-ends were in there and wanted them out. Thomas found the tobacco tin in a pocket and the pipe in a shoe box.

'There's a bottle of sherry in there,' said Maurice. 'And two miniatures.'

'Miniature what?'

'Gins.'

Both in a Wellington boot. Everything came back to the bed and Maurice drank one of the little Beef Eaters virtually in one.

'Where did you get 'em?' said Thomas.

'Cabinet. You want one?'

He didn't and went back to the window and looked out. Mrs Potts crossed the gardens with two dead rabbits. Maurice loaded his briar and lit up. When Thomas turned back to him he was shaking his head, a string of smoke coming out of his ear like a candelabra that had just been blown out.

'You don't wanna let it hang around on you,' he said.

'What?' said Thomas.

'Love,' he exhaled. 'Being in love with a girl.'

Thomas suddenly felt very happy. His whole body felt happy. Fuck the cigarettes, he was in love. He was in love with the prettiest girl in Broadstairs, and he was seeing her again tomorrow.

'Listen,' he said, returning to the bed, 'I'm sorry you're not feeling too pucker, but I'm just here to collect the pictures, then I gotta go.'

'Not so easy, white man,' said Maurice.

'Why not?'

'Because they're under the bed, and I can't get out of it.'

'What do you mean, not for a minute?'

'I can't, I can't stand up.'

'How do you get to the lavatory then?'

'I have assistance,' he said. 'If I get out of this bed, I'm on the floor.'

Whether Maurice's enfeeblement was real or imagined, it wasn't a sufficient deterrent to Thomas and he gave the mattress a couple of exploratory prods.

'Which end are they?' he said.

'Sort of in the middle,' said Maurice, pointing with the stem of his pipe.

'All right,' said Thomas. 'If I lift, you can hang on, OK?'

'What?'

'I'll just haul you up, grab the envelope, and lower you down again. You don't even have to get out.'

The bed was an ugly Victorian business with the mattress inside, like a bed in a box.

'You can't lift this.'

'Course I can,' said Thomas. 'Not a problem,' and indeed it was true. For his age his arms were particularly well developed, courtesy of the newspaper trade.

'You won't lift it.'

'I fucking will.'

'Anyway, what's the hurry?' said Maurice. 'They're safe under there.'

'Yeah, well, I don't know,' said Thomas. 'I'm worried about my grandfather. I don't know what's going to happen, and I don't like leaving them lying around, that's all.'

Maurice puffed reflectively at his pipe and seemed to understand. And then he said, 'What's happening with the other stuff?'

Thomas shook his head, confessed he hadn't really been looking. Maurice tugged the cork out of his Madeira bottle and wanted to know why.

'Because I can't. I can't get in. He's too ill.'

'Big error,' said Maurice. 'If it goes bad for him, you'll lose the lot, and that ain't doing him a favour, is it?'

He filled a medicine glass with his yellow booze and Thomas accepted it.

'It's a lifetime's collection, right?' continued Maurice. 'All brilliant stuff? And you don't wanna let that go too easy.'

'There's nothing I can do about it.'

'A statement you will live to regret,' said Maurice, plundering another swig from the bottle. 'You'll find in the long term you'll regret that, because if your mother gets hold of it, or even worse, your old man, that'll be that, won't it? They're not gonna hang on to it for you till you're "old enough", are they?'

'My old man might not be around.'

'How's that?'

'Probably getting a divorce.'

'Ay?' said Maurice. 'A divorce?'

162

As an inducement to more info he unscrewed the cap of his remaining miniature and added it to Thomas's sherry.

'Here, have a gin in it?'

Thomas swallowed a mouthful and gave a brief but comprehensive précis of the domestic crisis, including a somewhat embellished description of the events at Rob's bedroom window.

'Fuckin' Ada. Where is he now, then?' said Maurice.

'Back up there,' said Thomas. 'As soon as she'd finished throwing everything out, we collected it up, and took it all back upstairs again.'

'Did he thump her?'

'Nahh,' said Thomas. 'If he punches anyone, it's gonna be me. I tell you, he's walking around in a bad mood. I'm gonna need to get a fucking key for my bedroom door.'

Maurice knocked out his pipe on the leg of the bedside table, the solid taps underlining his conviction.

'There's only one key you wanna worry about, and you wanna worry about it quick. You have to try and think of it from your grandfather's point of view, hundreds of quims, right? Don't you think he's worried about it? After all, he'd rather you had it than they did, wouldn't he?'

'Maybe?'

'I'm fuckin' certain,' said Maurice. 'It's a lifetime's collection, right?'

'Yeah, you already said that.'

'Something you could never get again, not for love, not for money. You owe it to your grandad, and that's how you gotta think of it. If I were in your shoes, I would do *everything* I possibly could to protect that pornography, even to the point of asking him for the fucking key, and telling him why I wanted it.'

There was silence while Thomas considered his china's discourse. They both had another drink and looked at each other and started laughing. Why were they laughing? They didn't know. It was the booze, it was the quims, it was funny . . .

'I want those ducks,' said Thomas.

'You'll have to come back.'

'No, I won't. You just told me to protect them. I want them *now*.'

'Protect the *quims*, I said,' he said.

'It's up her quim.'

'No, it ain't,' said Maurice. 'It's up her arse.'

And for reasons best known to himself he exploded, crying with laughter: rolling around fighting for air and complaining of pain in the glands. Thomas hung over him, a similarly weeping head, laughing louder with every new lamentation.

'Hurts. Hurts,' gasped Maurice.

This protestation attracted an attack of hysterics, immobilising Maurice, who lay there weak and suffering it. He laughed till his tongue stuck out, and when he fought for an exit, Thomas was there filling it, roaring and insane, bearing down with fists either side of him for support. And they both laughed in each other's faces till agony in the gut muscles felt like it does when there's nothing left to spew.

'No more. No more.'

Maurice finally got his face out of the way and hung it over the edge to escape. Why were they laughing? They still didn't know. But it was probably the reason they were friends . . .

'All right,' said Maurice. 'I'll hang on to the side, and you can lift it up.'

'I'm arseholed,' heaved Thomas. 'I feel arseholed.'

'Come on,' said Maurice. 'I'm hanging on, lift it.'

Debilitated by tears, Thomas stuck hands down the side of the mattress and gave it a kind of preliminary weighing. It was heavy, and he said so.

'Go for it in one,' said Maurice.

All right, he'd have a go, and he got hold of it and hauled it up, and halfway there he started laughing again. On this occasion the stimulus was apparent. He was laughing because all the covers shot off and he could see Maurice's foot down the other end like a hook.

'Come on,' said Maurice. 'For Christ's sake.' His chin and eyes came over the bedding looking swollen and alarmed. 'Hurry up.'

Cackling with laughter, Thomas fought to gather strength, then in a single and enormous effort, suddenly wrenched the mattress upright. Simultaneously the door opened and Susan Potts made an entry with a dead rabbit. Although it all happened rather quickly, she was there with ample time to see Thomas wilfully toss her sick son out of bed. Maurice flew off into the sunlight, and as he vanished, Thomas barked with laughter.

There was the proverbial dull thud followed by a religious expletive from the floor.

'What on earth do you think you're doing?' demanded Mrs Potts.

Thomas swung round, and the shock of her, plus the murdered rabbit, tended to sterilise his merriment.

'Nothing,' he said.

'You just threw him out of the bed.'

'Not really,' said Thomas.

'Don't contradict me, you ridiculous boy, I stood here and watched you do it.' And it was unarguable: from her perspective, this is precisely what had happened.

'Help,' said Maurice.

'Put that mattress down at once,' she ordered, and thank God for that, because apart from the ducks there was a good clutch of moral-soiling magazines underneath. Thomas dropped the mattress and she thrust the rabbit at him, marching around the bed to get Maurice back into it.

'I'm astonished at you, Thomas.'

Thomas was in a nasty spot, and stood on it while Mother Potts hauled her son off the boards and packed him back into bed. There was a lot of pillow adjustment and feeling of the forehead. Maurice let her indulge it, flopping around like a twot. It was undeniable he looked awful, but unquestionable that this was caused by laughter more than anything else.

She was on the pulse now and looking at a watch. Maurice moaned and she oozed placations, had a look at his tongue that he shoved out willingly, and satisfying herself and finally him that no injury was discernible, she returned attention to Thomas.

Her face seemed larger than ever, like it had too many ingredients, and her eyes were full of anger and blame. Thomas looked back at her, holding the rabbit by its ears, and felt something move in his jaw that he hoped might resemble a smile.

'It was an error,' he said.

She wasn't interested. She was aware of the smoke.

'And I do think it dreadful you smoking in here.'

He shook his head, but what was the point. He protested nothing and neither did Maurice, the bastard, not a squeak in Thomas's defence. And far be it for Mum Potts to consider that the briar might belong to the second heaviest smoker in Thanet.

'If you don't know how to behave yourself,' she said, 'I'd rather you didn't visit again. Mumps is not a joke, you know.'

'I know,' said Thomas. 'I've had it.'

'Did someone come round and throw you out of bed?'

'Not that I remember,' he said.

'I'm *astonished*,' said Susan Potts.

That she might be but there was worse to come. Thomas saw it first, and then Maurice, and then everyone was looking at the bottle at the same time. This time, Maurice got up a feeble whisper. 'Don't forget your sherry,' he said.

And went back into relapse.

You cunt, thought Thomas. You utter treacherous cunt.

Susan grabbed the flagon and handed it on. Thomas was suddenly in possession of a Madeira bottle in his left hand and a dead rabbit in his right with instructions to get out the door.

Out of it he went and stood on the landing looking at the rabbit. He held it out in front of him, dangling by the ears. It was brown and big as a dog and he wondered why she carried them around the house.

After a minute or two she came out, closed the door with quiet precision and seemed to have calmed-off somewhat. Thomas's thoughts were a mess, struggling to work out the mechanics of viable apology.

'It was an error of judgement,' he said.

'We won't say any more about it,' hushed Mrs Potts. 'Maurice is sleeping now.'

She was already on her way down, Thomas descending a stair or two behind and every one of them a contribution to his ambition to get out of the front door. At the first-floor landing there was a framed photograph of Potts and a tall pygmy on the wall, and further opportunity for exchange.

'Excuse me, Mrs Potts.'

'Yes?'

'I wondered if you'd like your rabbit back?'

He held it up like an angler. She looked first at it, and then at him.

'The rabbit is for you,' she said.

'Is it?'

'Christopher told me you were here, we've just had a kill, and I thought your mother might like it.'

He looked at her blankly, trying to look grateful.

'Thank you,' he said.

'It's a buck.'

'Oh, is it?'

Why she cost it in dollars he didn't know, but said he'd certainly pass it on. On the last flight of stairs the afternoon that couldn't have got worse suddenly did. Potts burst through the front door under his eyebrows. On his way through he looked at Thomas and they exchanged curt acknowledgement, then at the kitchen door, Potts paused and looked back.

'Oh Thomas,' he said, 'I wanted a word with you.'

Thomas didn't want a word with him and this was everything he didn't want to hear. Moreover, whatever this 'word' was, it wasn't to be discussed in the hall, and he and his rabbit and bottle were obliged to follow the Reverend into the kitchen.

The temperature rose by about forty degrees – it was hot as hell, like the Belgian Congo. Steam condensed on the walls, pouring out of a kettle on a filthy old coal oven under a forest of saucepans and hooks. These were the table rabbit-hooks. Jumo looked across from the far end of the kitchen – he was skinning (clearly as a favour to Mrs Potts), and there were three undressed and another half-dozen still togged.

Potts whipped out a Player's, tapped it on the pack, and gestured Thomas to a chair at the opposite end of the table.

'You can sit down, Thomas.'

'I'm fine, thank you,' he said, and he kept the floor where he was.

'I wanted a word with you,' said Potts, fixing the cigarette to his lips. 'Because of something Maurice has told us.'

The 'us' referred to Mrs Potts and he put eyes across to include her. Thomas didn't know what Maurice had told them but already didn't like the sound of it.

'How is your grandfather?'

Oh, no, he thought, not the grandfather again, and he shook his head and didn't answer.

'I understand he's out of hospital now?'

'Yes, he is, but he's still ill.'

The Vicar's eyes and cigarette lit up concurrently. Thomas knew he was thinking religious and it dashed all hope he had of an easy out of here.

'Is he suffering at all?'

'Suffering?' said Thomas.

The Reverend's cheeks hollowed as the smoke went down, then billowed as the smoke came back, dragging a stifler.

'Yes,' he gasped, 'suff-er-ing?'

'I think the doctors have given him pills to stop the pain.'

Potts rolled the cigarette in his fingers. It was clear he wasn't enjoying it, in fact it was clear Potts didn't like smoking at all. They roughed him up and hurt his lungs. But because addiction demanded this procedure at least eighty times a day, necessity had forced the development of a technique. He cremated rather than smoked, ignoring pain, drawing as fast as was humanly possible. Within five drags he'd sucked the cigarette in half, leaving a super-heated prong of tobacco at its end.

'It must be very hard,' he wheezed, 'for your mother?'

'Yes, it is.'

On the ensuing drag he gagged at the sheer concentration of nicotine exploding into his throat. Nausea rummaged his face and for a moment his eyes vanished under the skull. There was something in his mouth. As his hand rose to his lips the tongue automatically presented itself like one of those old-fashioned coon-head money-boxes receiving a coin. Fragments of tobacco were removed, and the tongue then returned to the face for the cough, reappearing again as he struggled to breathe.

'And your grandmother,' he said. 'Hard on her?'

'Yes, it is.'

Mrs Potts joined in with an unspoken understanding, and at the other end of the table there was an unpleasant sound as Jumo parted a rabbit from its skin.

'Look here,' said Potts, 'I'll come to the point. Maurice has told us that your grandfather is having enemas.'

Thomas nodded in confirmation, didn't know where this was going, didn't see it was anything to do with them.

'Are you sure of that?' said the Vicar.

'Yes,' said Thomas. 'He's having them every day.'

Adjacent eyes made momentary contact and Susan took up the interrogation with an expression of no little concern.

'Why, Thomas?'

'It's his illness.'

'But who is giving him enemas?'

'My mother and grandmother.'

'Is there a nurse in attendance?' said Potts.

'No, my mother got rid of her.'

Potts heard this with some seriousness, pulled out a chair and Thomas was required to sit. He did so reluctantly, still clutching the ears and bottle. Seating himself opposite, Potts took a last smack at the cigarette and seemed grateful to put it out.

'Now, look here,' he repeated. 'I know this might be difficult, but I assure you of its importance. Are you sure, absolutely sure, they are giving your grandfather enemas?'

'Yes,' said Thomas, and he felt a kind of dizziness, realising he was drunk.

'But do you know?' said Potts, moving in behind his lenses. 'I mean, can you tell me exactly what an enema is?'

'Don't you know?' said Thomas.

'Of course, *we* know,' said Mrs Potts, joining them on the chairs. 'But we want to know if *you* know.'

'Why?'

'Because,' said Potts, instinctively reaching for his Player's, 'because of the potential seriousness of enemas in his condition. I'm not a doctor, but have had some medical experience, and in my opinion, and the opinion of Mrs Potts, who is a trained nurse, an enema, administered to a man in a condition so enfeebled, by, shall I say "amateurs", seems most inappropriate.'

'The enema,' offered Thomas, 'is the *cause* of his condition, and if it doesn't improve he'll have to go back into hospital.'

They both looked at each other again.

'I think you're confused, aren't you, Thomas?' said Mrs Potts.

'Confused?'

'Yes, yes,' said Potts. 'The boy's got it wrong.'

'I don't think so,' said Thomas. 'I'd better go now.' And he attempted to stand.

'Sit down,' ordered Potts. 'Now listen, I don't need details, but will you just tell me, roughly, what you know about an enema?'

Thomas felt unbearably uncomfortable – no way could he just sit here and describe so intimate a procedure in front of this duo. He put out a smile that went nowhere and was useless.

'But if you already know?' he said.

'Listen to me,' said Potts, getting quite stiff about it, 'we haven't got time to sit here playing games. This is important, and we demand to know what you know.'

Thomas looked at them, one either side of the table, Potts with palms down and almost out of the chair, and Mrs Potts, trying to get her face level with his and sort of nodding as if it would help with the description . . .

'Well . . . I . . . I . . .'

'Yes? Yes?'

'Perhaps a cup of tea?' suggested Mrs Potts.

'*Tea*?' snapped Potts. 'He doesn't want tea. He's not getting tea until he tells us all he knows.'

Thomas looked down, and they looked at him, and he could feel the pressure of their stares. It was clear he wasn't getting out of this kitchen until the question of the enema had been dealt with.

'Come on,' said Potts.

He could hear the blood in his brain, a cocktail of booze and embarrassment, and he thought if he looked at them he might laugh. Feeling almost faint with it, he took a deep breath and realised the words were already spilling out . . .

'The injection of some liquid, or gaseous fluid into . . .'

'What?' shouted Potts.

'The *anus*,' wailed Thomas, face up and purple with anxiety.

'My God, it's true,' said Potts. 'He knows,' and he took off down the kitchen towards Jumo. The black was still skinning, on his feet with a rabbit in the air like an accordion at maximum stretch. He was tugging in a frenzy, feet in one fist, fur in the other, separation somehow prevented by the animal's head.

'He don't want to come off,' said Jumo.

But as he said it, it did – the wretched thing flew apart and joined a pile of bloody others on the table. Thomas remained bent over the opposite end, throbbing with embarrassment.

'How long has this being going on?' whispered Mrs Potts, adopting the gentle approach.

He couldn't look at her.

'I don't know, I don't know,' he said. 'They've been doing it in private.'

'Secretly?' she said. 'You mean, secretly?'

'Yes, yes,' said Thomas, and he'd have said anything to get out of here.

Susan got up quietly and also made her way down the kitchen. Jumo had turned to wash hands and there was a rendezvous around him in the general area of the sink. Thomas couldn't hear what they were saying, at least what Potts was saying, because it was all in a low mumble as though some sort of religious conversation were taking place. Occasionally Jumo looked across at Thomas and said, yes, yes, yes, in quick succession. They were obviously filling him in. Finally Potts and Mrs Potts returned to the table, sitting again in opposite chairs. The Vicar's demeanour was grave.

'You were right to have told us about this, Thomas,' he said. 'It may be nothing, it may indeed be considered necessary for your grandfather's well-being.' Thomas nodded. 'But neither my wife, nor I, nor Dr Jumo, have ever heard of such a treatment carried out by lay people, at home, in a case such as your grandfather's.'

'Unheard of,' said Mrs Potts.

'And we feel,' said Potts, 'that it is our duty to speak to your mother about this. Not to interfere of course, we don't seek to interfere. But I have known your grandfather, albeit in a formal way, for many years, and it would be less than charitable of me not to put my mind at ease on his behalf. Don't you agree?'

'Yes,' said Thomas.

'Now, you mustn't worry about what you've said – leave it to us. You can go home and have no reason for recriminations over the very personal family matters you have chosen, quite rightly, to tell us about.'

Thomas stared at the rabbit and bottle in his lap feeling completely confused. It seemed, according to Potts, that he'd come into their kitchen, sat down, and of his own free will engaged in conversation and passed on intimate details about his grandfather's illness out of a sense of righteousness. There was something very worrying about that. He knew not what they might be, but was suddenly very concerned for the consequences.

'You're going to talk to my mother?' he said.

'Rest assured.'

'What will you say to her?'

'I will not *say*, I will *ask*. I will want to know why your grandfather is having so peculiar a treatment, for so serious an illness. Once a week would hardly seem indicated, once a day is astonishing.'

'I don't understand,' said Thomas.

'And neither do we, young man, that's why the Reverend intends to speak to your mother.'

'Just as soon as possible,' said Potts. 'Time is not on our side.'

'Pardon?'

'The end shall surely come, Thomas, come to us all. But no matter how intentioned, it is at the hand of God and not for mortals to decide.'

What the fuck was he talking about? What 'mortals'? It suddenly crossed Thomas's mind that this idiot thought his mother and grandmother were trying to murder Walter with enemas. A cigarette was in the Vicar's mouth and the first punishing drag vacuumed down. Jumo, who had been hovering at the peripheries, now took this 'mortals' business as his cue to move in.

'Whatever be resolved,' he said, 'grandfather must not be afraid of death.'

'No, no,' gurgled Potts. 'That would never do . . .'

A wheeze wiped out the rest of the sentence. He was still trying to speak, and again appeared to be on the verge, when incredibly, another great draft walloped into his lungs and asphyxiated him. Ripping the cigarette from his mouth he disappeared from view and came up fighting for breath over the rabbits.

'Are you,' he heaved, 'afraid of death?'

'Death?' said Thomas.

'Yes, death,' he said, recovering some wind. 'Are you afraid of death?'

'Yes.'

Floating on whites, Jumo's eyes rose to the ceiling, and with hands in pensive clasp he moved in with his God and accent.

'You must not be afraid of *salvation*. Fear of death poisons de joy of life. If life were de only importance, God would cease to exist, isn't am?'

Thomas looked at this blood-stained fanatic and didn't know what he was getting at.

'Life,' continued Jumo, 'is but a bubble hanging on a thread of faith.'

'Yes, yes,' said Potts, 'that's a good way of putting it.'

'Think of life as a soap-bubble,' said Jumo. 'Your bubble forms, your bubble bursts, but that does not mean God, aren't faith in that God, distroyed. We am not insects, isn't us?'

'No.'

'Do you understand what he's telling you?' said Potts.

'No.'

'No,' he repeated, at last losing the butt in the ashtray. 'At your age, death is difficult, I appreciate that.'

The boy's ignorance clearly presented a challenge. According to reputation, Potts was no spiritual half-wit, and wasn't short of penetrating analogy when faced with problems of the trade. (The parish magazine *Significance* had devoted space to his Christmas thesis, 'Santa Claus, The Profit of Greed', causing indignation amongst shopkeepers. He got into Sunday schools with stuff like this and put the wind up two hundred nine year olds. Letters appeared in the *Thanet Times*. One man said Potts had cut his cracker sales in half. But Potts triumphed, managing to persuade the flock that the man going up the hill was a reality, while the man coming down the chimney was a capitalist myth . . .)

'Let me see if I can put Dr Jumo's idea to you more simply,' he said. 'God blows the bubble pipe, God holds the pin?'

He raised eyebrows at his wife, seeking approval.

'Precisely,' she said, glad for the inclusion. 'The bubble is only temporarily ours.'

'I see,' said Thomas.

'We am not afraid when God blow through de pipe to create life; we must not be afraid when God choose to invoke de pinprick to take that life away.'

It was now impossible for Thomas to look at any of them, but all were looking at him, and it was apparent they expected some kind of answer.

'I'm not afraid of the pipe, or the pin,' he said.

'I wouldn't expect you to be,' said Potts.

'Why should he be?' demanded his wife. 'At fifteen your bubble is hardly formed.'

'Quite,' said Potts.

'De prick is a long way away,' said Jumo.

'My word, yes,' said Mrs Potts. 'When you're young, you just don't think about it. The prospect of the prick never entered my mind until I met the Reverend, and by then I was thirty.'

For a moment Thomas thought he was hearing things, and on the instant was assaulted with an overwhelming desire to laugh. She'd actually said it, but none of them seemed to realise what she'd said. Potts said something else but Thomas wasn't listening, he was fighting to keep his arse on the chair. For some reason Jumo and the Vicar were now conversing in Urdu. Thomas was convulsed with laughter, silent and agonising, a residual perhaps of his liaison with Maurice, but he was crying with it.

'Yes,' said Potts. 'Hip Hip, bandy bottle, goon hooter.'

It was amazing but evident that as yet the theologians were completely unaware of the turmoil going on in the boy. It took constriction of every muscle in Thomas's body to have a go at speech . . .

'I have to go now,' he said.

'Go where?' said Mrs Potts.

'Play darts,' said Thomas, rising hunched with his animal.

'Darts?' said Potts. 'How can you play darts?'

'I have to.'

Thomas couldn't look at him, his jaw was welded, his head nodding as laughter bombarded his stomach.

'But what about your grandfather?'

'What about him?' gasped Thomas, addressing the Reverend's boots. 'Will he get better?'

'Of course not,' said Potts. 'He's dying of cancer.'

'Cancer?' said Thomas. 'Cancer?' And that was it, full-blown hysterics right into the bastard's face.

'Good God,' said Potts.

He lunged aggressively and Thomas tried to strike him with the rabbit.

'Keep away from me, Vicar Potts.'

'Blimey,' said Jumo.

A bit of a scuffle was developing. Susan Potts chipped in.

'He threw Maurice out of bed.'

'What?' bellowed Potts.

'Threw him out,' said Susan.

177

'You little swine! You little spiv! How can you laugh at cancer!' And this delivered after him, 'Stay away from my son!'

Thomas wasn't listening. Swinging the bottle and dumping the rabbit, he was already halfway down the hall, laughing his head off as at last he hit the front door.

A DAY OR TWO IN SPRING

The situation at home had gone from bad to worse and Thomas started stacking saucepans inside his bedroom door. He was worried that Rob might come in in the middle of the night and smoke him with the Beretta. Saucepans would at least give him a chance. The plan was to go straight out of the window, no hesitations; as the saucepans clattered he'd be out. And if Rob somehow navigated the precautions and got in silently to club or choke, Thomas had a back-up. He kept a permanently wired Black & Decker under the bed with a three-eighths masonry bit in the chuck. If Rob got on top of him he would drill a hole in the back of his head. There was also a three-foot wood saw in case of power-cuts. While being strangled, Thomas would attempt to saw his father's legs off.

The fear that Rob might off him, indeed, snuff the lot of them while they slept, was very real. Fuelled by his continuing association with Ruby Round the Corner, there was an atmosphere of terminal hostility about. No one knew quite where it would surface next, but when this Potts business came along, everyone found a focus. Rob didn't give a fuck about religion, or Vicar Potts. But when the Reverend phoned and layed it on Mabs, there was a temporary lull in the divorce proceedings, and instead of talking through the dogs they talked to each other. You can't go on loathing the same person in the same room for the same thing for ever, and it was probable this was a welcome respite for them both. When Mabs got off the phone she was worked into something of a lather: said Thomas had all but accused her of trying to murder her father; said Thomas had laughed openly at his cancer, and tried to hit Potts with a rabbit.

'A rabbit?'

'He was drunk,' said Mabs.

Not an awful lot of ancillary information was required for Rob's eruption. 'I'll brain him,' he said, and walked up and down the living room as though waiting for an opportunity to do it.

'Brain the bastard.'

He looked at Mabs, and Mabs looked at him, and both of them looked away.

Of an evening, and this was an evening, it was Rob's practice to sink a gut full of Teacher's and sit in front of the TV massaging the Dobermann's balls. It was a common sight around here, a Scotch in one hand, balls in the other, and usually still in his shades. Why the dog backed up for it, why Rob did it, wasn't questioned. It was so normal it wasn't noticed, as much a part of the domestic landscape as the room itself and no one seemed to notice that either.

This room was a graphic manifestation of just how bad things had become. The dogs shat all over it and slashed up the furniture. Of late, various protections had been devised, giving the impression of some serious interior-decoration coming up. All chairs were draped with sheets and there was an enormous expanse of transparent polythene covering the floor. It 'gave' under your feet, and with carpet under it, felt like walking on sandwiches.

Policemen on the TV and a turd or two at the peripheries – it didn't seem to bother them any more. Except once a week the sheets had to be gathered in a clutch of gigantic unpleasantness and carried out to be laundered. They hung them on a hook in the out-house. It was Mabs' new Saturday Bag.

Thomas had spent the afternoon with his darling and had everything to feel happy about because he'd kissed her for the first time. The last thing he expected to walk into was the fall-out from Vicar Potts. By now Rob was arseholed on the sofa and didn't bother to get up. It was his mother that rose, her eyes the proverbial coals, her tongue an almost inadequate instrument for the tirade. The indictments were many. Thomas judged it better to hear them in silence. Mabs went through it, prefacing each new charge with 'How could you?' and when she'd listed the lot, went through them again putting 'How could you?' at their end.

Thomas winged it, aware of the gammon-coloured ball of fury in its collar – didn't want that fucker on his feet – and was therefore prepared to issue whatever apology was required to get out of here, and was on his way about it when Mabs put one in under the belt . . .

'He doesn't want you anywhere near Maurice,' she squawked. 'Ever again.'

'He can't do that,' said Thomas. 'Maurice is my best friend.'

'You threw him out of bed,' said Mabs.

'I did not.'

'Don't lie.'

'He fell out,' said Thomas.

'That's not what Potts told your mother,' said the rubicund ball, mouthing in for the first time.

'Potts wasn't actually there.'

'You were drunk on sherry, and threw him out of bed.'

Thomas tried a smile, failed, and shook his head.

'That's not true.'

'Don't argue with your mother.'

'I'm not arguing with her. She's arguing with me.'

A big mistake and Thomas realised it. Rob tensed, lard in the knuckles. 'Shut up,' he said, his facility for instant anger pushing up the volume. Thomas was perfectly prepared to follow instructions, and anyone with any sense would have let it go at that. But Mabs wanted more. Rage was her only currency with this man, the only communication she had, and she was obviously enjoying the chat.

'How could you lie like that about your grandfather's illness? How could you tell such lies about me?'

'I didn't.'

'*Don't lie.*'

'I love Grandad.'

She stuck her face into his and looked daft as the front view of a duck. 'I've spent months nursing him,' she wailed. 'Months changing his bloody bandages.'

'Listen,' said Thomas.

'How *could* you?'

'Listen, if you really want the truth . . .'

'Shut up,' snarled Rob, on his feet like some awful flesh engine. 'You're just a loud-mouthed lying little cunt.'

No slip of the tongue this, no spur of the moment either. This was a history of moments, an articulation of animosity reaching far back into Thomas's childhood. It was enunciated with such venom, such spite in the eyes, it took the breath out of everyone including, it seemed, even the man that said it, and it was the worst thing, now and for ever, that had ever been said to Thomas in his life . . .

There was a hideous silence. Thomas turned and walked out of the room leaving them alone with it. The silence was theirs again. The malice belonged to them again; it was theirs to share and they went back to it with a relish. Without further remark they sat in the black-and-white light, Rob drinking his whisky, and Mabs adjusting her glasses to watch some idiot bunch of actors pretend to be policemen on the TV.

Upstairs in his room, Thomas sat on his bed, his eyes stinging and he wanted to cry. Not because of what Rob had said, but because Mabs had sanctioned him saying it, engineered the environment and made not a sniff of protest in Thomas's defence. But there could be no tears, he could share nothing with Rob, and as always the sense of betrayal meant he could share little with his mother either. He felt again as he had as a child, a crushing humiliation, and with it resurrection of all those childhood fears. Memories of bitter days in Bristol, when he was five, and his father was never there. Where Rob had been and why he came back, sometimes after months, Thomas never knew. But he could remember the misery, acrimony and injustice, the clear sense of foreboding when he knew he was coming home. He could remember getting hauled out and beaten like a dog. But he never cried. He made a promise then and would keep it now. 'I will give you no tears. I will give you no laughter. To laugh because of you, or cry because of you, would be sharing something with you, and I will never share anything with you, for as long as I live.'

That was the promise and it was honoured on this day.

Thomas was hungry but determined to wait until they'd all gone to bed before descending to sort out some food. He went down at midnight. Dogs in their baskets and meat in the larder. He took a plateful of tongue and cheese back up to his bedroom, together with a roasting dish, forks, and assorted saucepans. He stacked the ironware inside his door and sat up in bed eating with his fingers and drinking a cup of milk. He was thinking about the Potts business, and thinking about his grandfather. Since Gwen had come into his life there had been a marked diminution of interest in the pornography. But if it was true Potts wanted a cessation of his friendship with Maurice, there would have to be an incentive to keep it alive. The one thing Maurice craved was the pornography, he'd always stay a friend for that, and Thomas was going to have to launch one last initiative to get it. Now was the time to look for the key, in the middle of the night when everyone was asleep. But not this night, he felt very tired, emotionally wiped out. It was about half-past midnight when he last looked at his watch, turned out the light, and slept.

It was about half-past two when the saucepans clattered, a terrifying jangle in the darkness. Thomas was out of bed before the last hit the floor.

'Keep back, keep back. I've got a drill.'

It howled at six hundred revs a minute, prodding indiscriminately at the gloom. Too dark to see Rob, but he was moving forward, trampling the forks. Thomas heaved to speak but got nothing. There was a high-pitched whine somewhere in his lung that overtook even the drill. The adrenalin was blinding him: he saw the stars of homicide, and thought he'd already been shot.

'I've got a saw,' he gurgled.

'Tom?'

'Spare me.'

'Thomas?'

It wasn't Rob. It was a girl.

'It's *me*, Tom,' and Bel turned on the light.

'What are you doing?' he said, fencing forward. 'What the fuck do you think you're doing?' He was still drilling the air in front of her, waving his saw. 'I thought you were in fucking Germany.'

'There's a train strike coming up, so we got an early flight.'

'It's *two o'clock* in the morning.'

'I know, we had to hitch. Got a lift to Ramsgate.'

The Black & Decker decelerated and Thomas stood staring at his sister. Bel was tanned from skiing, looked tired and pretty. She was clutching a couple of blankets that Thomas assumed must be something to do with her journey. With his heart still thrashing he turned away to relocate his weapons under the bed.

'What's all this?' she said.

'Just some saucepans.'

'I can see they're saucepans, but what are they for?'

He lifted eyes and shook his head, couldn't get into explanations now.

'It's for burglars. There have been burglaries. The police advised us to take precautions.' He stood up. 'I thought you were a burglar.'

She seemed to buy it, and quietly closing the door, advanced further into the room.

'Germany was wonderful,' she said.

'Was it?' said Thomas, but he wasn't in the mood for the travelogue. He retrieved saucepans and forks. Bel hovered with her blankets, looking around somewhat furtively before spotting uneaten cheese.

'Can I have that?' she said. 'I'm starving.'

'Help yourself,' said Thomas, and he switched off the wall-light in favour of a lamp by the bed. Two seconds later he was in it with the covers pulled up and eyes peering at her over the top.

'Does Mum know you're home?'

'No, I didn't want to wake her.'

'Don't mind waking me, though.'

'What?'

'I said,' he said, lowering the eiderdown, 'you don't mind waking me.'

'Sorry,' she said, chewing her cheese, trying to smile through a mouthful. 'I wanted to ask you a favour.'

'Why couldn't you ask it in the morning?'

'I want to sleep in your spare bed.'

'In *here*?' said Thomas, immediately suspicious. 'What's the matter with your bed?'

'Eva's in it.'

'Eva's in it? Why?'

'Because I couldn't put her in that room down the end. It's the horriblest room on earth.'

'It's all right if you're asleep.'

'It's got a *turd* in it.' This articulated in conspiratorial tone as though something astonishing had happened. But no surprise from Thomas who was acclimatised to such discoveries.

'It's so embarrassing,' said Bel. 'They're so hygienic, the Germans. I don't know what I'm going to say, Tom, the whole house smells of shit.'

'I know.'

'Why does she let them do it?'

He didn't know.

'I'll clean it up in the morning,' she said. 'Sleep there tomorrow. But I just can't face it now, I'm so tired.'

There was a yawn somewhere in all this. Thomas caught it and too exhausted to argue, nodded in reluctant acquiescence.

'All right, one night, and that's it.'

'Thank you,' she said, leaning in with a kiss. 'I'm sorry about barging in on you like that.'

'That's OK.'

'You've grown, you know?'

Dodging her affection he turned over, gesturing with his head. 'Careful how you sleep on that bed. It's an antique.'

Bel kicked off her shoes and he heard her undressing. Before she could get at the bed, the commode and various other bits and pieces had to be dealt with. There was a stuffed rook and a bag of rags and half a hundred gramophone records. His teeth clenched as she shifted them. These were very early recordings and would be extremely rare in the future . . .

'Tom?'

No answer.

'Tom?'

'What?'

'I'm sorry,' she whispered, 'but I've just got to ask. How's Grandad?'

'Not good.'

'What about "them"?'

'Not good either.' He rolled over and looked at her with one eye. 'Not a good time to have your friend here.'

'I know,' said Bel. 'I'm dreading it.'

'Has she got large tits?'

'What?'

'Are her tits gigantic?'

'No.'

He looked momentarily perplexed, then reaching for the lamp, rolled back in the direction from which he had come.

'If it's all right with you, I'm gonna turn out the light.'

Darkness resumed, together with a nasty sound of sliding vinyl. Thomas cursed her in silence. Still half dressed, Bel got into the bed and tried to make it on top of herself. There was much flapping of blankets and thumping about until at last she lay down, and then pumping violently in the pillow area, immediately got up again. Thomas knew he was in for more yak, and he was right.

'Tom?'

'What?'

'What shall I do with this?'

'What is it?'

'An old pot.'

Light on again, he swivelled, wide-eyed again and instantly out of bed. She was carelessly handling an eighteenth-century gravy-boat. This was one of his best pieces of porcelain, and he told her so.

'Put that down. That's Coalport.'

'Is it?'

'1760, worth at least twelve quid. More, with a lid on.'

It was snatched before she could give it and he vanished into a maize of furniture and bric-à-brac to secure it under his bed.

'You can't imagine how rare that is,' he said with a reappearing head. 'I bought it in Ramsgate, five shillings. The *idiot* didn't know what it was.'

Neither did she, and that was maybe what he meant. He clambered back into bed and glared at her. She looked up at him, contrite and imprisoned behind the bars of a dining chair.

'I'm sorry, it was under the pillows.'

No pity. No reply. No light.

A dozen or more minutes came and went and Thomas was at last on the nod. Not yet asleep, but in the business of blissful amnesia. He forgot about his armed father, and treacherous mother. Forgot the divorce and the dogs and the fear. And he forgot all about his sister, trampling in from Düsseldorf, who was still lying there wide-awake and worried in his room.

'Tom.'

No answer.

'Tom?'

'Yes.'

'Are you asleep?'

'Yes.'

'Sorry.'

'Sorry for what?'

'I've got to have a pee.'

Definite silence. Taut.

'I've got to have a pee. Tom?'

'Fucking Ada!' he snapped up, annoyed, awake, and loud. 'Are you gonna do this all night?'

'I can't help it, I can't get out. Can I have the light on?'

'No.'

188

'I can't see.'

He didn't care.

'I might tread on something.'

An observation that initiated a certain resentful compassion. 'All right, hold on.'

She heard him fumbling in the darkness and was suddenly blinded as the beam of a powerful flashlight hit her full in the face.

'Go on then,' he instructed. 'Get on with it, I'll steer you out.'

'Can't I take it?'

'No.'

Bel got up and followed the beam through the furniture. At the door she hesitated and looked back.

'I'll wait,' said Thomas.

Out she went and he killed the light and started waiting, and despite best efforts, started thinking again. He didn't want to think, he wanted darkness, wanted to dream. The thoughts came in no particular order and shared little but their morbidity. Mabs up first, and then Walter, and then Rob. What if it really had been Rob, barging in with the Beretta? Two terrifying flashes in the darkness, the first bullet through the palm of the extended hand, they always are apparently (he'd read that somewhere); and the second, a neat entrance hole in the left tit, searing pain, and the sound of a high-velocity .32 smacking into the wall behind you. It's very painful being shot, 'Body cavities cannot tolerate blood' (he'd read that somewhere else). Did he really think it credible that Rob might murder him? He considered it for several moments and decided he really did. That outburst in the sitting room was more than just incidental passion, no fantasy either, it was hate. Clearly there would have to be a rethink of securities. No hope of finding a key for such an obsolete lock. Why hadn't he put a bolt on? With a bolt he wouldn't have even had Bel in there. But then maybe it was a boon her clattering in, a piece of good fortune demonstrating catastrophic failure of the precautions? He was lucky it was Bel, he had her to thank for that, and where in God's name was she? This was the longest piss in history.

Downstairs the grandfather clock struck four so it had to be about three. His thoughts returned to his father, and he lay there in dingy torpor recalling highlights of Rob's aggression – the incident on the beach, for example, when Thomas was thirteen.

Running and running with Rob and his riding-crop and dogs. Rob always carried a riding-crop even though he didn't have a horse. From time to time on these loathsome marathons, it was Rob's practice to sprint up from behind with a fist of seaweed (the polished stuff, two yards long), and as he passed, launch this saturated and stinging mass hard into the back of your head. It was always a shock to receive it, always a laugh to give. Thomas laughed too, you had to, because Rob didn't like it if you didn't. But he didn't like what was coming next, and neither ultimately did Thomas. A cataclysmic error was imminent. Thomas did something he'd never done before: he picked up the seaweed and threw it back at Rob. This was all right in principle, but this particular clump was attached to a previously unnoticed portion of flint. The weed hit Rob square on the head and the flint, still travelling with considerable centrifugal force, spun around to the other side, and like some evil fucking bolas, clouted him in the opposite ear. Now this was a very cold day in January and it hurt. Clutching both ears, Rob sagged a bit, and spoke a few words like someone learning Korean. Thomas knew what was coming and ran for it as fast as he could, but there was nowhere to hide on this bleak stretch of beach so he ran into the sea – plunged in with Rob bearing down on him. When the waves were at his chest he felt his feet float up, and Rob beat him as he swam.

Thomas went further out into the North Sea and Rob went with him beating, swam at his side, ploughing through the surf in his shades and surgical-collar, the riding-crop reappearing through the firmament to beat with every stroke . . .

It was an appalling reminiscence, that riding-crop in the sea, but before reaching its fearful conclusion, the door silently opened and Bel crept in. He hit her with the light, ushering a suggested path back to the bed.

'Where have you been?' he said.

'Downstairs,' she whispered. 'I just nipped down to get some more cheese. And an apple.'

'An apple?'

'Sorry, Tom, I'm so hungry.'

She couldn't see his indignation.

'Don't talk,' he said.

'Sorry.'

As she got into bed the cheese came out and he noticed it had been secured between two slices of bread.

'You've made a sandwich?' he said.

She nodded, transfixed by the authority of his light.

'You were supposed to be on a *toilet*.'

'Sorry.'

'Jesus.'

Light out.

And then the eating started. An apple never sounded louder. He sprawled in frustration listening to every bite. And then there was glugging. She had milk. Obviously concealed a bottle on the way in. He heard it going down with the cheese. And then she belched, from deep in the throat, and he nearly got out and hit her.

'Be quiet!'

'Sorry.'

The silence got longer and turned into minutes, maybe five minutes before she started snoring. Thomas couldn't believe it, she'd come in here and given him insomnia, and now *she* was asleep. 'Quiet,' he demanded, but the impact of the protest fell upon himself. He was annoyed, and you have to be awake to be annoyed. He was both, the one fuelling the other in dreadful symbiosis. The iniquity of it all was overwhelming, so now was the snoring. She was cutting it up like a fucking chain-saw. He withdrew under the bedding to escape, but could hear it still – nothing changed but the simile – it was like someone mowing a lawn. Too hot to sleep under here of course, and anyway, he'd already abandoned any idea of that. The Ever Ready was still in his hand and he fired it at his watch. The brief but intense rush of light stamped his retina with purple circles that went green when he closed his eyes, and he did, blinking frequently until the phenomenon disappeared. It was 3.27 a.m. . . .

He was on the worry over Walter again, and thinking about the Vicar's dictum in respect of Maurice, when suddenly the obvious dawned. If he was going to have to make a final search for the key, why not now? What was there to lose? After all, there were only two requirements (to be wide-awake in the middle of the night and in possession of a torch); he was presently umpire of both. Why wait for another night to force himself into a position he was already in? Why risk an alarm clock, albeit buried in pillows, waking someone else? Plus with the kraut in the house you never knew, there could be unforeseen complications. Better surely to go now when Bel and her pal from the Ruhr were guaranteed to be asleep?

The proposition was instantly enticing and he got out of bed for it. To go or not to go, that was the question, but he was already going. Stifling light through his pyjama jacket, he put a last look at Bel who had her mouth open and was snoring like a man. He went through the door with the expertise of a ghost, sealing her carefully behind it. Even so, he could still hear her rasping until he was halfway up the corridor, many footsteps from his room. Out here were all the usual ingredients of the night. He passed the bathroom with its collective odours of flannels and disinfected things, its door ajar, and its interior illuminated with a faint blue of the water heater's pilot light.

At the end of the corridor he turned sharply on to the little landing. Years of familiarity with these premises meant his Ever Ready would not be necessary until he was inside his grandfather's room. As he climbed, a series of unavoidable creaks shoved up the adrenalin. He could hear his own blood, especially now, as in absolute darkness he felt the chill of a coal-black china doorknob in his hand.

This was unquestionably the most dangerous investigation he'd ever made – to be caught out here would be disaster – but to falter now would be to abandon the whole thing. It was too late for that, this really might be his last chance, and to that end he applied himself to the slowest twist this knob had ever had . . .

On resistance, he gathered the courage to push, and got an eye into the gap. There was a duo of egregious greeting, the one expected, the other not. First came the humbling of the nostril, an unequivocal capitulation to unwholesome wards of stale poultice with vigorous undertones of po. And second, the totally unexpected presence of moonlight. Had the sky suddenly cleared? This was the south side of the house and the moon was down on it, pressing at the windows and all over the floor. Was it friend or foe? Without alternative he was obliged to consider it benevolent. Moonlight would mean minimal use of the flashlight and that could only be for the good . . .

With meticulous caution he entered, fully opening and closing the door in one skilful manoeuvre. This most unnerving part was over without incident. He was in. For a minute or more he didn't blink, stood stiffly inside the door waiting to acclimatise his eyes. When focus came it was naturally on the bed where Walter lay sleeping with shallow sighs. Thomas fought his own tremulous inhalations, trying to get his breathing into synch with the old man.

As he calmed his confidence grew, the darkness thinned, and he sent eyes off on a rehearsal of the route he would take. Stop one was the wardrobe for a comprehensive search, and if no success in there, the infinitely more risky journey to the bedside table. This was a two-drawered affair with a cupboard, less than a yard from Walter's head. One slip could cause an avalanche. There was also a three-and-a-half-foot-high table lamp with a shade like a Turk's hat. If activity at the bedside was required this monstrous item would have to be removed.

Settling eyes on the wardrobe he struck out with the precision of a man on a high wire. Arrival felt like an eternity, but in fact he was on it prompt. It was *circa* 1930 with octagonal handles, a substantial but inelegant piece. The doors were identically veneered, featuring a pair of central knots with vertical lines bulging around them like a magnetic field. They were tightly closed but the key was in the lock and presented no problem. He put a glance back at his grandfather, all quiet in that department, and he eased one of the doors. Inside was a full-length mirror and a refreshing waft of camphor. On the various rails hung a fine-looking collection of suits, hats above, and some weird-looking shoes below. No light was necessary to check out the pockets. He found sixpence, bus tickets, and some ancient cigarettes. Nothing to detain him here and he sank to his knees to have a go at the more interesting collection of boxes. The first was cardboard packed with aluminium devices for stretching shoes. Another box revealed other such apparatus, some interestingly antique, one or two shaped like a whole wooden foot. (Were circumstances more favourable, he wouldn't have minded one of these.) He worked deeper and, risky as it was, was going to need the light. Shielding the lens he released a sliver through fingers, no drama from the bed, and he let out the lot. Brown shadows and several small suitcases. He withdrew the first, carefully censoring any snap from its locks: toiletries (including shaving-soap, blades, and denture cream, pyjamas, slippers, and a dressing gown, everything assembled for Walter's next trip to hospital). It was a depressing collection and he didn't trouble with it further.

Next case up was just as dull, as was the one after that. More rubbish in boxes, more ties and bow ties and socks patterned like wallpaper, unopened Christmas presents going back over years. In the depths of the case was a family of tins that on any other day would have fascinated – full of oddments and assortments, cuff-links, collar-studs, a frustrating selection of keys – but all were little keys and never the key he was after . . .

A stab of desperation brought him to his feet and for the next few minutes he was all over the cupboard again, fingers in shoes and hats and feeling at the hems. He went round the inner brim of a bowler hat and plunged to his shoulder blades in the lining of a coat. There was something down there, no question. It felt like a key and it was a key, but a Yale and not a Union. And that was it for the wardrobe. He was clammy with sweat and his anguish intense, plus his watch was catching up with the anxiety. He'd just caught a glimpse of it. Rob would be abroad in less than an hour and if anything went wrong in here this would not be a good place to be.

Closing the doors he turned once again to his grandfather, knowing he was going to have to tackle the bedside table and its dangerous set of drawers. His head craned in exhausted apprehension, eyes unwittingly on the ceiling. A crack fractured its way across like a portrait of lightning, and something not entirely dissimilar began to assemble in Thomas's head. Wait a minute, he thought, wait a fucking minute . . .

If Walter had something to hide he wasn't going to stash it where Thomas could easily find it. Walter was tall, Thomas was not, he's therefore going to exploit the physical disadvantage and stow it out of his reach. This ugly sod of furniture was over seven feet, tall enough to have an attic? A chair was procured, hardly high enough, and he mounted with trepidation, hauling himself a last inch or so to get eyes over the top. And there it was – at least, there something was – a green leather case with what looked like gold-plated clasps. He had to stretch till it hurt to reach it, got a finger round the handle and hauled it in. It was smaller and of much higher quality than anything below. Clutching it to his chest he descended, reopened the doors and almost got into the wardrobe with it. Flashlight on and a surprise: the clasps were solid gold, with a Birmingham hallmark (1922?). He was poised for the first when he noticed an inscription embossed into the lid of the case. It was his grandfather's initials, accompanied by a repetition of the design he'd seen downstairs on the Vicar's training ball: oak leaves, encircling two pairs of dividers. This was the kind of stuff he was after, highly concealed things and confidential property. It was also the most likely repository to date to contain a secret key. Securing his light, he again positioned the case for opening. It was locked. The bastard was locked and he almost groaned out loud, busted with the abhorrent realisation that to find one key he would first have to look for another. For a moment the will went out of him – it was pointless buggering about in here. There was only one solution, he was going to have to confiscate this case and get it into his workshop, sort out some alternatives. It was a simple-looking lock, all it wanted was a simple little key. Like the keys in the collar-box, for example? Optimism hit with the thought; with unexpected hope he disinterred the tins. If there was a God it had to be in one of these, and if it was any one, it was the obvious one, it was going to have to be the gold.

Bingo.

Excitement was making him clumsy. In his haste the second clasp snapped open with more volume than he would have cared for. And another noise in the darkness! There was movement somewhere and he crouched, shooting alarm at the bed. If Walter woke and spotted him, he'd cross the floor like a zombie, pretend he was sleep-walking, walk to the door, and walk out. He couldn't actually see Walter from here, but after an aeon of waiting there seemed little discernible variation in the breathing, and he again risked turning on his light . . .

The interior of the case was shared by two opulently lined compartments. The first sported a pair of white silk gloves with a tasselled scarf of the same material folded underneath. In the adjacent space was a peculiar-looking garment of shimmering fabric, heavy satin, almost watery to the touch. He shook it out: it looked like a kind of apron, oak leaves and fish embroidered at the edges and silver letters woven at its front: 'Most Holy Order of the Unveiled Prophets', the rest was silver stars. It was obviously valuable, at least, important, but what was it for? Thomas wasn't of a mind to care. Depressed at yet another false dawn he stuffed the apron back in the case. Its lid was about to go down when he noticed something (how he didn't miss it is anyone's guess, but he didn't). Sticking up by the hinge was a fragment of paper, so meagre a protrusion he had to use fingernails to get it out. It revealed itself as a yellowing business card with a central trademark that he recognised instantly. Staring out was an Arab's Eye, the same Eye as the one in the window of Madame Olanda's hut. Text was printed in confirmation: 'Madame Olanda – Fortune Teller – Reader of the Tarot –

Advisor of the Ball. Consultations daily. Telephone Thanet 346 (Nearest phone box on the jetty).'

Thomas studied the card and reversed it. Scribbled in pencil on the back: 'Dearest Wally, at any time convenient to you before eight o'clock, but not after for obvious reasons! Ever & for ever, your wandering love, Olanda.'

Your wandering love? Not available after eight o'clock for obvious reasons? But what reasons? For reasons of the Ball, or was it at eight that she began wandering about? He considered it and couldn't know and anyway there was suddenly something of greater importance on the agenda. This card revealed two things. The first, that his grandfather's relationship with the fortune teller was more intimate than he imagined, and the second, and of more significance, that there was another layer to this case.

He went at it, lifting a kind of tray. Nothing in here but a clutch of old letters done up with a rubber band. At first sight it could have been another disillusionment, but actually it wasn't. The very location of these letters invested them with an inherent distinction. Nobody's going to hide anything in a place like this unless something incredibly secret is going on and (astonishing as it is to report) Thomas momentarily lost interest in the key.

He went through the envelopes, all in the same hand, Olanda's hand, and all postmarked at around the time Walter first became ill and was forced to give up his business . . .

My dearest,

It was a pleasure to see you Saturday, and a sadness to see you so hurt. Please don't take it all upon yourself, I like you am grieved at the turn of events. You say you can never forgive, and I don't see you should, not because of her, love matters little here, but because of the boy. Silence is yours to do with as you like. Um̄ quotes silence as the divine dimension – existing before time and light – it is yours to use as you will. In this poor world, only love can be entrusted with the truth. Be well soon, Wally. Olanda.

The letter left Thomas blinking. He didn't understand it but was anxious for the next. It was hardly out of its envelope before a voice pole-axed him with shock.

'What are you looking for, Tom?'

He swung around, his torch delivering a random graph of panic along the wall.

'What d'you mean, in here? Nothing?'

Walter looked at him and looked like he'd been awake for a hundred years. His fingers clutched the sheets like roots and his voice was very frail.

'When you're out hunting secrets, make sure you're looking for the right one.'

Thomas didn't know what to say so he didn't say anything, crept to the end of the bed and stood speechless for excuse. There wasn't one. Nothing on offer but embarrassment. His grandfather was aware of his discomfort, and always a friend, changed the subject on Thomas's behalf.

'What time is it, Tom?'

'Ten-past four.'

'Come and sit down. Talk to me.'

If Walter wanted to let it go, Thomas was only too pleased. He pulled up a chair, and eager to keep the subject changed, said the first thing that came into his head.

'Bel's home, Grandad.'

'I know. I heard her.'

'Did you?'

'Got her friend with her. I heard them talking.'

'Her name's Eva,' said Thomas. 'I haven't met her yet.'

'Hoffentlich ist sie schön.'

'What?' No reply and Thomas asked again. 'What does

that mean? Is it German?' This got a nod and Thomas was impressed. 'I didn't know you could speak German, Grandad?'

'Not since the last time I died,' he said, and he barely had muscle to smile. 'Not since then.'

His face looked like he was wearing it, eyes peering out of it like it was a mask.

'I was in hospital for over a year, and they all used to come and talk to me, about the war, what we were all going to do after it. One girl from Dresden, she had her husband in an English hospital, in Bournemouth, that's how daft it all was. Anyway, that's how I learnt.'

'From nurses?'

'Yes.'

'Say some more?'

'Die Krankenschwestern waren sehr sympathisch.'

'What does that mean?'

'The nurses were very nice.'

His voice went away and he went somewhere with it. There was silence about. Somewhere outside you could hear the singing of the first bird.

'Can I ask you a question, Grandad?'

The old man's eyes came back.

'Is it true that you've got enema?'

'Enema?'

'Have you got it?'

'I don't know what you mean.'

'*Enema*,' insisted Thomas, like Walter, all but whispering.

'*Anaemia*? They say I've got *anaemia*?'

'What's the difference?'

'One's in your blood, and the other's up your arse.'

'And you haven't got one?'

'No.'

'Oh.'

This time the silence came from Thomas. He felt a shiver in his arms and not just because of the chill in here. Maybe he really had said something untoward in the vicarage, but if he had, whose fault was that? He didn't want to say anything, they made him say it. If anyone was to blame, it was Vicar Potts.

'Early for you?'

'Bel woke me up,' said Thomas. 'She's in my room.'

'How's that?'

'There's a turd in the spare room and she wouldn't go in there.'

'It's the Jack Russell,' said Walter. 'Useless, that dog. Fucking Crippen came through the window, he'd try and lick him. It's him gets the other two to mess in the house.'

'I don't know why they do it.'

'It's a protest, Tom.'

'What have they got to protest about?'

'Not the dogs. Your mother.'

'Mum? What d'you mean?'

It was a question that nearly didn't get answered. Walter looked at him and didn't seem entirely anxious to pursue it.

'She thinks she's getting shat on, so she's telling him with shit – talking through the dogs, like she does? All the dogs are doing is passing on how she feels.'

'With dog-shit?'

'That's right.'

'How do you know that, Grandad?'

'I know a lot of things,' said Walter. 'And some things are said better without words. No better way to say "I hate you" than a bayonet in the gut?'

This faltering hypothesis touched something in Thomas's psyche that he wasn't able to articulate. But it sounded like truth, so simple, yet so unexpected coming from the source it did. Walter knew a lot of things all right, but no chance of getting any further with it now, because once again the old man changed the subject . . .

'Your grandmother tells me you've got a sweetheart.'

Something else he didn't expect Walter to know.

'I told her that in secret.'

'That's how she told me.' He pulled in some breath. 'I'm happy for you, Tom. What's her name?'

'Gwendolin.'

'Is she pretty?'

'She's got very blue eyes.'

The light in the room was changing, moonlight into daylight; it was strange being here with his grandfather in the dawn. Thomas felt that he could talk to him about anything – Gwendolin, being in love, anything – things he could never say to anyone else, and that was probably true for Walter too. They were very alike, Thomas and he, liked the same things and thought in a similar way. Both were thinking about a girl with blue eyes.

'When I was your age, a little bit older, I was in love, Tom. She had the bluest, bluest eyes. She was the love of my life.'

'More than Grandma?'

'More than anyone I ever met. I never told anyone, but I can tell you, I've thought about her every day for nearly fifty years.'

'What happened to her?'

'The war, always the war.'

'Was she killed?'

'No, I was.' He smiled but his mask didn't. 'Before I went up the line, on that last day, she gave me a coin, a silver dollar, for good luck. And I was so afraid of losing it, I took it to the company blacksmith, had him drill a hole in it so I could hang it round my neck. And you know what, he drilled this hole right through the bit where the luck was, drilled the luck right out of it. I never saw her again.'

There was another lengthy silence and you wouldn't want to own the regret in Walter's eyes. After all these years, there was still the regret . . .

'You love her in the best way you can, Tom, because no one else will tell you this, but this is the best time, sometimes the only time? When you're young, you think it's yours for ever, your gift? But life goes so quick.' He would have smiled again if he could. 'Then one day you wake up, and girls you wouldn't have looked at twice don't look at you once no more. You take it from me, it's the best time, it's springtime, and you don't want to muck it up.'

'I won't.'

'You're after the wrong secret, Tom.'

It wasn't possible not to register how this was said, nor the penetrating look that came with it. After all the murmuring, his grandfather sounded curiously focused.

'What do you mean?' said Thomas.

Walter didn't answer and in the immediate context didn't need to. There was only one secret Thomas was after, and that was the secret of the filing cabinets. He felt the blood rising and feared an incriminating blush. Had Walter known all along, always been aware of his clandestine investigations? It seemed that he had, and if he had and the filing cabinets were therefore the wrong secret, it presupposed there was another secret that was right. What kind of secret was that?

'What is the secret, Grandad?' Again no answer from Walter, and Thomas let the lack of it evaporate before hazarding another question. 'Is the secret the reason you don't talk to Rob?'

Hard to read the silence, but you want to say there was more yes in it than no.

'We're very alike, you and me, Tom, not much education, but smart.'

Thomas agreed, praying he'd get back to the secret. But it wasn't to be. Walter closed eyes and shrank into the pillows until there was nothing left of him but a nose.

'I feel tired,' he said. 'More than tired.'

'Can I just sit here for a while?'

'As long as you like. I'd like it if you did.'

There was a burst of song-thrush in the gardens and another day expanding into the room.

'Grandad?'

'Yes?'

'How would it be if I moved the Morse key in here? We haven't transmitted for ages. I could wire it easily out of the bay tree, move the key up, and send you stuff when I got home from school.'

Walter replied but there was nothing in his voice and Thomas moved in closer.

'What did you say?'

'I'd like that.'

A long sigh and he was asleep. Thomas looked at him, mulling a confusion of thoughts including various kinds of guilt – guilt about sneaking in here in the first place, and guilt about staying here now. The truth was it was coming up to five and he didn't want to run into Rob. He also felt guilty about reading the letter (was it somehow a facet of the secret?). There was mention of a boy – was the boy him? He desperately wanted to read them all, but that was impossible now. Walter had every chance of telling him, but chose not to, and to pry further felt like betrayal. No way could he get back into that case. Nothing to do but reinstate it, and with hardly a sound he and the chair returned to the wardrobe and the letters went back into hiding.

'Tom?'

'What is it, Grandad?'

'I thought you'd gone.'

'No, no, I'm still here,' and he resituated himself at the bedside as evidence. Several slow minutes passed and the guilt went away: he was here for the right reasons now. He loved this old ruin of a man; above everyone in the house, he loved him. It was always Walter that looked out for him, let him steer the car and toot the horn even when he was a little kid. And now he was going to die. Death was all over him, every corner of his face, in his fingernails and eyes and hair. No point in pretending anything different. Very soon his grandfather would cease to exist and it made Thomas sad.

Outside he heard footsteps, someone walking the gravel, and he crossed to the window and looked out. White lilac all over the garden and the daffodils already gone. He looked down and saw Rob climb into the Wolsey on his way to work.

BOOKS AND OTHER ANGELS

Eva was planning to stay a month – she stayed less than a week. She was a squat prat with swarthy undertones and well-developed calves. Thomas couldn't fancy it, but Rob apparently did. He was all over her, grins and cigarettes, missing dinners with Ruby Round the Corner in favour of eating at home. 'Verstehen Sie?' he kept saying. 'Verstehen Sie?' and 'Ja, Ja,' she said . . .

'Verstehen Sie?'

'Ja.'

'It's so embarrassing,' confided Bel at the end of one of these dinners. 'She speaks fluent English, he knows about four words of German, and keeps saying "Verstehen Sie?".'

'What does "Verstehen Sie?" mean?' said Thomas.

'It means do you understand?'

It all kicked off OK. Day one they got the polythene up and Bel moved into the gloomy room. The dogs were kept in the kitchen and Rob started wearing a yellow cravat. Even so, Eva clearly didn't like the cut of the place. Thomas watched her at the edge of vision. She didn't like sitting in the armchairs and looked at her meat before she ate it. Day three she was taken up to meet Wol and that was the end of that . . .

Thomas wasn't actually there, he'd gone out to buy some pink wrapping paper, but from his grandmother's bulletin he managed to reconstruct the incident in his diary.

May Second: Spent the morning wiring the Morse key for Walter. He was asleep. That afternoon, despite Mum's protestations, Bel took Eva up to meet him. They'd picked him some flowers in the garden. Walter was out of it on some new pills and thought she was a *Krankenschwester*, and to Bel's amazement, started yakking at her in German. Mabs, and then Ethel (who'd just walked in) construed this as medicated gibberish. 'He's on a little morphine,' she said, 'for the discomfort,' and tried to shepherd everyone out. Bel said, 'He's speaking German, Mum,' and it was evidently directed at Eva. He had her isolated with a leer and there was some cycling going on with his feet. He sat up and said something that caused Eva to retreat with her eyes wide open. 'What's he saying?' said Mabs. Bel shook her head. 'I can't tell you,' she said. Wol was having a good time and said something else and the German ran. Bel rushed after her and there was a hell of a conflab on the landing, resulting in the first boat home to Düsseldorf.

That evening when she got back from the railway station, Thomas mustered with his sister in her room.

'What did he say?' he said.

'Oh, I don't know. Just nonsense.'

'What?'

'I can't really translate it.'

'What?'

'Remember when your arms were brown and beautiful things and your cock stuck up like a flagpole?'

'He said that?'

'He said, disinfectant gives me a hard-on.'

'A hard-on?'

'Einen steifen Schwanz.'

Bel's distress didn't appear to Thomas to be altogether authentic.

'He thought she was a nurse,' she said.

'He would do.'

'I didn't know he could speak German.'

'Didn't you?' said Thomas.

'Did you?'

'Oh yes, I've known for quite some time.'

Bel was still unpacking her suitcase. The framed photograph of Peter from Ramsgate came out, except it wasn't him any more. It was a blond youth with curly hair.

'What happened to the Vegetarian?'

'I met Wolff.'

'Does he know?'

'Yes, I wrote to him and told him.'

She hung blouses on hangers and went into the suitcase for more.

'Actually, if the truth be known, I'm glad she's gone,' said Bel. 'They were wonderful in Germany, didn't have her father oozing all over me. Did you see him with the Liebfraumilch? Made me sick.'

'She's divorcing him, you know that?'

'She'll never do it, she's just threatening him.'

'I don't think so,' said Thomas. 'She's got a dossier, she's gonna take it over to Canterbury.'

'I don't believe it.'

'It's true, I've seen the letters.'

'What letters?'

'The envelopes. She's had envelopes, from the court.'

Bel looked mildly surprised, and craning eyes over

208

a shoulder she vanished back into the wardrobe with footwear.

'Is he still seeing her?'

'All the time.'

'Old tart.'

'What's gonna happen if she does it, Bel?'

'I don't know. It's a madhouse.'

Thomas retired to his section of it, lit the oil-lamp and sat at his desk to wrap the present with some care. First pink tissue paper, then pink shiny paper. Pink was Gwendolin's favourite colour. He also had a go at it with a pink ribbon, but couldn't solve the mechanics of the bow and had to finish it off with sealing wax. It wasn't quite what he wanted but it looked all right, like a homemade cake with a jujube. Taking up his pen he inscribed it in rambling black letters, 'For My Darling Gwendolin, Happy Birthday, With Love From Thomas.'

Before the ink was dry the kraken awoke, reared spontaneously to nag in his head, and this time, for the first time, he heard himself saying it out loud. 'You're after the wrong secret, Tom.' Thomas had acknowledged this intelligence a dozen times a day since Tuesday and always got nowhere with it. He was about to re-examine it now and get nowhere with it again.

'You know where you went wrong?'

'Where?'

'You should have read those other letters.'

'I know I should,' he said.

'You might have to go back in there.'

'I can't,' he said.

'What about the secret then, you cunt?'

'What about it?'

'What is it?'

'I don't know,' he said. 'I don't know.'

Unquestionably, it was something to do with Rob, some unwholesome and enduring offence? Maybe there had been

209

tarts in Bristol, an agglomerate of scrubbers, maybe that's why he was never there? If Rob was constantly having intercourse, that would be reason enough for Walter not to talk to him – after all, Mabs was his only daughter. But then, why the mention of 'the boy' in the letter from Olanda? What did she know? Intuitively, Thomas sensed that he was involved in all this, but where did he fit in? Somewhere, he imagined, between love and loathing, Walter on the one hand, and Rob on the other . . .

With the latter in mind he got up and slipped the new bolts, blew out the lamp and into bed dragging a pillow down with him. For some minutes he lay there kissing it. 'Darling,' he whispered. 'Oh darling,' and he felt its tits and sort of fucked it for a while as he fell asleep, longing for the day after tomorrow . . .

When Saturday came Thomas was awake before it, set his alarm for just after four-thirty so he could be up and about when his father came out of hibernation at five. He told Rob he couldn't sleep, but the truth was he didn't want him barging at the door and discovering the securities. They drank the tea and got into the Wolsey and it was already day at the railway station, green and gaslit and warm. Bill Bing was now accompanied by a conked-out old effort called Sailor, who like Arthur before him wasn't cut out for this type of career. Two tons of newspapers were dealt with as usual, and by seven Thomas was wandering in sunlight up Pyson's Road on his way home.

He'd arranged to meet Gwen at eleven o'clock at the top of the cliffs overlooking the bay. The day could not have been more perfect: it smelt like holidays he'd had in this town as a child. The choice of rendezvous was significant. He stood at the gates of a huge castellated mansion with butter-coloured roses all over its walls. One hundred and ten years ago, Thomas's favourite author had lived in this house. The locals called it Bleak House (real name Fort House), and it cost 1/6d to get in. Halfway up its façade was a bust of the great writer, melancholy pink-granite eyes staring for ever out to sea. And it must have been days like this that brought him here, a whiff of salt and sweet tar in the air, and the ocean a dazzling blue.

Thomas hung over the railings looking down at the beach. The tide was on the turn and the sand shining like flat gold. He retraced steps to the gates, read the weather-eaten sign again. 'Charles Dickens House. Open to the Public, May to October. Teas.' In further distraction his watch came up, five more minutes gone. It was approaching eleven-thirty and he was getting a bit imaginative. Maybe she was waiting at a different house? Dickens had lived all over Broadstairs, every other residence had a plaque – he'd been up York Gate with *Copperfield*, and down the seafront with *Barnaby Rudge* – so many lodgings, there was even a house in Albion Street with an inscription saying: 'Charles Dickens Did Not Live Here.' But out of them all it was likely to be 'Dickens House' on the promenade, that was a museum too, and that, he convinced himself, was where she was waiting, sitting on a wall with no bike. They'd agreed to go bikeless so they could walk on the beach. A sting of anxiety propelled him from the gates, and clutching his present he was many yards into a scuttle when a voice called from behind . . .

'Thomas?'

He turned and looked at her and she looked like an angel. She wore a summer dress with lupins on it and white high-heeled shoes. He couldn't believe how grown-up she looked, how beautiful, or that she was his. Her hair was gathered in a pony-tail, and her lips so red, and her eyes so blue, when she smiled it made him dizzy.

'I'm sorry,' she said. 'Am I late?'

'No, no, not at all. I was just going down there for a minute.'

'Where?' said Gwen.

'There's a hole in the wall down there. I was going to have a look through it.'

Taking his hand she put an arm round his waist and raised her face to kiss him. It was a very different experience to the last. That kiss was his, this belonged to her, and it was a kaleidoscope of lipstick and red fingernails in his hair. He could feel her breasts pressing into his shirt and suddenly he was worried about his *Schwanz*. What if she could feel it like he could feel her tits? Gwen didn't seem to care about anything but kissing. Neither now did he. He wanted to absorb her, possess her, crunch her white teeth like hazelnuts. The very tip of her tongue pushed through his lips causing an overload of hormone in his vision. For a second or two he thought he was going blind. 'Oh darling, darling,' he said, and she looked up with melted eyes and moved her head to his shoulder. He was inside her perfume, inhaling her in a kind of delirium, and she smelt of something extraordinary, like rhubarb in expensive vinegar . . .

'Did you miss me?' she whispered.

'Oh yes.'

'Ever so much, or just a little bit?'

'Ever so much.'

At last they separated, and he aimed an index finger at the very end of her nose, pushed it like a button and regretted it as he did it. Why did he do that?

'Sorry,' he said.

'You are funny, Thomas.'

He realised the finger was a messenger of his vulnerability, her kisses were out of his depth. He wanted to touch her, but didn't know how, didn't know what to say.

'That's a perfume you've got on?'

'Don't you like it?'

'Superb.'

'It's Coty. My sister gave it to me.'

Presenting an opportunity to get his present up. He handed it to her with cautious modesty.

'It was supposed to have a ribbon on it, but I couldn't do it up.' Gwendolin smiled. 'It's not very much, I mean, really, it isn't much at all. I don't know whether you're going to like it.'

'I'm sure I will.'

'It's sort of, unusual.'

'Is it?'

'Not the sort of thing you probably think it is.'

'Isn't it?'

'Probably not.'

She peeked into the wrapping and went through an alluring pantomime of wondering what it was, listened to it and shook it a bit, and finally gave him a kiss on the cheek in receipt.

'I can't imagine what it is.'

'If you don't like it, I'll get you something different.'

'Of course I'll like it,' she said, her eyes widening in protest. 'I'll open it on the beach.' And she led the way for a hand in hand along the promenade.

Thomas couldn't remember feeling happier. He felt like gulls and fresh air, part of a huge celebration.

There were two hundred and fourteen steps to the sands; they knew it because they counted them, taking alternate tens. The beach was in every direction beautiful: nothing to disturb it but basking sand-flies and daft little oyster-catchers with long beaks. Gwendolin took off her shoes, wanted his off too, and they ran to the sea, scattering the birds, and laughing as they dared the waves. She flirted with them like she flirted with him, cheating the surf and then back to his side, hiding behind him and pushing him at the next breaker. His jeans got soaked and she held up her dress and there was a moment he'd remember for ever. Suddenly she was still, sun in her hair, sea all around her, and everything silhouetted against the gold.

'Shall we open my present?' she said.

'What?' said Thomas.

'Shall we open my present?'

They sat side by side warming toes in the sand. Was it for the sunshine or his eyes that her dress was so careless? She'd raised knees to re-explore the wrapping, revealing a comprehensive serving of thigh. Thomas didn't know what to look at, at her, her naked legs, or the gift. His expectations were if anything greater than hers; every tear in the paper was a sound of torment, and as soon as it came out he started apologising . . .

'I'm sure you won't like it.'

She wasn't yet sure what it was. It looked like a dirty old box. She opened the lid and it turned into a book – it was an old volume with a heavily stained title page.

'*The Personal History of David Copperfield*, by Charles Dickens. Chapman and Hall. London, 1850.'

'It's a first edition,' said Thomas, expanding on the apologies. 'Bound from the parts.'

She lowered eyes and journeyed a few chapters in, found a picture of spindly people that someone had thrown a cup of tea at.

'That's called foxing,' he said. 'It's quite normal for old books.'

'Is it?'

'Iron in the paper.'

He stared, waiting for the verdict. Although she didn't altogether say, it's what I always wanted, she did say, 'It's wonderful.'

'Are you sure?'

'Of course.'

'You're absolutely sure you like it?'

'I love it,' she said, 'I love antiques,' and she couldn't have said anything better.

'It's actually a *first* issue of the *first* edition,' said Thomas. 'There's a difference between the first and second issue. The first issue of the first edition has a dated pictorial title page, 1850.' He retrieved the book and showed her the date. 'If you get hold of a *second* issue of the *first* edition, the date won't be there. That's how you'll know. 1850 on the pictorial title page makes it much rarer.'

'Oh,' she said, leaving her lips in a pout.

'You *do* like it, don't you?'

The book was already closed, slender fingers clasped around its spine. The painted nails made it look ridiculous and were all the answer he needed. Why had he given it to her? (He'd considered toiletries and cursed himself.) She was a beautiful girl with naked legs and red toenails – this thing just wasn't on her agenda. Gwendolin put the book aside and nuzzled at his shoulder. Fingertips came out of nowhere, conducting a tantalising exploration of his ear.

'It's a marvellous present. Thank you.'

Clearly she wanted kisses, but he couldn't prevent his mouth waffling about the wretched fucking book.

'That's why I wanted to meet you up there,' he said. 'Outside Bleak House. I've never been in there, but that's where he wrote it.'

'Did he?' she whispered.

'In the room at the front. I've never been in there, but I've read about it.'

She wasn't listening any more, and neither really was he. Her lips were inches away, moving gently to kiss around his mouth. If the intention was silence, it was successful. Fingers were back in his hair and the embrace got heavy, not entirely in the romantic sense, but in its mechanics. She was almost on top of him and his heels were off the floor fighting gravity. This couldn't last and it didn't, they collapsed sideways into the sand. It was no interruption for Gwen. She lay in the shingle feeding red kisses, her lips teasing his like she teased the sea. Hands were on the move, one in his ear and the other burrowing into his shirt. He felt fingers spread on his belly, her little finger under his belt, sneaking to the hilt. And then her tongue was in his mouth – at first he didn't know if she knew it was in there – the last thing he'd had in it was an egg. What if she smelt it? A fried egg? As a precaution he started inhaling exclusively via his nose. This was successful but he was excited and worried that he sounded like a pervert. Gwen was breathing heavily too, her eyes half open, drowsy and blue as Minton china.

'Don't you want to touch me, Thomas?'

'Where?'

'You can touch me anywhere you like.'

To facilitate this most wonderful of invitations she lay back on his arm. Inside her collar he could see part of a silken shoulder strap, her favourite colour, and Christ, his colour too. Her knees were raised and her dress in a pool at the top of her legs. Like her brassière her knickers were pink. He felt giddy with desire. It was all his and all he had to do was take it. He pushed at her stomach and started kneading it. It wasn't what he intended or what she wanted, and her eyes opened. Stretched like a harmonica, his mouth sucked in a dreadful load of gawkish spit – Oh God, I've put her off! But apparently not. Gwendolin rolled closer and a button arrived under his fingertips. An attempt was made at it, and it seemed huge, the size of a dinner plate. He fumbled about, and failing to get it out of the buttonhole, abandoned it to more competent fingers. She undid it for him, plus the buttons above, and he didn't dare look down again until her eyes were closed. Breathless with expectation he ran fingers up her arm and slipped them inside her dress. She sighed. He felt around the back and then again at the front. In a wilderness of inexperience his hand wandered the peripheries of her brassière, until at last, with an audible snort, he forced it on to her tit. He held it like a component. This acme of static passion continued for some while before Gwendolin found a small whisper.

'You can move, darling.'

'What?'

'You can move about.'

He held her other tit. If anything it was more satisfying than the last, and over the minutes he moved it up and down a bit. He'd felt them both now and was working up a strategy for her knickers.

'Tom?'

'Yes?'

'Would you like an ice-cream?'

It was all over, and he sat up into a galaxy of wounded stars. Gwendolin also sat up, adjusting her dress to cover her thighs, then it was the turn of the buttons. He couldn't look at her. There was an arse on the coast and it was him. It was all lost, legs, tits, knickers, all his, and he just didn't have the nerve. Maurice would have had her dress off by now; worse, Shackles would have fucked her. Oh evil thought, oh evil, of that red bastard with his freckled neck and acne, probably scoured this very beach for his condom.

'Is something the matter?'

'No,' he said, avoiding her eyes.

She drew in her legs and kneeled next to him, an arm around his shoulder.

'What's wrong?'

'Nothing really.'

'Something's wrong?'

What was wrong was he wanted to ravish her, utilise her, mount her, but he couldn't tell her that, so he told her something else.

'I suppose I'm worried,' he said.

'What about?'

'I don't know, I've got so many it's hard to get them all in order. I've got *ten* major worries.'

'What are they?' said Gwen.

He shook his head and looked at her. Bits and pieces of a breeze shifted stray hairs on her forehead. When her next question came it was prefaced by a sympathetic pause.

'Is it because of your parents?'

'What about them?' said Thomas.

'Maurice said they might be getting a divorce.'

In the circumstances he didn't like the sound of this – not the divorce part – the Maurice.

'When did you see Maurice?'

'Yesterday.'

'In bed?'

'He was on his bike.'

Clutching handfuls of shingle he turned back to the sea. A long way out the cormorants were fishing.

'Yeah, they're one of the worries,' said Thomas. 'And so is Maurice, not much of one, but he's on the list.'

'Why?'

He sat back filling her in on the disaster at the vicarage, Potts, and Mrs Potts, and the black bloke with the rabbits, short-handing the lot into his principal worry, which was the iminent death of his grandfather, itself the precursor of his second greatest worry, the 'mystery' that might die with him.

'What is the mystery?'

'It's all very complicated. You don't want to hear all that.'

'Yes, I do,' she said, sounding like she meant it. 'I know I probably can't help, but sometimes it's a help talking about it.'

'I can't, because it's a secret.'

'I'll never say, I won't, I promise.'

'I mean, I can't tell you, because I don't know what it is. All I know is, it's something to do with me. I can't ask anyone because they won't tell me. The only person I can talk to is my grandad, and I can't ask him because it's *his* secret.'

Gwen didn't quite understand the machinations of all this and said so. Thomas went through the plot and sub-plot, told her about the case hidden on the wardrobe, the divine dimension, Um̄, and the secret of the letter. 'It's something to do with my father,' he said. 'My grandfather won't speak to my father, never has, and I know the secret is probably the reason why.'

'Can't you ask your mother?'

'My *mother*?' The concept raised eyebrows and he stood up under one of them. 'I can't talk to my mother about *anything*.'

It was time to be somewhere different; he grabbed shoes and offered his hand. 'Come on, I want to buy you an ice-cream.'

They retraced steps across the beach, cleared sand off their feet, and Gwendolin went back into heels. The stairs zigzagged up a wall of solid chalk, twenty to a flight, and after the second, Thomas was puffed.

'I wish we hadn't counted them on the way down.'

He leant over a balustrade to catch his breath. She joined him on elbows, staring at the same sea.

'Such a brilliant day.'

'It's your birthday,' he said. 'Wouldn't dare be anything different.'

'Thank you for my present, Thomas.'

There was a kiss about but he didn't take it, couldn't get into all that present-dialogue again. Instead he took her hand and led the way up the next flight.

'A hundred and seventy to go,' he said.

'Can I ask you a question?'

'Course.'

'You don't have to answer if you don't want to.'

'What is it?'

'None of my business, really,' she said.

'What?'

'Is it very upsetting, about your parents?'

'Upsetting?'

'Is it?'

Not the question he'd expected. There were two ways of answering it, and both dishonest. He could say he didn't care, which was a lie, or say he did, which was a bigger one. The truth was he did care in a one-sided way, because this marriage had trashed his mother, made her fat and value dogs more than people. Would Gwendolin be able to understand that? No, he didn't think she would. On arrival at the next landing he decided to answer as a plain statement of fact.

'They never loved each other,' he said.

'Never?'

'Not as far as I know. I've never seen them kiss.'

'Not even when you were little?'

'Worse then,' said Thomas. 'Well, actually better, because he was never there. The only memory I ever had of my dad was being frightened. Only time he ever touched me was when he was hitting me.'

'Why was he hitting you?'

'Don't know, he was always rushing around like the third world war.'

'How terrible,' said Gwen.

Thomas smiled, and meant it.

'Doesn't bother me any more, honestly doesn't. It used to give me asthma, but we're a hundred steps up, and I'm OK.'

'I can't imagine my parents hitting me,' she said. And if you wanted to know why, you only had to look at her. She was an angel. Thomas looked at her and felt proud.

'The thing that makes us different,' he said, 'is the damage that's been done to us.'

It was a satisfying assertion to throw her way. He climbed the stairs pleased at having said it (although in reality he hadn't thought of it, his grandfather had).

Her shoes clattered after him, a pretty sound, like a pink echo, and it went with her underwear.

'You're probably scarred,' she said, her face speaking a concern that wasn't remotely evident in his.

'I don't think so.'

'I mean, inside?'

'I don't think so.' And he dug up a grin. 'There's nothing left of it, just gone days now. When I was little, I used to have this fantasy that when I was old enough I'd get hold of him and bash him up. But I never think about it any more. I've got nothing left of being a kid, except a funny feeling about letter boxes.'

Her eyes asked the question.

'I don't like looking through them,' he said. 'I'd rather look through anything than a letter box.'

'Why?'

'Because of lots of things.' He shook his head. 'It's a boring story.' Plus he was out of breath.

'No, it isn't. I love you, Thomas, I want to know.'

'All right, I'll tell you what, I'll tell you when we get to the top.'

The ascent continued but she didn't have to wait. With sixty more stairs in prospect, Thomas needed another breather, and he leant back on the railings, supporting himself on hands.

'You know what Cubs is?'

'Of course I do, I was a Brownie.'

'When I was six, I wanted to be in the Cubs, and I pestered my mother, day in day out, for the uniform. She didn't have any money, but got it somewhere. It was a hat and a jumper, always winter. Every Tuesday night you had to go down to this hut and tie knots. I only ever went once. Our house was on a hill overlooking the road, and every Tuesday, I used to put on the uniform, go out the front door, cross the road, and get into the hedge opposite. And I used to sit there for hours watching the house, especially if my father was home, and then come back, and pretend I'd been to the hut.'

'Why?'

'Because I was afraid that if I didn't watch them they'd all move out when I was gone. I'd come back from the Cubs and get no answer, knock on the door and look through the letter box, and all the furniture, everything and everybody, would be gone.'

Thomas knew the story backwards but it was the first time he'd ever heard it out loud. It took the smile out of him, his sentiments towards those lousy memories getting a mirror reaction from Gwen.

'It sounds so miserable,' she said.

'I didn't think much of being a kid.' He looked up the next flight, then at her until the grin came back. 'Come on, I'll race you. No more talking till we get to the top, and when we get there, no more talking about this.'

Outspurting each other they ran all the way up to the esplanade. Thomas flung himself over the railings to resuscitate, and Gwendolin sat on the top stair. When she'd collected her breath, she looked up at him.

'You know what you should do?' she said.

'About what?'

'About your grandfather and the secret.'

'We said we weren't going to talk about it any more.'

'When we get to the top?' said Gwen. 'I've got another stair to go.'

Her smile was a mix of innocence and impudence and with a face like that you're allowed to break the rules.

'What should I do?' he said.

'Read all the other letters?'

An option that wasn't available. He shook his head.

'I can't.'

'Why not?'

'Because I can't. I would have done once, but I can't. It would feel like cheating. And even if I found out, what am I going to do with it? I can't tell him I've read his letters. Be like having money you can't spend.'

They started to walk, both thinking about the secret, neither focusing on the obvious. It was Gwendolin that finally did, inside the library at Bleak House. But that hadn't happened yet. They were still hand in hand on the cliff top, passing the great gates, when Gwen suddenly said, 'Let's go in?'

'You don't want to go in there?'

'I do.'

'What for?'

'I want to see where he wrote my present.'

She was already tripping up the path. Somewhere among the roses a head came out of a hatch. It was the property of an extremely old woman with orange hair and various bruises.

'Yes?' she said.

'We'd like to go in?' said Gwen.

'No children without adults.'

'We *are* adults,' said Thomas, rising with pith. Both of us are. How much is it to get in?'

'One and six,' said the old woman. 'Each.'

Thomas counted out and handed two piles of one and six across, and in exchange got a pair of yellow tickets with threepence written on them. As they shuffled in the hag vanished, reappearing at the other side of the front door.

'Tickets,' she said.

Thomas handed them over and she tore them in half and threw the bits in a bucket. She had an alloy crutch and bandage to the knee like lagging on a pipe. Maybe she fell over a lot? On her cardigan there was a badge saying 'The Friends of Charles Dickens', and clearly she could have been one.

'Follow the arrows,' she said. 'And no touching, no sitting, no eating.' Her nasty eye, the lower one, settled on Gwen, and for some reason she added, 'There's an American upstairs.'

This was a museum on a budget with brown paint and a smell of meals. An enormous Victorian staircase was under the auspices of the first arrow, and they climbed it looking at black-and-white pictures of characters from the books. Martin Chuzzlewit. Uriah Heep. Ebenezer Scrooge.

'Why have they all got such daft names?'

'Because they're all weird,' said Thomas, pointing at the next face up. 'He's a murderer, or got murdered, I can't remember. He's in *The Mystery of Edwin Drood*.'

'I'm surprised you've never been here,' said Gwen.

Thomas didn't answer but realised he was surprised too. This place was right up his street. Dickens must have gone up and down these stairs a thousand times thinking about Peggotty and Little Emily, and at the turn of the stairs, there she was, staring out of a gilded frame in a picture signed 'Kyd'.

'That's Emily. She's in *Copperfield*.'

'She looks a bit shifty.'

'She's actually much prettier than that.'

'How do you know?'

'In reality, she looks like you.'

Gwen wasn't sure of the compliment, dropped a glance at

Fagin and continued up. At the top of the stairs there was a choice of rooms, two out of three saying 'Private'. In a room overlooking the gardens there were candlesticks on a rococo sideboard, a green *chaise*, and a huddle of balloon-backed dining chairs of uneven quality. The walls were green flock, stained white in places by the sun. It could be the original wallpaper, it wasn't the original carpet. Charles Dickens never stood on this, no more than he looked at these paintings. A duo of repugnant oils hung either side of the fireplace – mahogany-coloured bulls in a Scottish swamp. A fiver for the pair, thought Thomas, and that was his general impression of the room. Everything had a kind of up-for-sale atmosphere, like the auction was over and the good stuff gone. Gwendolin wasn't fascinated and wandered down the far end to look out of a window.

'When did Dickens live here?'

'About 1850. He left because of an Italian playing a violin on the jetty.'

'Bit glum, isn't it?'

'Don't suppose he'd live here now. If he was alive now, he'd be in the back of a Jaguar, flat-out on the A2.'

She crossed the carpet and he didn't hear her footsteps until they were back outside on the stairs. Halfway up he suffered a pang of unwelcome speculation: what if Gwen thought her present was like this lot, worn out and morbid and worth about one and six? Suddenly this place felt like a mistake, and he was poised to disassociate the author from his dwelling when she turned back with a thought of her own.

'Did you hear about the play?'

'It's worth a *tenner*,' said Thomas.

'What?'

'Nothing, nothing,' he said. 'I'm sorry, I was thinking about something else. That was just my mouth.'

He smiled with it and she repeated her question,

looking bemused. 'Did you hear about the play?' she said.

'What play?'

'The school play.'

He hadn't.

'Waldron got your part.'

'Waldron?'

'And Margaret Ruther got mine.'

'Waldron and Margaret Ruther?' The billing was appalling. 'How could she cast Waldron and Margaret Ruther?'

'I suppose because they're the tallest.'

'They can't act,' said Thomas. 'They'll just stand there looking enormous.'

'She offered me Louka.'

'Don't do it. I wouldn't touch it. There's plenty of other parts.'

'What parts?'

'Professional parts. You could be an actress, and play any part you like.'

They had arrived in a room they weren't yet aware of, sunlight cascading on to a red carpet.

'I want to be a receptionist, Tom.'

'What?'

'In a big hotel.'

He could see her behind the desk with the headphones, receiving orders for dinners with full garnish. It would work of course, but surely she thought she was worth more than that?

'What about you?' she said.

'I don't know, I haven't quite made up my mind. Either a poet, or an antique dealer.'

It was with eyes of the latter that he looked around. This was more like it, this was the library/writing room and there was some decent stuff about. Portraits and clocks, and framed letters. Almost all the walls were floor to ceiling with original glass-fronted bookcases, and more glass at the end of the room in a huge pseudo-Gothic bay window with spectacular views of the sea.

This was floor to ceiling too, and facing it, on a slightly raised dais, was the great genius's writing desk. *Circa* 1830 and highly polished, it was a mesmerising piece of furniture, exuding like an altar, but more important than any altar because its holiness wasn't fake.

Thomas stood staring at it, all he could do not to bow at it, but recognising it as the most important antique in the house, he rejected it, enhancing its magnificence by deciding to leave it till last . . .

With Gwendolin like a bright little apprentice, he conducted an audit of the books. Case after case. Though they looked the part, crumbling bindings preaching authenticity, this show was of dubious provenance.

'Nothing you'd want to read in there,' he said.

'They're very old, aren't they?' said Gwen.

'Period's right, but they're junk.'

'What about these green ones?'

'Library Edition,' said Thomas dismissively. 'Not worth a thing. You could buy that lot in Ramsgate for a couple of quid.'

'Really?'

'Old doesn't necessarily mean much in terms of books.'

As he said it he realised the implications. What about the dirty old gravy-coloured bugger he'd given her?

'There's only *one* old book worth anything in here.' He didn't mean to say it all again but couldn't stop himself. She got another earful of dates and pictorial title pages. 'I'm sure they'd give anything to have your *Copperfield*. It's very rare.'

'I know.'

'I'm sorry, I know I've already told you all that.'

'I don't mind,' she said. 'I like you telling me.'

'Do you?'

She nodded.

'Well, what's amazing,' said Thomas, 'is he wrote it over there.'

It was there, he explained, that Dickens sat, month after month, with his hair sticking out and his fingers covered in ink.

'It took him two years.'

'For *one* book?'

'There was a lot of imagining to do.'

Gwendolin seemed genuinely susceptible to the magic, although she probably couldn't see the ghost.

'Who taught you about antiques, Tom?'

'I taught myself. I like furniture.'

He moved on, peering at a framed letter. It was brittle with age and almost torn in half.

'I've just thought of something,' she said. 'Do you know who wrote the letter?'

'It doesn't say?'

'I mean the *secret* letter, to your grandfather. Do you know who wrote it?'

He'd never considered the other correspondent, but now he did it was obvious where she was going and he looked at her and nodded.

'Then why can't you write to him?' said Gwen.

'It's a her.'

'All right, a her. Why can't you write?'

'Saying what?'

'Saying . . . I don't know . . . you'd have to make something up. Make her think you already know. If she thinks you already know, you're halfway towards finding out.'

Thomas thought about it, wondering why he'd never

thought about it. Of course he could write to Olanda. It was a good idea. But it wouldn't work.

'The person in question doesn't like me.'

'You *know* her?'

'Yes.'

'Why doesn't she like you?'

'Well, it's not actually me, it's my father. She *hates* my father.'

'Why?'

'It's complicated.'

'That can only be a help, can't it?' said Gwen. 'If she doesn't like your father, she'd probably be pleased of the opportunity to tell you why, and why is probably the secret.'

It wasn't and she was way off course. Thomas knew why Olanda didn't like Rob. But that said, the idea of writing was gaining currency . . .

'I'll have to think about it,' he said.

She left him to speculate, climbed a couple of stairs, and made a tour of the writing desk. It was little wonder the books were a marathon. This thing wasn't constructed for short stories, it was ten feet long and solid as a bank. There was an accompanying chair, polished with age, arms gleaming in the sunlight.

She pulled it out and looked across at Thomas.

'Will you sign my book?'

'What?'

'Sit where he did, and sign my book?'

Opening the precious volume she positioned it on the desk. Thomas felt reluctant but didn't know why. If the idea was anything, it was surely charming?

'All right,' he said, and he sat in the special chair, found a pen in his pocket, and wrote: 'For My Darling Gwendolin, On Her Birthday, May 26th, 1959. With Love For Ever, From Thomas.'

'Shall I put kisses?'

'Yes.'

Three kisses, and another as he stood up. She didn't want the present now, she wanted him. It started clumsily with too many mouths. Gwendolin sat on the edge of the desk and pulled him towards her. He was standing between her legs, right between her legs, with her dress in retreat and getting closer all the time. All sorts of stuff was touching, she could feel it this time, no question of that, wanted to feel it, and pressed herself further forward. 'I love you, Thomas, I love you,' and he whispered the same thing too. He did love her, and she was intoxicating him, pressing her sex into his. No more kisses, but the embrace endured, and the next time, the next time, he swore, when the next time came, he would make love to her . . .

THE SECRET OF THE BALL

It had been threatening for days, and on the first day of June, it hit. A gale came out of the north-east, crossing England at its most easterly point, which was Broadstairs. Thomas heard it before he heard it on the wireless. Gale warning, they said: 'There are warnings of severe gales in sea areas, Dogger, Dover, Thames, Viking, North Utsire, South Utsire, German Bight.'

Broadstairs wasn't mentioned, but it was right in the eye of it. It came in the middle of the night; by dawn it was gusting at ninety miles an hour. Slates flew off and windows rattled. There was a high G-note in the bathroom, and sudden changes of pressure all over the house. Even indoor doors banged. The BBC said sea-walls had been breached at Whitstable, and at Dover, the port was closed. They also said a Spanish tanker was aground off the Goodwins carrying over fifty thousand tons of oil. They'd tried to get a helicopter out, but couldn't. A lifeboat was standing by.

When Bel came down for breakfast in her pleated skirt and school tie, Thomas told her all about it, reconstructing a background to the impending tragedy.

'There's forty hands on board,' he said. 'Haven't got a hope in hell. I should think the majority have already gone over the side.'

She was accustomed to his dramatics. Even so she said, 'I hope not.'

'You wouldn't last five minutes in this.'

On her way to the larder, Bel detoured for a look out the back door. The lilacs were hysterical, like a bunch of mad dancers doing voodoo.

'It's a tempest,' she said.

'They tried to get a Lynx out – couldn't get anywhere near it.'

'A what out?'

'A Sea-Lynx,' he said. 'Air-sea rescue helicopter. Waste of time in a breeze like this?'

He thought he sounded rather RAF.

Bel sat at the table with Weetabix.

'How dreadful to be on a boat.'

'I'm going down there for a dekko,' said Thomas.

'I wouldn't go near the jetty, you'll get washed off.'

'I'm going to North Foreland, have a look from the light-house. You can see right across the Goodwins from there.'

'What about school?'

'I'm excused. I've got an appointment.'

'With who?'

'I'm not in a position to discuss it,' he said, snatching a look across the gardens himself. 'I might be able to tell you later, depending on how it goes.'

He turned back expecting further inquisition, but there wasn't any.

'Can I ask you a question?' he said.

'All right.'

'What do you know about the rhythm-method?'

'What?'

'Have you had any experience of it?'

'I don't know what you're talking about?'

'I'm talking about "sexual intimacy".'

'Mind your own business.'

'What *is* the rhythm-method?' he said.

Her answer was no answer.

'I think you should go to school, Thomas.'

He went out of the back door instead.

Riding a bicycle to North Foreland was practically impossible. The wind was astonishing. It sucked the breath out of his head and pounded the earache in. Even going down hills he had to pedal, and on the flat, had to push. Everywhere the gale was in its fury, the roads littered with broken trees, and sad it was to see these gigantic canopies in the ruins of their final spring.

North Foreland stuck out into the weather, a chalk promontory of cliffs and turnips, its ancient lighthouse high in the farmland, supervising one of the most dangerous waterways on earth. Thousands of ships had gone down on the Goodwins. On autumn days, when the tide was lean, you could see some of the masts, some a hundred or more years old, someone had once told Thomas . . .

He arrived at the headland, wheeling his bicycle along a rutted track that would eventually bring him to the lighthouse. Hedgerow either side gave a phoney sense of protection. But at the end of the path the wind was back and he saw what it was doing to the sea. It was yellow and insane. He'd never seen the sea look like this before. It was the biggest event he had ever seen in his life.

Clutching binoculars, he climbed to the highest point of the Big Light's foundations, pressed himself at the wall to avoid getting torn off. These were quality lenses, forty-power Zeiss, even so it took a while to find and get focus on the ship.

The waves out here were wide as streets, thirty, fifty feet high, colossal water pulled apart in the air, collapsing into troughs and bottomless cisterns filled with drowning. Inside this sea was the stricken ship, black and red, visible but

intermittently as the gale boiled it like a lobster ...– – –...
But no hope out there ...– – –... This one's another mast,
thought Thomas . . .

'Hey, you! You there!'

If the binoculars hadn't been on a cord around his neck
he'd have dropped them. The voice was stern and angry.
He looked in its direction but it had gone somewhere else
in the wind.

'Get down, I say! You there!'

Expecting grief from a lighthouse type of person, Thomas
descended and an unexpected face appeared from under the
metal stairs. Maurice grinned, his hair stuck up on end, like
a pot of chives.

'Hello, Cock Hole.'

'I might have known it was you,' said Thomas.

'But you *didn't*, did you?' Still grinning, Maurice retreated
into a rusted porch, lighting up before he re-emerged. 'I saw
you coming,' he said. 'Saw you turn off.'

'Were you already here?'

'Nahh, coming up from the beach. I was hoping I might
find a body.'

'Has one of them gone over?'

'Fuckin' all of them.' He put smoke through a nasty smile.
'But all into a lifeboat, unfortunately. Only the Captain and
some other twat left out there.'

Thomas fought his way back up the stairs with Maurice
in pursuit. His cigarette glowed in the gale.

'Let's have a look,' he said, and he grabbed the binoculars, forcing Thomas up more stairs with him. 'Can't see
nothing.'

'You have to focus. You have to wait for the waves.'

'Got it,' said Maurice. 'Got it.' He held the cigarette
between teeth, breathing around it, exhaling with the butt
still in place. 'Jesus fucked,' he said.

'What is it?' said Thomas.

'The fucker's snapped.'

'Gimme the binoculars.'

He'd already taken them, readjusting for Maurice's lousy vision. For a moment the tanker was hidden, then it rose, and Maurice was right. It seemed to have broken at the stern, its giant superstructure flailing on the sea like a hinge. And something had happened to the waves. The spume at their crests had changed colour. It was brown.

'She's leaking oil,' said Thomas.

No reply and he lowered the binoculars and Maurice had gone. He was momentarily visible under the lattice heading back for the shelter of the porch. By the time Thomas got down to join him he was firing up a fresh smoke.

'I assume you don't want one?'

He assumed correct.

Like the rest of the lighthouse the alcove was white, an iron door in a metal frame sweating rust into the paint. They squatted with backs to it, staring across ploughed fields and on into the raging sea.

'Wish the wind would blow west,' said Thomas.

'Why?'

'It's putting out oil.'

A topic for which Maurice showed a singular disinterest.

'No school?' he said.

'I've got an appointment.'

The smoker raised eyebrows but didn't ask what.

'What about you?' said Thomas. 'When you coming back?'

'I reckon I'll get another week out of it.'

'You don't look ill.'

'Exercising, aren't I?'

'Are you?'

Maurice smirked, took a shattering drag allowing smoke

to escape around his knuckles in a classic policeman's hold.

'Did you know?' he said, 'that one good wank is equal to a seven-mile run?'

Thomas didn't.

'I'm probably doing over a hundred miles a week. Keep meself fit.'

He sniffed.

Thomas raised the binoculars, scanned the foreshore and cliffs. The wind rampaged over everything, tore wings off birds and flung seaweed into the air like wigs.

'Fucking gulls out there,' he said. 'I don't know how they fly in this.'

'They ain't gulls,' said Maurice. 'They're storm petrels.'

'How do you know that?'

'They're in the Bible. A very bad omen, petrels.'

'Are they?'

'The worst,' said Maurice. He stubbed his cigarette and stood. 'My old man says they're an omen of extreme ill.'

It was unlikely Vicar Potts had any other type of omen. Thomas didn't want to talk about Potts, but seeing Maurice mentioned him, asked how his father was. Implicit in the question, of course, was Potts' attitude towards Thomas's last visit . . .

'He'll get over it,' said Maurice. 'Makes me laugh, he refers to you as "The Corrupting Influence".'

'Does he?'

'The *Penman* Boy.'

'It wasn't my fault.'

'Brought up like vomit, you were.'

Maurice was amused. Thomas wasn't. Together they barged into the wind, Maurice's hair back on end, his homemade scarf flying.

'Cold for June?'

236

'Yeah,' nodded Thomas. 'Where's your bike?'

'Walked, didn't I?'

And he walked with Thomas back along the track until they were out on the Bay Road. Thomas got on his bicycle; the wind was with him now, he'd virtually be able to sail into the town.

'I'll tell you what,' he said, his nonchalance barely disguising the agitation, 'you know those "protectives" you've got, do you think I could have one?'

Maurice converted a neutral expression into the most salacious fucking grin Thomas had ever seen in his life.

'Getting on all right, are we?'

'Can I have one?'

'Is that who your "appointment's" with?'

The grin maintained. Thomas shook his head. So did Maurice.

'I've used 'em all,' he said.

'Used 'em all on who?'

'Wanking.'

'Wanking?'

'Southpaw with a Durex – you get a better wank.'

Thomas looked at his watch, about to be gone.

'You'll have to have a yodel in the canyon,' said Maurice. 'She'd like that.'

Thomas rose on a pedal and took off, not daring to ask what that meant. Gwendolin was far too pure to be thought of in sexual terms by anyone other than himself. Ten minutes later he was back in Broadstairs, parked his bike on the seafront and did the last couple of hundred yards on foot. No one about. No one would come out on a day like this unless they had to. The gale went for coloured lights on the promenade, and across the beach was having it out with the jetty . . .

He arrived in the environs of his destination. Looked at his watch. He was early. She'd said any time after eleven on any weekday; if he came on a weekday, he'd be sure to get in.

For some minutes he loitered outside the hut. There were sepia representations of the Sphinx and Pyramids, and the signed photo of the celebrity. Black curtains filled in the rest together with a list of charges. The Ball was most expensive at five bob. Tarot, three and six. Palms, half a crown. Next door was a boarded-up fish-fryer with a similar set of charges. If you didn't want the Ball you could have a Cod. Or a Hake for three and six. Thomas was instantly worried about money. What if she said he had to have the Ball? He had enough for a Tarot or a Haddock. Coming here began to feel like an error of judgement – he wouldn't have considered it had it not been for Gwen – and if she'd known the repository of the secret was Olanda, she probably wouldn't have considered it either . . .

He walked back up the front and sat on a bench with his collar up. There were further worries. Olanda hated Rob, and when she saw his son walk in, might she not refuse an audience? What value was it anyway? He didn't actually need the psychic side, he needed answers, and answers weren't what she did. He was the wrong type of client, he knew enough about the fortune teller to know that. She was an expert in the occult who had an occasional word with the dead. Her customers, by and large, were perishable ladies whose fate was obvious – not many septuagenarians think they're going to get shagged by a moustached Italian – births and weddings never came into it, substantially narrowing Olanda's field. But she never got the deaths wrong. All summer she handed out Swan Songs for three and six. They gave her the money, she gave them a date. 'But not yet,' she would say. 'Not for a long while yet.' And they'd leave happy with ninety-one under the belt, and like the rest of the refugees, tramp inland through the dreary streets to their bed and breakfasts, to all the Sea Views that didn't have any, and Four Winds that only got one, from the east, with rain in it . . .

Thomas knocked at the hut's door. 'Enter,' said a voice, and he did.

It was like walking into a filthy old cinema, same kind of darkness, same kind of smell. Darkness enhanced the proportions of the place and any sense of being in a garden shed was gone. The air was rank with steam; where it came from, or what it meant, he wasn't sure. He wasn't sure where the fortune teller was either. All walls were draped in black curtain – he assumed her to be behind one (perhaps observing him through a small hole).

'Sit,' said the voice.

He sat awkwardly on the only chair. Was an *eye* on him? He didn't know, but felt a surge of discomfort, as though in the presence of great authority, like Enright or the police. In front of him was a table swathed in black, and on top of it, the Ball. It was smaller than he imagined, no bigger than an onion, supported on a tripod of ebony and brass. Next to it, a saucer spilled smoked ends, cerise lipstick in the fag ash . . .

Suddenly a face appeared, holding curtains around its chin. 'I will be available momentarily,' she said, and disappeared again. Thomas realised the place was divided in two, steam coming out of her side. She was boiling something in there.

'Do you have an appointment, young man?'

He stared at the curtain, didn't like conversing with it, but said, 'Yes, I telephoned. Eleven o'clock?'

Wind howled about the hut, and as his eyes became accustomed, he took a tentative look at its interior. What light there was escaped the eye sockets of an ape's skull, and above, fairy lights curled around a piece of tyre. It was carved into an ear and painted pink. All sorts of rubbish was nailed up. There were dromedaries in frames, sacks of leaves, and pictures of Red Indians spreading hands at red-and-yellow dawns. Dominating all, and somehow attached to the curtains, was a portrait of an evil-looking pisser with too many arms and an eye in the middle of his forehead. *The Pope of the Underworld*, it said. *Um̄*.

More activity behind the curtains and Olanda came out in her entirety carrying a mug of tea. She was under the turban in a velvet robe, wore nail varnish, red as matches. Half of them struck. There was a toke left in her full-strength Abdulla which she hit before delivering the butt to the ashtray.

'What is it that brings you to me?' she enquired.

The voice was puffy, with tints of Wolverhampton. Thomas didn't know quite how to phrase it.

'I wanted to know something.'

'From the Ball?'

'I don't know,' he said. 'I thought I'd leave it up to you.'

She sat far side of the orb looking at him, and he looked at her. Did she recognise him? He felt confident she didn't. Except in half-light (and very occasionally at the depot), they barely saw each other. Even so he was nervous of curses. She'd given one to Rob, and he didn't want one himself.

'You won't mind my tea?'

'No,' said Thomas.

The mug came up and she took a gulp. This was the first time he'd seen her close up. Her face was horrible, hairs stuck down her nose like insect legs. Despite the tea there was a strong smell of rum about. It was eleven in the morning and she was cut.

'What's your name, boy?'

'Christopher.'

'Christopher?'

'Christopher Bantock?'

There was too much question mark in his reply; he realised it as he said it. Olanda looked across like he'd given her short change.

'You're not here at the behest of anyone else?'

'Oh no.'

'Because not a few of the *misguided* traverse my portal, like some might cross that of a doctor, and there, describe *symptoms*, attributing them to *another*, when it is *they*, themselves, who are suffering.'

'Oh no, not me. I haven't got any symptoms.'

She looked at him hard enough to make him shift eyes.

'What is it you seek, Christopher Bantock?'

'There's a secret?'

'Of what matter?'

'Family stuff.'

'I think you speak of a death.'

'I do.'

'Of a loved one?'

'It is.'

'With whom you wish to speak?'

'No, not really, he isn't dead yet.'

There was a long silence, morbidly orchestrated by the wind.

'Move closer,' she said. 'Give me your hand.'

He offered it with reluctance; she took it for examination in hers. These hands were worse than her face, heliotrope in tone with grotesquely long fingers, knotted here and there like bamboo. One wore an encrustation of diamonds on a ring that manifestly was several sizes too big. To prevent loss, it was secured above the index knuckle with a washer of blackened chewing gum.

'You will live a very long life,' she said, and that seemed to be that, and Thomas looked at her expecting her to ask him for three and six. Finally, she released the hand, and gave off more.

'But there is turbulence?' she said.

'Yes,' he agreed.

241

'I see portents,' she whispered. 'Of great ill.'

'Ill?' He felt a sour chill of adrenalin plunging in either thigh. She was the second person to see ill in the space of one morning. 'What do you mean?' he said.

'I must use the Ball.'

Striking a match she lit a candle and snuffed the monkey. The hut fell to darkness. Although here with no anticipation of an oracle, Thomas was transfixed. All eyes were on the crystal.

'I must go back,' she said, moving hands towards the Ball as if to lift it. 'Back, Back. When were you born, Christopher?'

'July the 1st 1945.'

'It is November the 1st, 1944'.

Some part of the wind found a way into the premises, billowed in the curtains releasing fresh steam. Whatever was out there, it was still boiling.

'I see a *woman* . . . I see a *wife* . . . there is an assignation, in the West End of London . . . A dark secret . . . It is *you*.'

'Me?'

'I see a hotel . . . kisses on the stairs . . . *uniforms* . . . I see your father in an *army* uniform.'

'He was in the RAF.'

'*Army*,' she said, confirming it with the Ball. 'He was in the American Army.'

'Rob?'

Inadvertent reference to the forbidden name was but a momentary distraction, barely noticed by either.

'Your mother was in love with the American Army.'

'All of them?'

'One of them.'

'But my mother was married in 1943.'

'Adultery!' she crowed, fingers stretched. 'Adultery rears in the West End of London . . . there is love, there is a pregnancy, there is a problem . . . tears, tears . . . your mother bears the

242

fruit of one, but is married to another . . . tears and lies . . . lies and lies . . . walking the streets of lies and houses of lies . . . living the lies and lying the lies . . . years of lies . . . until at last, there is *truth*!'

She raised arms suddenly like she was at the end of a conjuring trick. Thomas nearly gasped. Her eyes wobbled circuitously to the ceiling with his following, and while up there she said, 'I speak of eyes that look, but do not see, ears that listen, but do not hear, tongues that lie, but are silent for the truth.'

A protracted and dramatic silence ensued, with nothing about its business but the gale. When she spoke again, it was within the parenthesis of a whisper: 'With an hourglass of tears are measured these days.'

And then the eyes came down, bulging like specimens, and the mouth reanimated, talking faster and faster, spittle flying as her auguries welled into a mesmerising stratosphere of inevitable crescendo: 'Truth,' she intoned. 'Truth, to be stuck to the underside of lies, despised and denied its time, truth, with a broken heart in the suffocating darkness, *truth*, too terrible to speak, that dare not speak its name . . . but speak it shall, shall shout it out loud . . . its name is *Thomas* . . . its name is *Thomas Penman*!'

'Ahhh!' interjected Thomas. '*Ahhh*!' backing off on unsteady feet. 'Oh God, Oh God, you *know*!'

She came around the table, hardly bothering to stand for the journey. 'Sit,' she ordered. 'Sit, and listen to me.'

'Will you curse?'

'Sit. Sit.'

He collapsed backwards into the chair with his tongue gone huge. 'I only told you I was Bantock,' he gurgled, 'because you don't like Rob, and I thought if I'd come in here as Rob's boy, you wouldn't have seen me.'

'I'm not talking to Rob's boy,' she said. 'If you were Son

of Rob, you would not be welcome here. I am talking to the grandson of your grandfather.'

'What's the difference?' heaved Thomas.

'You see this?' Olanda plunged fingers down the front of her garment and whipped out an amulet. Solid gold on a golden chain. It was a configuration Thomas recognised: a crucifix with a ruby at its centre surrounded by oak leaves . . .

'What is it?' he said.

'The Holy Order of the Unveiled Prophets. It was given to me by your grandfather, as a symbol of affection, and trust.'

'Who are the Unveiled Prophets?'

'He's one, and I'm an Honorary.'

'Is it religious?'

'It's Masons. You know what they are, don't you?'

'No.'

'A Mason is initiated with a noose around his neck and a dagger at his heart. You can *trust* a Mason.' She sat before saying more. 'You can trust a Mason to tell you the truth, and I'm going to tell you the truth, if you're ready for it.'

'I am.'

'I know you are, and you've come to me just in time. You don't know this, Thomas, but I've discussed you on many occasions.'

'Have you?'

'With your grandfather. Your grandfather and I were very close before he was ill . . . Do you trust your grandfather?'

'Yes, of course.'

'Then you must trust me. You have come to me, because on the morning of this great storm, there was nowhere else to be. You do understand that, don't you?'

He supposed he did, and nodded to that effect.

'And you have a secret,' she said. 'Built on damnable offence. So let us now cut down the suffocating years of deceit and shame, and throw you into the light.'

'All right,' he said.

'Your mother loves another man.'

'My mother?'

'Another man is your father.'

'What do you mean?'

'You will know the truth, but never your true father.'

'It's *Rob*.'

'It isn't.' Her eyes returned to the Ball. 'Come back with me, Thomas. Lay your hands on the table, and come back.'

It was clear he wasn't keen.

'You needn't be afraid,' she said, pitching it low and Wolverhampton. 'I shall speak of two things, and two things only. Love and Light.'

She reached for his hands and he let her take them, laying each carefully on the table like a couple of side plates.

'And truth, Thomas, I shall speak of truth. Love and truth are indivisible. Put truth to darkness and love will perish, for what nourishment is there in this concord of denial and corruption? What could flourish here but the slanders that sustain it? Lies feeding on lies, one bloated falsehood suckling another? It is a purgatory without light, a hole within a hole, an eternity of holes, and in each hole, a prisoner.'

'What prisoners?'

'Your parents, Thomas, they are prisoners in the holes, and you are a prisoner of the imprisoned, tearing at your shackles, and howling in the darkness of their deceit. For where love is denied, there is protest, in the bowels of the darkest night, there is protest, as you must have protested in your innocent years.'

'I don't think I did.'

'Oh, yes, yes, you did, a protest most vile. But not with words, you wouldn't have had the words. We're going back, Thomas, back to the beginning, where words there were none, where love denied was a filthy substance, soiled and punishing, the currency of the sewer, and perhaps the only language they would understand.'

Did she mean shit? It sounded like shit. She was back on the Ball.

'Let's have a look at some dates. It's 1943. In 1943 your mother married?'

'Yes.'

'It was winter.'

'It was summer.'

'That's right,' said Olanda, making seasonal adjustments to her orb, 'it was summer, but raining and cold?' Facts Thomas could neither confirm nor deny. 'Hard rain on London pavements, a wind moaning, like the wind today, and so cold, some said it *felt* like winter? She wedded Rob in a red-brick building on the ground floor, and soon after, he was away to the war, off in the RAF.'

'Yes.'

'He was a pilot?'

'He was a navigator.'

'He was a navigator *close* to a pilot?'

'Yes, in the same plane.'

'It's 1944. September, 1944. Does the 15th mean anything to you?'

'No,' said Thomas.

'It was then she met a Man.' (A single eye was briefly raised with all the forensic acumen of her craft.) 'A Man with dark hair, green eyes, and unusually large ears. An American Man, a handsome soldier. She was swept off her feet, and right there and then, there was a night of love.'

A magnetic silence followed during which she moved closer to the oracle. It seemed she had spotted something of moment.

'Oh dear, oh dear.'

'What?' said Thomas.

'September the 21st? Rob home for a week. Fate held its breath. November. December. Tears at Christmas?'

'Christmas?'

She gave a startling résumé of that awful season, Rob gone, the Yank back, and Mabs in the bath with a coat-hanger and bottle of gin . . .

'Too late. Too late. The seed was sown. 1945. A letter from Rob? How should she answer? The war was over, she was pregnant, it was to America she would go. April. Apple-blossom. The war ended in tears. The American left suddenly, packed for Chicago in the dead of night. She was abandoned, with child by another, and Rob coming home. What could she do? A desperate plight wanted a desperate solution. This unrighteous conception coincided with one of his leaves, it could have been his. Why couldn't it be his? It *was* his. She handed him the baby.'

If Thomas felt anything, he didn't know what. All he was aware of were his ears, listening.

'All was well,' continued Olanda. 'As these things might well be. And then came the letters. Indecorous letters, letters from America. In 1948, he found out. It wasn't his baby at all! Lies and tears. And now the plight was Rob's, his turn to decide what to do. Should he stay, forgive, bring up baby as his own? Or should he protest his injury, too much pain to bear, and go? He did neither. He neither forgave, nor left. Her treachery was his revenge. He hated her and punished her by punishing the child, denied it rights to a loving father, and a loving mother too. Your mother stands accused. So deep was her shame, she could never protect you. You were a walking affirmation of her guilt. A living betrayal. The secret, Thomas, is you.'

Thomas realised he was holding his breath. Even the shadows were still. After what amounted to a considerable silence, she blew out the candle and relit the ape. The wind meandered, troubling the curtains, releasing more steam. Thomas sat staring at the crystal, and then up at her. He'd wanted to uncover the secret, but didn't anticipate anything like this. Coming out of this witch, such an indictment was on the frontier of unbelievable. She had axes to grind. Yet somehow, he did believe her. It was fortunate perhaps, he was still numb.

'So many things to think about,' he said.

'Not really, your best plan's to focus on the one.'

'Why did you tell me?'

'You came to me, and asked.'

'Yes, but I didn't expect all this.'

'Would you have preferred another lie?'

He had nothing to say so said nothing. Except he heard himself saying something about the steam.

'My primus,' she said. 'Would you like some tea?'

'No.'

'Some advice then?' She stood up. 'When you're fighting devils, you're better off with one sword in your hand than the weight of ten.'

'What do you mean?'

'You're free now, Thomas, you have the truth. It's all the weapon you'll need.'

And his turn to stand, hands in pockets, fumbling for words and change.

'How much do I owe you?' he said.

'You owe me nothing. You owe them nothing either.'

It was an extraordinary thought, but at this moment he felt closer to this ugly old bitch than his mother.

'I'd better go.'

He looked at the door, went about getting through it with the eyes of the Soothsayer on him.

'Are you courting, Thomas?'

'What?'

'Seeing a lass?'

'Yes.'

'Then you must take care,' she said. 'Be aware of the words of Um̄. For as the Prophet says: What has gone before, will almost certainly go after.'

What did she mean? He couldn't handle another autopsy and didn't stay to ask. He started walking and was halfway home before he realised he was meant to be on a bike. Too late to go back, and better to walk anyway, it gave him time to think. Olanda's revelations were astonishing, but he couldn't truthfully say he felt astonished. Battling the weather up Ramsgate Road he deciphered a probable reason why. You can't feel astonished unless you can pass it on, tell someone else and make them astonished too. Astonishment only has value in its communication. But if what Olanda said was true, they already knew it all, and he couldn't possibly discuss it with them anyway. So what value was it? He'd gone in there to dig out one skeleton and got up another (as a matter of fact, hadn't even asked about the Trappist relationship between Walter and Rob). The secret had become a secret. It was like discovering penicillin and having to keep it to yourself. What did it matter if Rob was, or wasn't, his father? If the Ball was right he was never going to find out. And whoever the other cunt was, he must have been an awful cad to slope off and leave Mabs in the lurch like that. What a horrible choice of fathers.

The difficulty, clearly, was separating information the fortune teller had amassed via Walter from information given by the Ball. The Ball said Mabs had got into a bath with him and a bottle of gin. It would have been Gordon's. It wasn't until his thoughts shifted to his mother that any of this felt painful. If Olanda was right, it meant Mabs had started rejecting him before he was even born – not only a bastard, but an escaped abortion – no one could feel comfortable with that.

For a mile or two he felt depressed: it was too big a calumny to take. And then of course, coming with it, there was the contradictory and entirely novel hypothesis to be considered, that perhaps Olanda had made it all up. She despised Rob, and was perfectly capable of concocting the whole thing out of malice. He hated her too. Hated her birds. He'd mocked her husbands. Maybe she was working revenge over that?

As he approached the house, his eyes automatically rose to an upstairs window, knowing he was going to have to find out.

There was only one person who knew the truth and was also capable of telling it, and that was Walter. He was going to have to go in there and confess everything, tell him he'd read the letter, tell him why he'd read it, tell him he was after the pornography, tell him the truth . . .

Ethel was on her way downstairs as he walked in. Wind caught the door and slammed it behind him. His intention was to go straight up and it would have happened if it hadn't been for the expression on his grandmother's face. Something was up, and it was the subject of his question.

'Your grandfather's bad,' she said. 'I've already phoned the doctor once. I'll have to call again.'

'I'll go up and see him,' said Thomas.

'Not now. He's just asleep.'

She continued into her sitting room and he followed. Ethel wasn't very competent with the phone. She didn't like it, and dialled with lips moving as though trying to remember instructions. Until recently, this phone was kept in the hall, and that's how she thought of it, like a visitor, a stranger to be talked to at the front door. When the surgery answered it was obvious the voice that worked there made her uncomfortable. It was evidently a different receptionist, and Thomas listened as she went through it all again.

'He can't seem to settle,' she said. He was 'seeing things'

and didn't seem to know her. Yes, he'd had his pills, but he was complaining of pain. She was sorry to be a worry, but would it be possible for the doctor to come right away?

Ethel heard the excuses down the line, apologised again, and replaced the receiver as if it belonged to someone more important than herself.

'They say he'll come as soon as he can.'

'Is Mum up with him?'

'No. She's out.'

'Where?'

'Ask no questions, you'll get told no lies.'

She sat in her armchair to wait. When someone's waiting, you can't do much but wait with them, and that's just about how the afternoon went by. Long silences and long thoughts. Thomas was as anxious for the doctor to arrive as was Ethel. Clearly, until that eventuality, there was little chance he was going to get in to see Walter.

'Couldn't have come on a worse day,' said Ethel.

Thomas nodded without thinking about what she'd said. His thinking, in fact, was all over the place. He was back at the beginning and starting all over again. A lot of what Olanda said made total sense of course, a lot was demonstrably true. But what was all that stuff down the sewer about? 'Soiled and punishing?' 'A protest most vile?' Did she mean he shat himself because Mabs didn't love him? As far as he could remember, he shat himself because he liked it. It was one of his few great pleasures. But then, what did he know? Maybe that bag was some sort of protest? Maybe he was punishing her in a peculiar sort of way? The thought, like the rest, went nowhere. He couldn't find the words to sort the mechanics of that one out – which in a sense reiterated what Olanda had said – you wouldn't have had the words, she said . . .

'He should be in hospital, really.'

The voice was full of age and trouble, spoken as if part of

some ongoing conversation, and indeed, that's what it was. Thomas looked at her, realising half an afternoon had passed, and for every moment of it she'd been sitting there worrying exclusively about Walter. After all these years there was still some love, and it made him feel guilty and sad.

'It'll be all right, Gran.'

'Couldn't have come at a worse time,' she said.

A car pulled up outside and Ethel stood to get an angle out of the window. It wasn't the car she wanted. It was Rob.

'He's home early,' she said.

And not a minute later, Bel was home too. They heard her dump her satchel in the hall and go straight upstairs. Ethel took her glasses off, sat down, and put them on again.

'I was hoping it was the doctor. Or at least your mother back.'

'Where is she, Gran?'

'Canterbury.'

It was a reply out of distraction more than anything else. Thomas was on to it instantly.

'Canterbury? What's she doing in Canterbury?'

Ethel realised something was out the bag, but didn't know quite what. Didn't know how much Thomas knew. Clarification was simultaneous.

'Is she over there divorcing him?'

There was an apprehensive hiatus. Her reticence was innocent.

'It's nothing to do with me, Tom. I don't get involved.'

Thomas was on his feet, moving in, keeping it friendly.

'You can tell me, Gran. I already know all about Brackett, and Ruby Round the Corner. And the Assizes. Is that what she's gone to Canterbury for?'

'If she has,' said Ethel, 'you haven't heard it from me.'

A thumb relevant to Rob went over Thomas's shoulder.

'Does he know?'

'I don't know.'

'Well, he *must* know? What's the point of divorcing him if he doesn't know?'

'I don't know, Thomas, I've got enough on my plate. I'm staying out of it.'

With timing that wasn't far off poignant, the Anglia appeared in the drive. Thomas saw it coming and felt his hair stand on end. No way did he want to be about when Mabs came back. If the bigamist went animal, that's their affair, their marriage, and their divorce. He was going to be behind bolts.

'I'm staying out of it too, Gran.' He turned, already halfway out the door. 'I'm going to talk to Bel. Will you let me know when the doctor's been?'

He took the stairs in twos. Music was coming out of his sister's room. He almost went in, but didn't. Why should he tell her? He wasn't going to tell her, she probably knew. He saw her this morning and she didn't tell him. Better to keep your mouth shut until the full implications evolve? He elbowed her door and went through his own. Framed it and bolted it and nothing happened for over an hour.

There was a knock on the door.

'Who is it?' said Thomas.

'It's me. Bel.'

The dread of the moment was dealt with. They both knew, and they both knew they knew.

'When did she tell you?'

'Half an hour ago.'

'Does *he* know?' said Thomas.

'Yes.'

'Did he punch her?'

'Neither of them have said a word about it.'

Wind shunted up the back of the house. They shared an available expression of disbelief.

'I don't give a bugger,' said Bel. 'I'm much more

worried about Grandad. The doctor's going to give him an injection.'

'When did he come?'

'He's in there now.' She carted hair off her face. 'Anyway, she sent me up to tell you dinner's ready.'

'Dinner?' said Thomas. 'What do you mean?'

'It's a fry-up, on trays.'

'Is Rob having a fry-up?'

This was apparently the case.

Thomas looked speechless, but actually wasn't.

'She's gone out and divorced him and come back and cooked him fucking dinner?'

Bel nodded, and somewhere a door slammed.

'I don't believe it,' said Thomas. 'I don't want any.'

'If they're not saying anything, why should we?' His sister took a pace or two up the corridor. 'Come on, let's just get down there and eat it.'

It was still being cooked when they walked in. *In Town Tonight* on the TV and Rob in his shades. He had a Scotch on the go. By convention, Thomas's place was at the other end of the same sofa. He sat down and could smell the eggs. The Dobermann came up for its squeeze. Looking at Rob (although he wasn't looking at him), it was obvious, there was no physical resemblance at all. Rob was blond and a rhino, Thomas dark and a weed. They were what they always had been, strangers whose fortunes happened to put them in the same house. News up next, it was another normal evening. Nothing different, except his father wasn't his father, and wasn't even married to his mother any more.

Mabs came in with the first of the trays. She was wearing a buff woollen suit and court shoes and had had a hair-do. There was a curious expression of satisfaction about her, hard to put your finger on, but she seemed somehow pleased with herself. Typical of her to get smug over the attention of legal twots, 'Let me just sniff your arse.' The polythene was back and squelched under her feet. Rob didn't look at her but around her, to keep eyes on the TV. As she approached, she clipped a turd off at right-angles with the side of her shoe. It was expertly done, conducted with such deft indifference, Thomas was surprised she'd even seen it. It was perhaps an old one, previously spotted, and she was already of a mind to have it out of the way? It shot under the television set.

Rob got his tray, a variety of fried things, including eggs, and mushrooms exuding black water. As the rest of the trays came in, he finished his whisky and started eating with eyes still on the TV. Thomas's attention was with the turd under it; he was ruminating on what his grandfather had said. 'She thinks she's being shat on, and she's telling him with shit.' That's what he said, something like that, anyway? Walter knew everything. What Walter said made sense. And what Olanda said seemed to make sense too. The present environment was a profound endorsement of the impotence of words, their worthlessness. Were the opportunity to arise (and such was inconceivable), Thomas couldn't think of a single thing he would say to either of them. And yet, there wasn't space left in his brain for the turmoil he was struggling with. He wanted to get up and shout at them, stuff those fucking mushrooms down their throats. Who the fuck do you think you are? What the fuck do you think you're doing? How can you just sit there with your crummy divorce and mushrooms? You know what I'm going to do? I'll tell you what I'm going to do. I'm going to make a ton of fucking explosive, ten fucking tons, and I'm going to wire this fucking shit-house up, and blow the bastard to bits.

He ate his bacon, and egg on top of the fried bread. Inadvertently, he looked across at Bel. Whose side was she on? Not theirs, that's one consolation. But did all this mean she might not be his real sister? The best she could be was his half-sister. He needed to see Walter quickly. He needed to know who he was.

At the back of the news there was a piece about what everyone could see out of the window. There was a gale in Kent. There were pictures of waves crashing over sea walls at Dover. The newsreader also mentioned the stricken Spanish tanker, but they didn't have any pictures of that. 'It's on the rocks,' she said, meaning she knew nothing about the Goodwin Sands. 'Leaking thousands of tons of oil.' That was the news. But some better news out of the hall. Thomas heard the doctor leave. He watched him walk down the drive holding his hat on, and get into a yellow Vauxhall.

Ten minutes later, Thomas was heading upstairs. He would have gone straight into his grandfather's room, except Ethel was again in the vicinity.

'Don't go in there now, Tom. The doctor's given him something to sleep.'

'Just for a minute? I just want to see him for a minute?'

She looked at him without sentiment, too much fatigue in her face for that.

'It'll only be a minute, Gran?'

'Don't say anything about Canterbury.'

'I won't.'

Ethel found the banister, shook her head at it all, and went on her way. There was a strange smell on the stairs, intensifying as he slipped quietly into Walter's room. It was a smell of sweet metal. A smell like babies, except the opposite of that. It was a complex odour Thomas had never encountered before, but he realised at once what it was, it was death . . .

Wind trampled the roof, shuddering curtains that were half closed. Outside the evening was becoming green. A chair was already in place. Thomas moved it closer to the bed and sat looking at his grandfather. Walter lay on his back, swathed in blue-and-white-striped pyjamas, silver stubble on his unshaven face. His eyes were open and staring up. He made no acknowledgement of Thomas at all, not even after he'd repeated his name.

'It's me, Grandad.'

Reaching out, he took the old man's hand, or rather, settled a hand on top of his.

'Can you hear me?'

All Thomas could hear was Walter's breathing, hesitant and slow, like the air hurt. After what built into an interminable silence, Walter turned his head in the boy's direction.

Yes, it seemed probable he could hear him.

'I need to ask you something,' whispered Thomas. 'I'm sorry to ask you now.'

Walter stared with such lack of expression, it was as if he didn't see. His eyes were a failed industry, so deep in his skull he looked like a rotting bird.

Thomas repeatedly found something to clear in his throat, still fumbling for the right way to unload it all . . .

'I went to see Madame Olanda this morning. You know, the fortune teller. She told me all sorts of stuff about before I was born. She told me some weird things about Mum and Rob.'

No change in the expression, or Thomas's faltering tone.

'Olanda hates Rob, because of the pigeons. And I wanted to know whether what she said was true.'

He went on to tell him the story, almost word for word, as Olanda had told it to him. Told him about the adultery in the West End of London, about the American man who went to Chicago, even told him about the bath and bottle of gin . . .

'You said I was looking for the wrong secret. Is this the right one? Is it the reason you don't talk to Rob? Not because of Mum? Because of me?'

During all this, Walter hadn't moved. Not an eyelid. Thomas was worried that he didn't even have the strength to hear.

'You're the only one I can ask, Grandad. No one else will tell me the truth. It's not because I want to blame anybody, I just want to know who I am.'

There was another silence filled up with the wind. Involuntarily, he felt his hand close on Walter's, and there was a response. Whatever life was left went into the movement. Walter held his hand too.

Although he couldn't say it, Thomas knew his grandfather loved him, and he sat holding on to the old man until the room was dark, and there was nothing else to listen to but the gale.

THE SINS OF THE FOREFATHERS
PART II

There were skylarks over North Foreland, so high you could barely see them, but each had its own room of song. Chalk paths crossed the farmland and there was an aroma of hot weeds. It had been stifling all day; even now, in late afternoon, the fields were shimmering.

Gwendolin wore a blue cotton dress and a funny-looking straw hat that seemed too big for her. It had cherries and tiny painted apples on it. She'd taken her shoes off and given them to Thomas to carry, walked a little way ahead of him picking the big daisies. They had held hands and they had kissed, but they'd hardly talked all day. She told him she was 'three-quarters' through *Copperfield*, but it was obvious she wasn't past page 26.

He smiled but didn't say anything.

'You seem so distant, Tom.'

'Not really.'

'You are.'

'I've been trying to work out a poem,' he said. '"Chocolate Beach". But I can't seem to get the words in order.'

And then they'd sat for a while in the meadow, eating biscuits she'd made, drinking lemonade, and lying on their backs in the scarlet poppies, looking up at the sky and listening to the larks. It was the second Sunday in the month. Across the headland, they could hear the bells ringing at Holy Trinity . . .

Thomas was filled with misgivings, a foreboding he kept to himself. It wasn't so much a presentiment that something dreadful was going to happen, but that something dreadful was already in process. More than once, Gwendolin had sat up to ask him what the matter was.

'Just thinking,' he told her.

'Why don't you think out loud?'

He took her hand.

'Is it your parents that's worrying you?'

'No. I'm not thinking about them.'

'Then what?'

It was pointless telling her what he would never know himself, so he lied, said he just didn't really feel like talking much today, there wasn't really much the matter at all. It was a lie of some dimension. He was in a jungle of anxious thoughts. All this had to go somewhere, surely? He couldn't live the rest of his life with this? It was like a feeling of regret, of guilt almost, without knowing the felony. Had there been some kind of deal done with Rob, a contract to 'be his father', that was broken? He would never know now. Walter was dying and hadn't spoken for a week. Neither had his parents, hadn't said a word. What was going to happen to them? He imagined they would stay together for the newspapers. They didn't need a 'marriage' for what they had, just an endless awful road with no stops. And if they ever ran out of fuel, they'd get out and fucking push . . .

'Thomas? Come on?'

Gwendolin had wandered a long way up the path in front of him. She turned and stood clutching a swathe of daisies, her hat at her side, the sun inside her hair. He looked at her and loved her, thought they would always be together, he and her, although this was the last day he was ever going to see her in his life.

A wall of ancient flint crumbled into cow parsley. Gwendolin sat on it waiting for him, knees tucked under her chin. Her dress had collapsed up her legs, her smile was sweetly promiscuous.

'I've got a present for you.'

He climbed the wall and sat next to her to take it. She'd torn the string out of her hat and tied it around the daisies.

'They're to cheer you up.'

He made a big thing of sniffing them, of getting cheered up by them, and realised he was a bit breathless.

'You're sweating, Tom.'

'It's hot.'

He felt a zip of perspiration running down his cheek. Gwendolin leant in and kissed it, touched it with her tongue. He wasn't at all sure he liked her doing it.

'Why did you do that?'

'I wanted to,' she whispered, her lips still very close. 'It tastes like seaweed.'

'When did you eat seaweed?'

'You taste like the sea.'

They kissed again, her fingers searching a way into his shirt. And his hands were all over her. He could smell heat in the nettles and the aromatic in her hair. She was wearing the same perfume, like vinegar mixed with roses. At the periphery of the kisses he could see her naked thighs. He thought about it, and thought about the thought, and then he didn't think about it and just did it. He put his hand up her dress. A pulse of raw adrenalin hit him in the brain. It was a moment of exquisite crisis whose penalty was reward. Gwendolin opened her legs and let him touch her. He put fingers inside her knickers. It was without prohibition, no censure but the elastic across his hand.

Gwendolin kissed him, complete, luscious kisses her mouth wouldn't satisfy. 'We could do it, Tom?' she whispered. He felt her heart beat, the contour of her breast. Everything she was was his, and everything he could ever want was her . . .

'I love you so much,' she said.

'I love you so much too.'

'We could do it, darling?'

A divine anaesthetic drenched his senses. She abandoned the wall without letting go of his hand and he followed in a kind of dream. They were going to make love. He could hear crickets in the field, and a cuckoo in the wood. They walked towards it hand in hand, up a gentle slope away from the path.

There were bluebells here, spilling from the trees, washes of indigo stewing in the sun. They lay down together, and what he wanted was her pleasure to approve. But it was different this time, this time he was to love her without error. She guided his hand, he touched where instructed, kissing with her enthusiasm. Her dress was open at every button, lifted and relinquished; she wore no brassière. Whatever else was her underwear was lost about her legs.

Her mouth called him darling, and he was kissing the word. Then, with unexpected abruptness, she put an end to the embrace, sat up and knelt in the flowers. Thomas looked at her with a *frisson* of doubt: had he done something wrong, had he hurt her?

Staring at him all the while she reached for the hem of her dress, lifting it in one simple movement. When her arms were stretched above her head, with her breasts raised, eyes looking into his, she paused for the smallest moment. It was an expression of breathtaking femininity, so beautiful, she looked like a spell, blue eyes and bluebells behind her like ink. She was completely naked now, except ribbon in her hair, her knickers pulled down and useless around her thighs. Yet not a trace of embarrassment or disconcertion; were it not for the imposition of her sensuality, she might have been alone.

Still kneeling, she took the remnant of what she wore past her toes, dropped it like a little pink handkerchief next to her dress. She was looking at him, one knee slightly turned in and the only symptom of modesty. Thomas was bewitched, knelt facing her, trying to still the arousal in his breathing. She touched his lips with her lips, but it wasn't a kiss. Diligent fingers unbuttoned his shirt, let it fall from his shoulders. He felt the sun on his back and didn't move. The same fingers undid his belt, and the buttons underneath. She opened his jeans. With sweetest care, she slipped fingers inside his pants, gently moved them away from him, lowering them with one hand, while caressing him with the other. 'I want you to take your clothes off.' He barely heard her, but did as he was told. They undressed him together, Gwendolin discarding his clothes on top of hers.

She put her mouth to his, again it was no kiss, the tip of her tongue choosing which lip to touch. There was something in his head as dangerous as a blush, but it felt like a kind of radiance. Now naked as she, they lay down once again in the flowers.

'I love you, Thomas.'

Reckless caresses, tingling like sherbet, one found a way to his sex. She teased at first, hardly touching, endearing with the back of fingers, as if to soothe. He felt a shudder in her blood as his fingers returned to her. She was liquid and ravishing, kissing properly with her legs very apart, and rubbing him firmly now. He belonged to her, and she to him, and he knew she wanted him where his fingers already were.

He could smell the hot earth, bluebells and her hair. Her eyes were closed. There was a catch in her breath as he moved on top of her. He pushed where he thought, but couldn't get inside.

'Let me, darling, I've done it before.'

'Have you?' he said, and felt foolish saying it.

'Lots and lots of times, but never with anyone I love like you.'

So it was the first time, and she was helping him.

'There. There. Push now.'

He pushed inside her. She felt like light. A stench of bluebells, vanquished in ruthless joy.

He could feel her racing heart and, as he began to fuck her, something cold going up his arse. Was it her? It wasn't. It was a dog, a fucking Corgi, sniffing and licking his bottom. He had paws on Thomas's back, and was trying to mount him.

'Branwell! Come here!'

Thomas saw the dog skid off, but didn't see its outraged owner. Her name was Penelope, and she was fifty-eight years old. She walked briskly away, tugging the ridiculous animal on its lead. Shortly after, she was followed up the path by her son, the maths guru and Rotary Club member, Gordon Norris. He was some distance off, but near enough to recognise the lovers.

He watched them, for perhaps longer than was necessary, to get the gist of what was going on.

'Come along, Gordon.'

She had scarpered up the wall, her fat arse following towards the side-car.

Norris followed her.

Gwendolin and Thomas were still fucking. She was full of light. It was coming out of him, and he fucked it into her.

After love they lay naked until the evening came. She nuzzled in his arms; it was still incredibly hot. She was a part of him that would always be, and he a part of her.

He would remember this night for ever, the moon rising in its yellow room of heaven, her nakedness in the broken flowers.

There was singing in the darkness, but in this infinite darkness, there was light. He could remember her name, hear her laughter in a plait of burning stars.

She was the love of his life.

It was a morning of miracles. You don't need the list, but the sun was on its way and the roses full of dew. Outside on the chimney pots, a bird was singing sweet as jam. And at ten-past eight, on this morning of miracles, Thomas's grandfather died.

There was no shock of course, and very little fuss. Rob went to work and a pair of young undertakers came round to take the body away. It was all done very quickly. Thomas didn't want to look at him when he was dead.

'It's a blessed relief, really,' said Ethel.

There were relatives to inform, and at last, a phone call was put into Vicar Potts. The Reverend had 'popped out' and Susan took it, offered condolences, very sympathetic, but better to speak to Michael, 'Yes, yes, he'll be home in a minute.'

She cradled the phone and was already on her way back upstairs. She carried a fat can of white paint, and a pair of ancient brushes still melting in a jar of turpentine. It had been a long winter, and what with Maurice ill for most of it, a bit of belated spring-cleaning was in order. She was going to do the landing and his room.

Just then, the Reverend appeared in the hall, his sunlight harsh on a polished wood floor. Susan leant over the banisters, and shouted down the news of Walter Furseman's passing.

'All right, I'll give Mrs Penman a call.'

'I'll need your help in a minute,' she said.

'For what?'

'I'll need your help to move the bed.'

Precisely fifty-five minutes later, Potts sat at his kitchen table with the pornographic photographs and accompanying literature. There were various dirty magazines, including something called *Razzle* and another by the name of *Spick and Span*. Almost all of it was pretty girls climbing over gates, showing their stocking tops and underwear. Lewd, but innocuous stuff compared to the photographs.

How could anyone refer to that monstrous aberration as 'Eve'? And this complementary, male indecency with hair slicked down, given the name of the finest, first sentient creature of God?

'It's an iniquity,' thundered Potts. 'An outrage.'

But curiously, he wasn't as offended by the Duck and Apple as he was by the pages that came out of the same envelope. It was a story – or part of a story – about a fifteen-year-old boy at a boarding-school, and his relationship with a nymphomaniac matron. Some of the lines were as unhappily unforgettable, as they were unforgivable . . .

Viz . . .

One of the older boys, Watson, a blond little homo, who had sucked him off in the bath house, told him to look out. 'She's got a cunt like a leprechaun trap,' he said.

And . . .

With womanly vigour she got hold of his wanking-piece, stropped his member, and whipped his balls.

And . . .

She brought in Mrs Herbert, an enormous hagiographer who taught divinity. 'I'm going to put you to the breast,' said Matron, and he was forced to suckle a tit with a nipple the size of a lolly.

'It's iniquitous!'

The Reverend exhaled, flattening another butt in the ashtray.

'Might I read it?' said Susan.

'I'm not at all sure you should.'

'He's my son too, Michael.'

An undeniable truth; even so he hesitated before handing the pages across. They were in no particular order. She sat at the table to read, and he definitely didn't like her doing so . . .

The boy went up and knocked on her door. 'Come in,' said a cultured, slightly husky voice. And he did go in. It was raining softly against french windows, a small coal fire in her grate. She was sitting at her writing bureau. She didn't look up at him. 'Take your blazer off, and go and stand by the fire. I don't want you to get cold.' 'I'm not cold, Matron.' 'Do as you're told,' she said. She continued writing, he could hear the pen scratching, smell her perfume from here. She wore a full-skirted, very tailored black dress, a single row of pearls, and black high-heeled shoes. She also wore glasses which she took off. It was possible, that, not so long ago, she was very beautiful . . .

Susan turned over and found the next page in correct order.

The furniture in the room, or *chambre*, as it seemed, seemed to be sort of old French furniture . . . gilded chairs. He took his blazer off and stood in the firelight, it was the only light. She at last walked over to him, slim, handsome legs, a taut bosom that seemed too full for her. She sat in a gilt armchair, discreetly pulling her frock quite high over her knees, and him towards her. 'You are a strong boy?' she said, eyes on his legs and her hands shortly after following. They examined him, calves and thighs, gliding up and down, ever inquisitive, exploring, from time to time, right up inside his blue serge, schoolboy shorts. Although engaged to make legitimate examination of his legs, the back of her fingers touched lightly several times in a more private area. 'I know you are a new boy,' she said. 'Shy? But from reports I have of you, you seem very bookish. Handsome little boys like you shouldn't have their noses in books. You should be out on the playing fields, and in summer, swimming naked in the river.' 'I don't like sports, Matron,' said he. 'There *must* be a reason for that,' she replied. Uncrossing her legs, she sat back. Her dress seemed to have moved higher. There was a glimpse of something that might have been a white suspender. 'I think we better get you undressed,' she whispered . . .

'My word,' said Susan, looking up. 'It's spicy.'

Potts slammed his hand on top of it all. He would have no more of this. She would read no more. He snatched the pages, and would deal with this when Maurice came home.

An eventuality that happened at half-past four.

The wrath was deep and instant. While his mother stood silently by, the Vicar puts oaths in the air. Maurice had never seen his father so enraged, a thrashing seemed imminent, there was but one way out . . .

'They're not mine,' he said.

'They were under *your* bed,' bellowed Potts.

Maurice shook his head, trying to look amazed.

'They're not mine,' he repeated.

'Then whose are they?'

'I don't know.'

Potts moved in and grabbed him with some emotion.

'Now listen to me, I want the *truth*, boy. If they're not

yours, what are they doing under your bed? I want to know who put them there.'

Maurice looked to his mother for support, but didn't get it. The arsehole was freaking out. He didn't want to drop anyone in it, but was reluctantly impelled into that desperate arena of last resort, known in the trade as, 'Wouldn't you?'

'It might have been, Thomas,' he offered.

'*Penman*?' boomed Potts.

It was possible?

After a bruising moment, Potts released the arm, staring hard at his son. He wanted to believe his innocence, but couldn't quite accept it, not, that is, until Susan reminded him the Penman boy had been round in March, inexplicably lifting Maurice's bed.

Suddenly it made sense. An ingratiating smile from Maurice. Suddenly he was off the hook.

'Yes, that must have been when he done it.'

'Penman. Penman,' said Potts. A youth already banned from this house. It was Penman.

The situation had ameliorated itself remarkably in Maurice's favour, but Potts was still furious. His immediate inclination was to get on the phone to Thomas's parents, but in view of the call he'd just had from them, it wasn't appropriate.

But he wasn't going to let this go. He would take this matter further.

He took it to Enright.

'You are to go and see Matron.' Matron had to see all the new boys. One of the older boys, Watson, a blond little homo, who had sucked him off in the bath house, told him to look out. 'She's got a cunt . . .'

Enright raised eyes with a dozen pages read, perhaps a dozen left to go? He sat behind his desk, Potts and Norris at its other side, looking back at him. The headmaster made a note on his pad and, skipping a page or two, continued to read. The atmosphere was grave . . .

'I think we better get you undressed,' she whispered. 'I've got religious prep,' said the boy, in alarm. 'All lessons for you,' said she, 'have been cancelled today.' Elegant fingers reached up, unknotting and removing his tie. There were a deal of resistant buttons, first those of his shirt, then those of his shorts. She took his shorts down, and beckoned him to step out of them. He realised she was French. He was now wearing only small black gymnasium shoes, underpants, and a little vest. She told him to hold it up. Conscientious fingers examined his chest and tummy, they tickled so, and to his horror made his penis rise. She turned him round and pulled his pants down to examine his bottom. 'Just loosen your legs for me?' she said. He felt fingers slip between, a hand delicately cupping his testicles. She held him quite tightly. A tiny clock struck five on the mantelpiece, he felt a flood of shame. And he had a funny feeling in his penis – meek – but rude. He knew she was going to turn him back to her . . .

Enright took glasses off, stuck a little finger into the corner of his eye. He'd had enough of this, and addressed himself to Norris.

'Where is he?' he said.

'Outside, waiting in the corridor.'

'All right, let's have him in.'

'With respect, Headmaster,' interjected Potts, 'I know it is repugnant reading, but I do think you should finish, just the last page or two?'

Enright had been into shady dormitories of teenage sodomy, abuse through the pockets of trousers, down throats, and up corsets of a 'Ladies' Paradise'. He shook his head, caring for no more, but Potts insisted, and he deferred to the Reverend's judgement . . .

She turned him back to her, his shame exploded. His pants were around his knees, and he was in full cock. 'I think we've found out what the matter is,' whispered she. Her fingertips fell down his penis like the petals of a collapsing rose. She turned him sideways, carefully escorted his male up to full erection, like a terrier's tail at an important show. And then, like her trained little pet (as soon he was to be), he was turned again to face her. 'You may ask permission to remove the rest of your underwear.' He asked, and permission was granted. 'And now, I want you to go over to that little table, and bring me what's in the drawer.' Wearing only shoes, he did her bidding, stood in front of her while she opened a small black velvet case. 'Put your hands behind your back, and push your bottom forward.' 'Please, Matron,' said the boy. 'If you don't want it smacked, push your bottom forward.' From the scented pouch, she produced a lead and tiny collar, like a dog collar, and secured it around his member. 'It's very tight, Matron.' She looked up, delicious red lips in a smile of charming sympathy. 'I know,' she said, 'I'm sorry, it might have to be just a little tighter.' And it was, and the lead was connected to the collar with a click. She stood, tugging him gently after. 'Come along, I'm going to take you to the infirmary.' 'For what?' he said, in further alarm. 'I'm not ill.' 'To bathe you, and milk you, and no more questions.' She put a finger across her lips, and opened the door. 'What boys like you need is discipline, and affection, and you will find I have an abundance of both.' He followed her out, the head of his penis throbbing like a turkey's heart. With his lead

271

attached, she led the naked boy, silently, along the chilly corridor . . .

And that really was it, for Enright. There were more pages, but he wasn't having any more.

'Bring him in, Mr Norris.'

Norris momentarily disappeared into the corridor, came back with Thomas following. He didn't seem to know quite what was up. But then he saw Potts, and the pornography, and he knew. All sat, except he, and they were all staring with expressions of thankless contempt. It was a committee of moral men, Potts, Norris, Enright, the latter pacing himself to get through it all. His eyes raised, Thomas was so panicked, he could barely follow the indictment.

Here was a boy, according to Enright, who was a seasoned pornographist, a masturbator, with a predilection for loitering in girls' lavatories. (Had Enright not beaten him for that, but some few months ago?) But worse, there was worse, so much worse than that. Loathsome as these photographs were, there was so much worse to come. For here was a boy, this rueful 'peeping Tom', who had taken a girl into a field, a mere child of fifteen, and had illicit, underage, and criminal sex.

Potts cleared his throat.

'Mr Norris saw you in a field at North Foreland with Gwendolin Hackett.'

Was it a statement, or a question? It was both. Clearly, what they were all looking at was a fully formed, full-blown, adolescent pervert. There was an execrable silence before Enright spoke again.

'This is a matter of utmost seriousness. I have spoken to your mother, who, of course, informed me of the unhappy situation with your grandfather. It is the reason we have waited some days before bringing you in here. And because of the circumstances, I don't intend to deal with this from a disciplinary perspective now. But dealt with, it will be. Let me assure you of that.'

The Reverend nodded in sombre agreement. Enright continued.

'For now, I will only say this. I spoke to Gwendolin's parents at some length on Monday, and her mother again, on Tuesday morning. You may, or may not have noticed, that she hasn't been in school.'

'I haven't been in school myself, sir.'

'What?'

'I haven't been in school myself.'

'Quite so,' said Enright, correcting himself. He unleashed his glasses, wiped them with a clean white handkerchief, and put them on again. 'There was a consideration of making Gwendolin a Ward of Court. It has been decided, however, that she will move to Edinburgh, live with her aunt, and complete her schooling there.'

Thomas was mortified, felt like he couldn't breathe.

'Why?' he said.

'Why?' echoed Enright. '*Why*? I don't think you realise the seriousness of your situation. You are the owner of these detestable photographs. They are odious and despicable. This sort of material is *criminal*, Penman. Do you realise that?'

'I suppose so,' faltered Thomas.

'Then why bring it round to my son?' demanded Potts.

'Where did you get it?' This question was from Norris, in similar tone.

Thomas shook his head and didn't answer.

'You are an utterly degenerate boy, Penman.' He rapped fingers hard on the photographs. 'I can't imagine where you got this filth, but it is utterly repugnant. And now you ask *why* Gwendolin Hackett has been taken by her mother to live in Scotland. Do you consider yourself a fit associate? Do you? The girl is *fifteen* years old.' He said it like it was an accusation. 'Let me tell you, Penman, if it wasn't for the regrettable circumstance of your grandfather's death, I would be referring this to a different authority. Are you aware that intercourse with a fifteen-year-old girl is rape? An imprisonable offence?'

'Answer him, Penman,' said Norris.

'No, sir.' He looked at him but could hardly talk. 'It wasn't rape, sir.'

'Don't contradict me,' snappped Enright, his eyes inflamed behind the spectacles. 'I'm dealing with the world as it *is*, not as you might wish it to be. It is rape. Statutory rape.'

They were, this committee, what pornography is, making something beautiful into something that is vile. Hot tears pushed around Thomas's eyes and streamed down his face. Not so much in sadness, but in rage. And yes, in overwhelming sadness too.

'I love her, sir,' he said.

Enright looked at him through a long silence, and replied with all the dismal authority life had invested in him.

'You don't know what love is.'

He stood up and walked around his desk, slapped Thomas hard across the face.

'I shall be writing to your parents. Some measures will have to be taken as a result of all this. When they are decided on, you will be informed.' He opened the door. 'Now, get out.'

Thomas got out of the office, got his bicycle out of the sheds, and got out of the school. The day was hot, he walked with the bike, he was in no hurry to get anywhere. Only one thing for certain, he would never go back into that ugly fucking building for as long as he lived. They would have to kill him and carry him in dead to get him back in there.

He threw his hat into a hedge, all sorts of tears still around. Scotland couldn't last for ever? He hoped Gwendolin didn't feel alone and sad. There would have to be a way to get her back. He would go there, walk there if necessary, walk to fucking Scotland and get her back . . .

He walked in the general direction of his home, a headful of clouds developing grandiose schemes of rescue, one involving horses and a rowing boat on the Clyde. If Gwendolin wanted to, they could run away together, get married if necessary. Gretna Green was in Scotland. He felt the loss of his grandfather; Walter was the only one who would understand, have the right advice. They buried him yesterday, that third-rate Christian with the eyebrows had buried him, he'd gone into the same plot as Old Moules. Thomas wasn't asked to the funeral – it would be too upsetting for him, they said – and for once they were probably right. He was so upset he didn't see the street. He hated Walter being dead, he was gone for ever, the truth buried with him. No chance of any truth now. He could ask Ethel, it was a possibility, but he knew she would never tell. 'You'll have to talk to your mother,' that's what she would say. Ethel stayed out of things, that's how she got by . . .

Christ, he had a headache.

He had arrived without realising it and turned into the drive. Smoke hung over the gardens, lines of blue light through the apple trees. Thomas peered over the wall and could see his father, chaperoning a blaze at the edge of the little orchard. He had a wheelbarrow of pornography, photos of nude girls scattered in the grass. It was another funeral of sorts, and in some organic, inexplicable way, the end of Thomas's childhood.

Shards were rising in the heat, pages on fire as they went up. Rob fed the flames with handfuls, glancing occasionally at the pictures and smiling to himself as he tossed them on. Thumbing through one small volume, he hesitated. It disappeared into his trouser pocket. Otherwise, he burnt the lot, came out with another load. He destroyed everything, and when he'd finished burning it, he got into the Wolsey, and Went Around the Corner.

Thomas sat upstairs thinking about all those tedious hours he'd spent filing keys. But he was already sad enough to feel sad for that, and actually felt nothing. How was it the keys were so readily available to Rob? He hated adults and was becoming one. In three days he would be sixteen . . .

That night in his room he wrote a letter to Gwendolin. Told her he would always love her, that she was the love of his life, and that no matter what happened, he would find a way for them to be together. He wrote her address in Queen's Road, and 'Please Forward' in a corner of the envelope.

In the morning he would post it.

In the morning he got up early, just after dawn, and went down into the gardens. It was glistening and warm already. For a moment he looked around like he didn't know where he was going. Where was he going? He was going to get all the keys out of his workshop and throw them in the sea. He was going to throw all the detonators in, and the half-made bombs. They were childish things and he wasn't a child any more – all that was past; he knew his life had changed irrevocably . . .

Crossing the vegetable gardens, he made an unscheduled detour through the orchard. There was a vague smell of burning still in the air. The bonfire was a grey heap, like mould on batteries. He kicked gently at the ashes, stirring up bits of a brassière catalogue, and the charred remains of what might have been a book. Only the top part survived, page numbers, and a few chapter headings. 'Halibut', one said, and 'Dover Sole'. It fell to bits in his hand and he let it drop. Something else in the ashes? He picked it up. It was a coin, an American silver dollar with a hole drilled in it. He rubbed it with his thumb until the metal shone through. It was Walter's unlucky coin.

Thomas put it into his pocket and went into his workshop. He found a piece of sacking and spread it on the bench, gathered all the keys and explosives, tying the whole thing up in a bundle. He was on his way out when he noticed something white at the edge of his vision. It turned his head so sharply it almost hurt. There was a tape, a long transmission out of the Tishman. Where had it come from? Dumping the sack, he tore it off to read

. ...– .–. –.– – – .... .. –. – – –. – – – .–.. .– – –. –.. .– ... .–
.. –.. .. ... – .–. ..– .

The message was astonishing, from a dead man, and Thomas was so moved by it he couldn't move at all. It must have taken every last bit of Walter's life to work the Morse key.

It said: 'Everything Olanda said was true.'

Birds were singing outside. Thomas continued to read.

.–.. – – – ...– . .. ... – .... . – – – –. .–.. –.– – – .–. . .– .–..
– .–. ..– – – – .... – – – .. .–.. – – – ...– . .–.– – – – –

'Love is the only truth, Tom. I love you.'

Thomas stood for a long time in the silent workshop, relishing sweet tears. Walter loved him and never let him down. He could feel the love of the old man, and felt more loved than he ever had in his life.

He put the transmission in his pocket and walked out, down through the empty town and down to the sea. The jetty was deserted to sunlight, it wasn't yet six o'clock. At its end, he stopped and leant over the balustrade. The tide was on the turn, beginning to expose the rock pools, ruined waves coming in the colour of shit. There were many dead birds along the shoreline, everything was choked with oil. You could smell it, but couldn't really see it in the pools. It was the same colour as the seaweed. 'It's like chocolate,' Gwendolin had said. 'Petrels in oil?' said Thomas, feeling smart. If only he could have that day again, and do it differently. They would have been at North Foreland so much earlier if he hadn't sat here, trying to write her a poem. And yet, it was the best day in his life.

He'd forgotten to bring the keys and bombs, but felt in his pocket for Walter's coin. Stepping back, he threw it as hard and as far as he could into the sea . . .

'Fuck it,' he said.

And he stuck a fag in his mouth, and turned back to the town, with nothing much to look forward to, but life.